TRAGEDY AT LAW

ff

TRAGEDY
AT LAW

Cyril Hare

faber and faber
LONDON · BOSTON

To J.A.F.

First published in 1942
by Faber and Faber Limited
3 Queen Square London WC1N 3AU
First published in this edition in 1985
Reprinted in 1987 and 1990

Printed in England by
Clays Ltd, St Ives plc

British Library Cataloguing in Publication Data

Hare, Cyril
Tragedy at law.
Rn: Alfred Alexander Gordon Clark
I. Title
823′.912[F] PR6053.L29/
ISBN 0 571 13657 5

Chapter 1

NO TRUMPETERS

"No trumpeters!" said his Lordship in a tone of melancholy and slightly peevish disapproval.

His words, addressed to nobody in particular, produced no reply, possibly for the reason that no reply to a statement of fact so obvious was possible. Everything else that man could devise or tradition dictate for the comfort or glorification of His Majesty's Judge of Assize was there. A Rolls Royce of cavernous size purred at the door of the Lodgings. The High Sheriff, faintly redolent of moth balls but none the less a shining figure in the full-dress uniform of a Volunteer Regiment long since disbanded, strove to bow respectfully and to avoid tripping over his sword at the same time. His chaplain billowed in unaccustomed black silk. The Under Sheriff gripped his top hat in one hand and in the other the seven foot ebony wand, surmounted by a carved death's head, with which the county of Markshire inexplicably chooses to burden its Under Sheriffs on such occasions. Behind, the Judge's Clerk, the Judge's Marshal, the Judge's Butler and the Marshal's Man formed a sombre but not less satisfying group of acolytes. Before, a detachment of police, their buttons and badges gleaming in the pale sunshine of October, stood ready to ensure safe conduct through the streets of Markhampton. It was an impressive spectacle, and the lean stooping man in the scarlet robe and full-bottomed wig who was its centre was well aware that he was not the least impressive part of it.

7

But the fact remained, odious and inescapable. There were no trumpeters. War with all its horrors was let loose upon the earth and His Majesty's Judge must in consequence creep into his car with no more ceremony than an ambassador or an archbishop. Chamberlain had flown to Godesberg and Munich and pleaded for them, but in vain. Hitler would have none of them. The trumpeters must go. It was a distressing thought, and the look on the High Sheriff's face might be interpreted as meaning that it was a trifle tactless of the Judge to mention such a painful subject at such a moment.

"No trumpeters!" repeated his Lordship wistfully, and climbed stiffly into the car.

The Honourable Sir William Hereward Barber, Knight, one of the Justices of the King's Bench Division of the High Court of Justice, as he was described on the cover of the calendar of the Markshire assizes, had been known for obvious reasons, in his early days at the Bar, as the Young Shaver. As the years passed, the title was generally abbreviated to "the Shaver". More recently a small but growing circle had taken to calling him among themselves "Father William", for reasons with which his age had nothing to do. He was, in fact, a man still under sixty. In civil dress he was, it must be admitted, nothing very much to look at. His clothes always hung badly from his lanky frame. His manner was jerky and abrupt, his voice harsh and somewhat high-pitched. There is, however, something about judicial garments that gives consequence to any but the most undignified figure. The ample robes concealed his gawkiness and the full-bottomed wig that framed his face enhanced the austere effect of his rather prominent, aquiline nose and disguised the weakness of his mouth and chin. As he settled back upon the cushions of the Rolls, Barber looked every inch a Judge. The little crowd that had gathered round the door of the lodgings to see his departure went home feeling that, trumpeters or no trumpeters, they had seen a great man. And in that, perhaps, lay the justification of the whole ceremony.

Colonel Habberton, the High Sheriff, was less fortunate in his costume. The Markshire Volunteers had never been a particularly distinguished or warlike body, and it was difficult to believe that the designer of their uniform had taken his work seriously. He had been altogether too generous with his gold braid, too fanciful with his treatment of the shoulder straps and had given fatally free rein to his imagination when it came to the helmet which was perched uncomfortably upon its owner's knee. In its best days the uniform had been a gaudy mistake. In the age of the battle-dress it was a ludicrous anachronism—besides being damnably uncomfortable. Habberton, his chin smarting from contact with its high, stiff collar, was uneasily aware that the titters which he had heard coming from the crowd had been directed at him.

Judge and Sheriff eyed each other with the mutual distrust of men compelled to associate on official business who are well aware that they have nothing in common. In a normal working year Barber encountered anything up to twenty sheriffs and he had found that by the time he had discovered anything of interest about any of them the moment had always arrived to move on to another town on the circuit. He had, therefore, long since given up the attempt of trying to make conversation with them. Habberton, on the other hand, had never met a judge in his life before his appointment and did not care if he never met another when his year of office was over. He scarcely ever left his own estate, which he farmed seriously and efficiently, and held the firm opinion that all lawyers were crooks. At the same time he could not help being impressed by the fact that the man before him represented Majesty itself and the recognition of this feeling caused him no small annoyance.

In fact, the only occupant of the car who was entirely at his ease was the chaplain. The assize sermon having, like the trumpeters, been sacrificed to the stern necessities of war, nobody expected him to say or do anything. He could, therefore, afford to sit back and regard the proceedings with an amused and tolerant smile. This he accordingly did.

"I am sorry about the trumpeters, my lord," Colonel Habberton observed at last. "I'm afraid it's because of the war. We were instructed. . . ."

"I know, I know," said his lordship forgivingly. "The trumpeters have other duties just now, no doubt. I hope I may hear them again the next time I am on the circuit. Personally," he hastened to add, "I don't care anything for all this paraphernalia." The wave of his hand seemed to include the car, the footman on the box, the escorting policemen and even the Sheriff himself. "But some of my colleagues take a different view. I can't think what any of my predecessors would have thought of an assize without trumpets!"

Those who knew Barber best used to say that whenever he was particularly faddy or exacting he invariably excused himself by referring to the high standards set by his colleagues or, in their default, his predecessors. One had a vision of a great company of masterful beings, in scarlet and white, urging on the modest Barber to abate no jot of his just dues in the interests of the whole judiciary of England, past and present. Certainly Barber usually showed no reluctance in obeying their summons.

"The trumpets are there all right," said Habberton. "And I had the tabards made with my own arms on them. It seems rather a waste."

"You can always have the tabards made into fire-screens," suggested the Judge kindly.

"I have three sets of those fire-screens at home already—my father's, my grandfather's and my great uncle's. I don't know what I should do with another pair."

His lordship pursed his mouth and looked discontented. His father had been a solicitor's clerk and his grandfather a barman in Fleet Street. At the back of his mind lurked a secret fear that strangers would find this out and despise him for it.

The Rolls Royce crawled on, keeping pace with the bodyguard of police.

"Damn this stick!" said the Under Sheriff genially, as he wedged his wand of office with difficulty between himself and the door of the car which he shared with the Marshal. "I've done this job for ten years now, and how I haven't smashed it every time, I can't imagine. It ought to have been put into cold storage for the duration along with the trumpeters."

The Marshal, an ingenuous-looking, fair-haired young man, looked at it with interest.

"Do Under Sheriffs always have that sort of thing?" he asked.

"Good Lord, no! It's peculiar to this loyal and stick-in-the-mud city. Is this your first assize?"

"Yes, I've never seen one before."

"Well, I expect you'll have seen quite enough by the time you've finished the circuit. Though it's not a bad job for you—two guineas a day and all found, isn't it? *I've* got to keep an office going with both my partners and half my staff called up and this Punch and Judy show to attend to as well. I suppose you know the Judge well, don't you?"

The Marshal shook his head.

"No. I'd only met him once before. He happened to be a friend of a friend of mine and offered me the job. Marshals are hard to come by just now, I suppose." He blushed slightly and explained. "I was turned down for the Army, you see. Heart."

"Bad luck."

"And as I was keen on the law, I thought it was rather a chance. I suppose the Judge is a very great lawyer, isn't he?"

"M'm. I'll leave you to answer that one when you've seen a bit more of him. You ought to get some useful experience anyhow. My name's Carter, by the way. I don't think I caught yours?"

The young man blushed again.

"Marshall," he said. "Derek Marshall."

"Of course, I remember now. The Judge mentioned it—'Marshall by name and Marshal by occupation!' Ha, ha!"

Derek Marshall laughed rather feebly in agreement. He was beginning to realize that he was going to hear quite a lot of this jibe before the circuit was over.

Not every car can move so smoothly as a Rolls when constrained to keep pace with policemen marching at regulation pace. (In point of fact, as Barber was at that moment pointing out, his predecessors in office would have scorned anything less than mounted men. Habberton turned the knife in the wound by recollecting that his grandfather had provided twenty-five javelin men in livery.) The hired vehicle in which Marshall and Carter were riding ground and jerked forward uneasily in its noisy bottom gear.

"It will be all right when we are through the Market Place," observed Carter. "We catch them up there, so as to get to the Cathedral before them. . . . Here we are! Get ahead, man, get ahead!"

The car shot forward, scattering the loiterers who had gathered in the narrow square to watch embodied Law pass by.

Beamish, the Judge's clerk, was feeling thoroughly pleased with the world. To begin with, he was on the Southern Circuit, which for many reasons he preferred to any other. Secondly, he had succeeded in recruiting a staff —butler, marshal's man and cook—who seemed thoroughly amenable and would not be likely to question either his authority or any little pickings which might come his way while they were associated. Lastly and immediately most important, it was evident that the Under Sheriff of Markshire was a Real Good Sort.

Under Sheriffs, in the eyes of Beamish, were either Mean

Bastards, Decent Gentlemen, or Real Good Sorts. They declared their quality at the very first moment of the first day of an assize. When the cars drew up at the doors of the lodgings to drive to church and thence to open the assize, it would be found that a Mean Bastard had provided no conveyance for the Judge's clerk. He was left to scuttle through the streets on his flat feet—and Beamish's feet were very flat—or to hire a taxi for himself, and the Lord knew that it was hard enough to square the circuit accounts without such extraneous expenses. A Decent Gentleman, on the other hand, offered Beamish a seat in his car, beside the chauffeur, so that he arrived at his destination in comfort, if not in dignity. But a Real Good Sort, who understood something of the importance of a judge's clerk in the scheme of things, provided him at the expense of the county with a car of his own. Such was Beamish's happy position at this moment, and his fat little body quivered with pleasure as he followed at the tail of the procession through the streets of Markhampton.

Beside him sat Savage, the butler, a depressed, elderly man, with a permanent stoop as though his back had become bent through years of deferential attendance on generations of judges. He was reputed to know every circuit town in England and he had never been heard to say a good word of one of them. On the floor, between the two men, lay an odd variety of objects—a pouch containing his Lordship's notebooks, a tin box which held his short wig, a rug for his Lordship's knees and an attaché case from which Beamish could produce, when called upon, sharpened pencils, a spare pair of spectacles, a box of throat lozenges or any other of a dozen necessities without which justice could not be properly administered.

Beamish was giving his last instructions to Savage. They were quite unnecessary, but he enjoyed giving instructions and Savage did not appear to mind receiving them, so that no harm was done.

"As soon as they've put me down at the Cathedral I want you to take this lot up to the Court."

"I only hope they've done something about the draught on the bench," interjected Savage mournfully. "It was something cruel last spring assizes. Mr. Justice Bannister complained about it something dreadful."

"If his Lordship finds himself in a draught there'll be trouble all round," said Beamish, almost gloating at the prospect, "*Big* trouble. Did you hear what he did on the Northern last year?"

Savage merely sniffed. His manner suggested that nothing that judges did would ever cause him any surprise and that in any case it never made any difference whatever they did.

Beamish began to fuss round the car as they neared the Cathedral.

"Now, have we got everything?" he said. "Black cap, smelling salts, Archbold—where's the Archbold, Savage?"

"Under your foot," said the butler, and produced that indispensable compendium of the criminal law.

"That's all right, then. Now about his Lordship's tea and biscuits this afternoon——"

"I've told Greene to see to that. It's his place."

Greene was the Marshal's man. Why it should have been the place of such a functionary, and no one else, to attend to the Judge's tea did not appear, but Savage's gloomy tones left no room for dispute in the matter. Beamish decided to defer to his greater experience. So long as he did not have to demean himself by getting the tea, it did not signify who did.

"Very well, so long as you've arranged it between you. Begin as you mean to go on is my motto. Here we are! Send the car back for me. Sharp, now!"

The Mayor and Aldermen of the City were awaiting the Judge at the great west door of the cathedral. So were several press photographers. The Corporation bowed respectfully. The Judge bowed back. After some preliminary hesitations, which gave the photographers a good opportunity of shooting the Judge from various angles, and Beamish of making sure that he was well in the picture, the procession finally sorted itself out and moved up the nave to the strains of the national anthem.

Outside, the police stood at ease, standing in line from the cathedral entrance, facing northwards. Opposite them, facing southwards, was another line of police, ready to take on the duties of escort from the service to the court. The Judge's lodgings being in the City of Markhampton, it was the duty of the city police to protect its august visitor. The assizes being uniquely the affair of the County of Markshire, it was equally the duty of the county police to keep watch and ward over them. Rivalry between the two forces had been acute and even at times violent, until a solemn conference between the county authorities and the city fathers —under the presidency of no less a being than the Lord Lieutenant—had produced an acceptable compromise: from the lodgings to the cathedral the Judge belonged to the city; from the cathedral to the courts to the county. On the second and subsequent days of the assize, the county relieved the city at a place approximately midway between the lodgings and the courts. Such are the complexities of local government in Markshire.

The Chief Constable of Markhampton stood at the head of his men and being gifted with a sense of humour, winked solemnly at his opposite number, the county superintendent. The superintendent winked back, not that he saw anything amusing in the situation, but because it was evidently the proper thing to do. Presently a small, dark man in a shabby blue serge suit made his way out of the crowd and approached the Chief Constable. He muttered a few words in the other's ear, and then turned away. The Chief Constable appeared to take no notice, but as soon as he had gone, beckoned to the superintendent, who came forward to join him.

"That fellow Heppenstall," he said quietly. "He's about again. My fellows lost trace of him last night, but he's in the town somewhere. Just mention it to your Chief, will you?"

"Heppenstall?" echoed the superintendent. "I don't think I know—what's he wanted for?"

"Wanted for nothing. We've got to keep an eye on him, that's all. Special Branch tipped us off about him. Tell your Chief, he'll know all about it. And if the Judge—— Here they come! Party, '*Shun*!'"

The procession emerged into the sunlight once more.

The Shire Hall at Markhampton, where the assizes were to be held, was an eighteenth century building, the architecture of which Baedeker would undoubtedly have classified as "well-intentioned". Both within and without it was in the uncared for condition into which the best-intentioned of buildings are liable to relapse if they are only occasionally used. If the authorities had dealt with the draught on the bench which had so disturbed Mr. Justice Bannister, that was all that they had done by way of improvements for a long time past. At all events, Francis Pettigrew, leaning back in counsel's seats and studying the ceiling, found his eye caught by the patch above the cornice where plaster had peeled off, and recognized it for an old acquaintance. He fell to wondering rather drearily how many years it was since, holding his first brief on circuit, he had first observed it. The thought depressed him. He had reached an age, and a stage in his profession, where he did not much care to be reminded of the passage of time.

On the desk in front of him lay two briefs, no more interesting and little more remunerative than the one which had given him so much pleasure as a youngster all those years ago. They would just about pay his expenses for coming

down to Markhampton. Beside them was a packet of papers
—printers' proofs at which he had been working overnight.
He glanced at the title page, which was uppermost. "*Travers
on Ejectment.* Sixth Edition. Edited by Francis Pettigrew,
M.A., LL.B., sometime Scholar of St. Mark's College,
Oxford, sometime Fellow of All Souls, sometime Blackstone
Scholar in Common Law, of the Outer Temple, Barrister-
at-Law." The reiterated "sometime" irritated him. It
seemed to have been the keynote of his whole life. Some
time he was going to be successful and make money. Some
time he would take silk, become a Bencher of his Inn.
Some time he would marry and have a family. And now in
a sudden rush of disillusionment, from which he strove to
exclude self-pity, he saw quite clearly that "some time" had
become "never". "There was a cherry-stone too many on
the plate, after all!" he thought grimly.

Looking back at the confident, and—he could fairly say
it now—brilliant young man who had opened his career at
the Bar beneath that self-same flaking plaster ceiling, he fell
to wondering what had gone wrong with him. Everything
had promised well at first, and everything had turned out
ill. There were plenty of excuses, of course—there always
were. The war, for one thing—that other war, already being
shouldered into oblivion by its successor—which had interrupted his practice just as he was showing signs of "getting
going". A bad choice of chambers, burdened by an idle
and incompetent clerk, for another. Private difficulties
which had kept his mind off his work at critical moments—
the long drawn out agony of his pursuit of Hilda, for
example. God! What a dance she had led him! And,
looking at it dispassionately, how extremely sensible she had
been to take the decision she did! All these and other things
he remembered, the friends who had let him down, the
promises of support unfulfilled, the shining performances
unrecognized. But to be honest, and for once he felt like
being honest with himself, was not the over-riding cause of

Francis Pettigrew's lack of success—no, if he was to be honest why not call things by their proper names?—of his failure, then, simply something lacking in Francis Pettigrew himself? Something that he lacked and others, whom he knew to be his inferiors in so many ways, possessed in full measure? Some quality that was neither character nor intellect nor luck, but without which none of these gifts would avail to carry their possessor to the front? And if so, how much did he, Francis Pettigrew, care?

He let his mind go back to the past, indifferent to the growing clamour and bustle in the Court around him. Well it hadn't been a bad life, taking it all round. If anybody had told him, twenty-five years ago, that middle age would find him eking out a precarious practice by the drudgery of legal authorship, he would have felt utterly humiliated at the prospect. But looking back on the road he had travelled, though it had had some uncomfortable passages, he found little to regret. He had had some good times, made some good jokes—just how much his incurable levity of speech had told against him in his profession was luckily hidden from him—made and kept some good friends. Above all, the Circuit had been good to him. Circuit life was the breath of his nostrils. Year by year he had travelled it from Markhampton right round to Eastbury, less and less hopeful of any substantial earnings, but certain always of the rewards that good fellowship brings. Of course, the old Southern was not what it was. The Mess was a dull place now in comparison with the old days. When he had first joined it, there had been some real characters in its ranks—men of a type one didn't see nowadays, men who bred legends which he, Pettigrew, and a few old stagers like him, could alone remember. That race was long since extinct. Those strange, lovable, ferocious oddities belonged to a bygone era, and his successors would have nobody to remember who was worthy even to father a good story on.

So mused Pettigrew, all unconscious of the fact that in the eyes of every member of the mess under forty he was already a full-blown "character" himself.

There was a stir in court. Outside, where in the days of peace should have sounded a cheerful fanfare, were heard the shouted commands of the superintendent of police. A moment later Pettigrew, in common with everyone else in court, was on his feet and bowing low. If anybody had happened to look at him at that moment, he would have surprised on that lined but genial face an unusual expression of antagonism, not unmixed with contempt. There were few people alive who could bring that expression on to Pettigrew's normally kindly features, and unhappily Barber was one of them.

"Silence!" roared an usher to an assembly that was already as mute as mice.

Beamish, standing at the Judge's side, then proceeded to declaim in a peculiar warbling baritone of which he was inordinately proud, "All manner of persons having anything to do before My Lords the King's Justices of Oyer and Terminer and general Gaol Delivery in and for the County of Markshire draw near and give your attendance." Nobody moved. They were all in attendance already and a posse of ushers made sure that they should draw no nearer to the fount of justice. "My Lords the King's Justices do straightly command All Persons to keep Silence while the Commission of the Peace is read."

All Persons continued to keep silence. The Clerk of Assize then took up the tale in a thin treble, "George the Sixth, by the Grace of God. . . ." After Beamish's elocution his performance was somewhat of an anti-climax, but the formalities were got through without disaster. The Clerk bowed to the Judge, the Judge to the Clerk. At the right moments His Lordship perched upon his wig a small three-cornered hat, and for a few delirious instants looked like a judicial version of MacHeath. The vision passed all too quickly and the hat was laid aside, to be seen no more until the next circuit town.

Beamish boomed once more. This time his target was the High Sheriff, whom he commanded to be pleased to deliver the Several Writs and Precepts to him directed that My Lords the King's Justices might Proceed Thereon. With the air of a conjuror, Carter produced a roll of papers, tightly bound in pale yellow ribbon. This he handed with a bow to Habberton. Habberton handed it with a deeper bow to Barber. Barber, with a bare nod passed it down to the Clerk of Assize. The Clerk put it on his desk and what became thereafter of the Several Writs and Precepts nobody ever knew. Those all important instruments were certainly never heard of again.

The little procession filed out once more, and reappeared a few minutes later. This time His Lordship was seen to be wearing his bob wig and had abandoned his white-trimmed scarlet hood. It was a sign that the time for mere ceremony was over and that the grim business of criminal justice was about to begin. To Derek Marshall, experiencing his first contact with the criminal law, it was an august, a thrilling moment.

There was a brief, whispered colloquy between Judge and Clerk, and then:

"Let Horace Sidney Atkins surrender!" piped the Clerk.

A meek, middle-aged man in a grey flannel suit climbed into the dock, blinked nervously at the magnificence that his wrong-doing had somehow collected together, and pleaded guilty to the crime of bigamy.

Markhampton Assizes were under way at last.

Chapter 2

LUNCH AT THE LODGINGS

"Marshal!" said the Judge in a hoarse whisper. It was
his Court whisper, something quite different from any tone
normally used by him—or indeed by anyone else.

Derek, in his seat on the Judge's left hand, started somewhat guiltily. Despite his enthusiasm for the law, he had
found a succession of the small cases taken first on the
calendar intolerably dull. Casting about for some occupation, he had seized on the only literature immediately
available—the Testaments provided for witnesses taking the
oath. Markshire not being a county much inhabited by
Jews, except for those too wealthy to be often encountered
in the criminal courts, the Pentateuch was little in demand
for this purpose; and Derek was deep in the Book of Exodus
when the imperious summons reached him. With an effort
he dragged his mind away from the court of Pharaoh to the
far less interesting court in which Barber was dispensing
justice, and bent his head to catch the great man's orders.

"Marshal," the whisper went on, "ask Pettigrew to lunch."

It was the second day of the assize. The hour was
12.30 p.m. and Pettigrew was just tying the red tape round
his second and last brief before leaving the court. Barber, if
he had so desired, could have sent his invitation at any time
after the sitting of the court that morning. By delaying it to
the last moment he must have known that he was combining
the pleasures of dispensing hospitality with the maximum
of inconvenience to his guest. Such, at least, was Pettigrew's

21

first reflection when, having bowed himself out of court, he finally received the message in the dank and cheerless cell that served as counsel's robing-room at the Shire Hall. He had planned to catch the only fast train of the afternoon to London, which left at one o'clock, and lunch on the way. If he accepted he could hardly avoid spending another night in Markhampton. Moreover, the Judge had expressed his intention of dining with the mess. Two meals in Barber's company was more than enough for one day. On the other hand, there was nothing to make his presence in London necessary. Barber, who was quite alive to the state of Pettigrew's practice, knew this also and would be certain to take a refusal as an affront. And that, Pettigrew reflected, would mean that he would have his knife into him for the rest of the circuit. He pondered the alternatives, wrinkling his nose in a characteristic fashion, as he tenderly folded his wig into its battered tin box.

"Lunch with his Lordship, eh?" he said at last. "Who else is coming?"

"The High Sheriff and the Chaplain, and Mrs. Habberton."

"Which is she? The rather pretty, silly-looking woman who sat behind him? She looked as if she might be quite good value. . . . All right, I'll come."

Derek, a little upset at the cavalier treatment of a quasi-royal command, was about to leave, when another member of the Bar, a contemporary of Pettigrew's, came in.

"I'm just off," said the newcomer. "Will you share a taxi down to the station?"

"Sorry, I can't. I'm staying to lunch."

"Oh! Father William's invited you, I suppose?"

"Yes."

"Sooner you than me, brother. So long!"

Derek, greatly mystified, made bold to ask, "Excuse me, sir, why did he call him Father William?"

Pettigrew regarded him quizzically.

"Have you met Lady Barber?" he asked.

"No."

"You will shortly, no doubt. Do you know *Alice in Wonderland*?"

"Of course."

> "*In my youth, said his Father, I studied the law,*
> *And argued each case with my wife;*
> *And the muscular strength——*

Look here, you'd better be getting back to court, or the Judge will be rising on you unawares. He must be pretty nearly through his list. See you at lunch, then."

After the young man had gone, Pettigrew remained for a few moments alone in the dingy robing-room, his lean face puckered in thought.

"Silly of me to talk to the boy like that," he murmured. "After all, he may *like* Barber. And he's certain to like Hilda. . . . Oh well!"

He fought down a twinge of remorse. At this time of day, it wasn't as if he need have any fine feelings so far as *she* was concerned!

Pettigrew, who had walked up from the Shire Hall, arrived at the Lodgings just after the other guests. He entered the drawing-room just in time to hear Barber repeating, "Marshall by name and Marshal by occupation," and the burst of girlish laughter that signified Mrs. Habberton's appreciation of the jest. Her laughter was not the only girlish thing about her, Pettigrew observed, as introductions were effected. Her manner, her clothes, her complexion, were all designed to foster the illusion that although she could not have been less than forty by the calendar, she remained essentially no more than nineteen—and a somewhat callow nineteen at that. And yet, he reflected, "designed" was hardly the right word. Nobody quite so obviously brainless could be properly said to have designed

23

anything. The truth seemed to be that it had never entered Mrs. Habberton's fluffy, still pretty head that she was in any way different from the fluffy, pretty girl who had married from the schoolroom twenty odd years before. And one had only to glance at her husband to see that he did not notice any difference either. In a few years time she would probably be a rather pathetic spectacle. Meanwhile she retained a certain kittenish charm which Pettigrew acknowledged to be not without its attractions. Barber appeared to share his opinion.

Marshall, still rather pink about the gills from the echo of Mrs. Habberton's laughter, dispensed sherry with an unsteady hand, and a moment or two later Savage flung open the door and announced, with a deep curvature of the spine, "Luncheon is served, my Lord!"

Mrs. Habberton moved towards the door, but the Judge was there before her.

"Forgive me," he grated, "but on circuit it is customary for the Judge to take precedence of everybody—even of ladies."

"Oh, of course! How silly of me, I forgot!" tinkled Mrs. Habberton. "You are the King, aren't you? How very naughty of me! And I suppose I ought to have curtsied when I came into the room?"

Barber's voice floated back through the doorway.

"Personally, I don't care for all this sort of thing, but some of my colleagues. . . ."

It was a very substantial lunch. Rationing was then still in the future and Mrs. Square, the cook, had been nurtured in a tradition which was not to be disturbed by such minor matters as a war. Mrs. Habberton, to whom housekeeping was a perpetual nightmare, twittered with envy and excitement as she surveyed the menu. She saw, disguised in Mrs. Square's idiosyncratic French, fillets of sole, lamb cutlets, pancakes and an untranslatable savoury. Her eyes sparkled with childish delight.

"Four courses for lunch!" she exclaimed. "In wartime! It's a revelation!"

As usual, she was conscious, too late, that she had said the wrong thing. Her husband reddened, the Chaplain coughed awkwardly. The Judge raised his eyebrows abruptly, as abruptly lowered them again, and took breath to speak.

"Now he's going to talk about his colleagues again," thought Pettigrew, and plunged desperately in to the rescue. As usual, he said the first thing that came into his head.

"The four courses of the Apocalypse, in fact," he remarked.

In the silence that followed he had time to reflect that he could hardly have said anything worse. There was, it was true, a brief splutter of laughter from the Marshal, but this subsided instantly under the Judge's stare of disapproval. Mrs. Habberton, for whose sake the sally had been made, showed an expression of blank incomprehension. The Chaplain looked professionally pained. The High Sheriff seemed to find his collar tighter than ever.

His Lordship, in the exercise of his royal prerogative, helped himself first to fish, still in ponderous silence. Then he said pointedly:

"Let me see, Pettigrew, are you prosecuting in the murder trial this afternoon?"

("He knows damn well I'm not," thought Pettigrew. It was some time since an Attorney-General's nomination on circuit had come his way, and privately he considered that Barber had not a little to do with this.) Aloud he said suavely, "No, Judge, Frodsham is leading for the prosecution. Flack is the junior, I think. Perhaps you are thinking of the Eastbury murder, where I am to defend."

"Ah yes!" replied Barber. "That is a Poor Person's Defence, is it not?"

"That is so, Judge."

"It is a wonderful system," the Judge went on, turning to

25

Mrs. Habberton, "by which nowadays the poor can obtain the assistance of even experienced counsel at the expense of the State. Though I fear", he added, "the fees allowed are sadly inadequate. I think it shows great unselfishness on your part, Pettigrew, to undertake such a case. It can hardly be worth your while to come so far for such small reward, when you might, no doubt, be earning far more substantial sums elsewhere."

Pettigrew bowed and smiled politely, but his eyes were glassy with anger. All this heavy-handed irony at the expense of his poor, shrinking practice by way of revenge for one feeble joke! It was typical of the man. The Eastbury murder was a case of considerable difficulty and likely to attract fairly wide attention even in the middle of a war. Pettigrew had looked forward to its giving him some welcome publicity, which might extend beyond the confines of the Southern Circuit. Now he realized with a sinking heart, that if Barber could so arrange matters it would prove to be merely another flash in the pan. He found time, too, to wonder whether his client would be hanged merely because the Judge had a down on his counsel.

Meanwhile Barber continued to pontificate.

"Undoubtedly the system is an improvement on the old days," he pronounced. "But I'm sure I don't know what some of my predecessors on the Bench would have thought of it. They would have seen something very illogical in an arrangement by which the State, having decided that a man should be charged with an offence, should go to the expense of paying somebody to endeavour to persuade a jury that he was innocent. I think they would have considered it part and parcel of that sentimentality which in many directions is becoming far too common nowadays."

Colonel Habberton murmured sympathetically. Like many another honest man, he lived by catchwords. "Sentimentality" was linked with "Bolshevism" in his mind as the root of all evil, and there were few reforms, social or poli-

LUNCH AT THE LODGINGS

tical, that did not come under one heading or the other.

"This outcry against capital punishment, for instance," said the Judge, and the conversation which had been in danger of becoming a monologue instantly became general. Everybody had something to say about capital punishment. Everybody always has. Even the Marshal produced some ill-digested recollections of what he had once heard someone say in a college debating society upon the subject. Pettigrew alone remained silent, for very good reasons of his own. He knew quite well that his turn was coming, and he had not long to wait.

"Sentimentality is a disease that particularly affects the young," the Judge remarked. "Pettigrew, for instance, used to be a most violent opponent of hanging. Isn't that so, Pettigrew?"

"I still am, Judge."

"Dear, dear!" Barber clicked his tongue sympathetically. "The illusions of youth die hard with some of us. Personally, so far from abolishing the death penalty, I should be in favour of extending it."

"Stretching the stretching, in fact," Pettigrew murmured to Derek, who sat next to him.

"What did you say, Pettigrew?" said Barber, who was not nearly so deaf as all judges are popularly supposed to be. "Oh! Ah! yes! Well, you will have your joke, but some of us consider the subject a serious one. I should be strongly in favour of the execution of far more criminals to-day. The habitual thief, for example, or the reckless motorist. I should hang them all. They are better out of this world."

"And in the next," said the Chaplain unexpectedly, "they may be sure to find Justice."

Of all the solecisms at this unhappy lunch party, this was undoubtedly the most devastating. A man of God had actually presumed to make a public profession of his beliefs—beliefs, moreover which hinted at the existence of a justice superior to that dispensed in the High Court! It

27

put a summary end to a discussion which, if never very profound, had at least been lively, and cast a complete pall over the rest of the proceedings. Thereafter conversation languished and died in spite of intermittent efforts to revive it. Mrs. Habberton, in an attempt to make the party "go", put her foot into it once more by asking the Judge whether he thought the prisoner in the case for trial that afternoon had really "done it", but apart from this nothing was said worthy of record. Savage, reinforced for the occasion by Greene, bustled to and fro with the admirable dishes. Behind the door a mysterious individual known as the house-butler was occasionally to be seen handling bottles and plates. But the best of food, drink and service could not disguise the fact that the lunch, as an entertainment, was a failure. Everybody was relieved when Savage announced that the cars were at the door and Barber retired to assume his wig before returning to Court.

His expression still sullen and morose, the Judge was walking through the hall of the lodgings on his way to the door when Beamish handed him a letter.

"Excuse me, my Lord," he murmured, "but I found this just now. It must have arrived while your Lordship was at luncheon."

Barber looked at the envelope, raised his eyebrows and opened it. The message inside was quite short, and he read it through in a moment. As he did so, his face cleared, and for the first time that afternoon he looked positively cheerful. Then he handed it to Derek.

"This will amuse you, Marshal," he said. "You'd better give it to the Chief Constable when you get to Court."

Derek took the flimsy, typewritten sheet, and Pettigrew, standing behind him, read it over his shoulder. It ran as follows:

To Justice Barber, alias Shaver:
Justice will be done, even to judges. Be sure your sins will find you out. You are warned.

There was no signature.

"Now that is the kind of thing that cheers up an assize," said Barber genially. "Good-bye, Mrs. Habberton, it has been a great pleasure to meet you. So long, Pettigrew. I shall see you in mess this evening. Are you ready, Mr. Sheriff?" And he drove off in high good humour.

Pettigrew, looking after him, had to admit to a certain feeling of admiration.

"Damn it all, the old brute has guts!" he murmured.

None the less, he did not greatly look forward to his dinner in mess that evening.

Chapter 3

A DINNER AND ITS SEQUEL

It was unusual for the Judge to be entertained by the Bar at the first town on the circuit, but this departure from custom was being made at his own request. Pettigrew, who was a stickler for tradition, strongly disapproved, but the rest of the mess saw no objection. One evening was as good as another for a mild jollification. Besides it was known that Lady Barber would be joining him for the rest of the circuit, and it seemed only fair to give the Shaver an evening out while he could have it. It was an excuse to finish the champagne which had been quite long enough in the cellars of the Red Lion, and they struggled into their stiff shirts with a good grace.

Barber had insisted that it should be an informal evening, and he marked the informality by driving Derek down to the hotel in his own car, waving aside the offer of the Sheriff's Rolls Royce. He was still in the genial mood that had come over him immediately after lunch. The afternoon's work had been unexpectedly light. The prisoner, midway through the case for the prosecution, had, upon a broad hint from the bench, offered a plea of guilty to manslaughter, which was promptly accepted. Derek, who had been looking forward to hearing his first death sentence in the sickly state of excitement of a tourist at his first bullfight, felt a mixture of disappointment and relief at the tame conclusion. The Judge, despite his bloodthirsty conversation at table, had shown every sign of satisfaction at the result and imposed a sentence which erred, if at all, on the side of lenience. Derek, who was not wholly devoid of brains, came to the conclusion that his outburst at lunch was no more than a mild attack of exhibitionism, and further that the presence of Pettigrew had something to do with it.

· About a dozen men in all comfortably filled the small room allocated to the mess at the Red Lion. (It was rumoured that there were women members of the Southern Circuit, but apart from paying their entrance fees, they were not encouraged to take part in its activities. The local solicitors were conservative folk and saw to it that no hope of briefs should tempt them to disturb the ancient masculinity of the mess.) The chair was occupied by Frodsham, the only leader present, a plump, affable man of no great attainments, but gifted with an air of success and prosperity that was rapidly making him successful and prosperous. The Judge sat on his right and Derek opposite the Judge. On Derek's left was the Clerk of Assize, a tremulous old gentleman with a weakness for taking snuff. Pettigrew, whether by accident or design, had placed himself as far as possible from Barber, on the left of the Junior, who as custom prescribed, sat at the foot of the table. Here the younger members present had naturally gravitated. Pettigrew enjoyed the society of the young, and he was aware that they enjoyed his, although he was beginning to suspect that they regarded him rather as a museum piece than as a human being like themselves.

The Judge's good humour lasted through dinner, and, assisted by an adequate supply of champagne, communicated itself to the rest of the company. He gave his views upon the war, which were no better or worse than anybody else's views in October 1939. He told, inevitably, a number of anecdotes of his early days at the Bar, and as the evening wore on, became mildly sentimental about old times on the circuit, which he hinted, was not what it had been. Pettigrew, who was in the habit of thinking exactly the same thing, listened to him with barely concealed scorn. One of his minor grievances against Barber was that he had never been a true circuiteer. As soon as he possibly could he had deserted the rough and tumble of the assize courts for the flesh-pots of London. For years before his appointment to the bench he had been a member of the Southern in name only, requiring exorbitant fees to tempt him into the country, away from his ever-growing practice in the Strand. No harm in that, Pettigrew conceded. He too had dreamed of a rich metropolitan practice in his time. But he loathed hypocrisy and he had his own reasons for loathing this particular hypocrite. It enraged him beyond measure to hear this impostor pretending to those who knew no better that he was a true heir to circuit traditions and a repository of circuit lore.

They had reached the stage of brandy and cigars, when the Judge rose to his feet.

"There are a lot of fine old circuit customs which are in danger of being forgotten," he observed. "Here is one that may be new to many of the younger members present. Indeed I think that I am probably the only person here old enough to remember it, and I should like to revive it. It is the old toast which used always to be proposed by the senior member of the mess at the first Grand Night of the Michaelmas Term. I give it you now—Fiat Justitia!"

"Wonderful what a lot the Judge knows about these old customs," his neighbour observed to Pettigrew, after the toast had been duly honoured.

"Wonderful," said Pettigrew drily. The toast should have been "Ruat Coelum", and it was drunk at the end of the Summer Term, and was proposed always by the Junior. These trifling exceptions apart, Father William had got it perfectly. But it didn't matter. As the old fraud had truly said, circuit customs were in danger of being forgotten; and Pettigrew had by now drunk enough not to care greatly one way or the other.

"By the way, Marshal," remarked his Lordship to Derek as he resumed his seat, "did you give that *billet doux* of mine to the Chief Constable?"

"Yes," said Derek. "He seemed to take it—well, rather more seriously than you did."

"It's his business to take things seriously. Besides, he hasn't seen so many of them as I have. It is extraordinary", he went on, turning to Frodsham, "how many anonymous letters a Judge receives in the course of his career. One takes no notice of them, of course. You'll need to cultivate a thick skin when you arrive on the bench, I assure you."

"Oh come, Judge, my ambitions hardly go as far as that, you know," said Frodsham in a tone which made it very clear that they did. "What was this particular letter about?"

"It was merely a threat of the usual vague kind. Rather more offensive than usual so far as I remember. What did the Chief Constable say about it, Marshal?"

"He didn't say very much. He just looked rather glum and said, 'That will be Heppenstall, I shouldn't wonder.'"

"Heppenstall?" said Barber sharply.

"It was some name like that, I think. He seemed to know all about him."

The Judge said nothing for some time after that, but he helped himself liberally to the brandy.

The cessation of the flow of reminiscence from the head of the table seemed to put a momentary damper on the high spirits of the evening, and Frodsham was quick to notice it.

"Mr. Junior," he called down the table, "will you kindly designate some member to entertain us?"

This was a tradition of the mess that everybody knew. On being designated to entertain the company, the chosen member was bound forthwith to contribute a song, story or impersonation upon pain of a substantial fine. If his contribution failed to entertain, the penalty was equally substantial and decidedly undignified.

"I designate Pettigrew," replied the Junior without hesitation.

Pettigrew stood up and stood silent for a moment, his nose contorted in wrinkles that lost themselves between his eyebrows. Then he said, in crisp professional tones,

"Mr. Junior, I beg to contribute the story of Mr. Justice Rackenbury and the case of indecent assault tried at these assizes in the Hilary Term of nineteen hundred and thirteen."

There was an anticipatory burst of laughter. Everybody present had heard of the story, most were familiar with more or less garbled versions of it, and Pettigrew had told it at circuit dinners half a dozen times at least. That made no difference. This story was a legend, and legends do not lose their potency by repetition. Rather, in the hands of accomplished bards, they gather with the years fresh accretions which add to their value as part of the inherited lore of the tribe. The mess sat back in confidence that they would be well and truly entertained.

It was, in fact, for the time and place, a good story—mildly obscene, highly technical, and told at the expense of an amiable company lawyer whose incompetence as a criminal judge had long since passed into history. Pettigrew told it well, his expression never varying and his voice maintaining throughout the dry tones of an advocate discussing some unexciting point of procedure. He appeared to be unconscious of the gusts of merriment around him and when the tale reached its indecorous conclusion seemed quite surprised to find himself on his legs and the centre of hilarious applause.

In fact, so familiar was the story to him that he had for the most part recited it almost absentmindedly, while his thoughts were busy on another plane. Once launched on the well worn grooves of the famous dialogue between Rackenbury and the prisoner awaiting sentence, he could safely leave his tongue to take care of itself. His brain, meanwhile,

34

was occupied with half a dozen different things, mostly trivial enough. Presently, however, one question came to occupy it to the exclusion of all others. This was, quite simply, "What on earth is the matter with the Shaver?"

For the Shaver was not laughing with the others. More, he was not listening. He was sitting glumly regarding the tablecloth and from time to time helping himself to another liqueur brandy from the bottle which had somehow become anchored at his elbow. Characteristically, Pettigrew's first anxiety was for the brandy. "There's not too much of that 'Seventy-Five left," he reflected. "I must remember to tell the Wine Committee at the next meeting. Of course, we'll never be able to get any more as good as that, but we must do the best we can. . . . Sickening to see the Shaver hogging that grand stuff. Not like him, either. He'll be tight if he isn't careful." He found that he had finished the story and sat down abruptly.

Barber was not tight, but he had certainly had enough to drink, and if he went on at the rate he was going it would not be long before he would have had too much. Something of the kind seemed to have occurred to him, for the laughter that crowned Pettigrew's efforts had hardly subsided before he suddenly pushed away his glass and said across the table, "Marshal! It's time we were getting home."

Derek was not a little disappointed. The night was still young and he was just beginning to enjoy himself. But obviously there was nothing to be done about it. The distinguished guest rose from table and the party automatically broke up. Derek retrieved their hats and coats and they went out into the hall. Frodsham and one or two others accompanied them out. Looking round to say "Good night" to these, Barber saw amongst them Pettigrew, also dressed for the street.

"What are you doing, Pettigrew?" he asked in surprise. "Aren't you staying here?"

"No, Judge, I'm stopping at the County."

Barber might not be a good circuiteer, but he knew enough to understand exactly what staying at the County implied. The Red Lion was not only the regular hotel for the mess, the place to which "letters and parcels for gentlemen of the Bar" were ordered to be directed by the circuit notices, it was the only first class establishment in Markhampton. Everybody stayed there as a matter of course. Everybody, that is who could afford to. To stay at the County, which in spite of its name was a miserable pothouse, was a confession of dire poverty. The Judge took a quick look at Pettigrew, at the shabby overcoat and the frayed trouser legs which showed beneath them.

"The County, eh?" he said after a pause. "How are you getting there?"

"I shall walk. I like a bit of fresh air after dinner."

"Nonsense. I'll give you a lift. It's on my way."

"No really, Judge. I'd much sooner walk."

Outside it was pitch dark and a steady rain was falling.

"You can't walk in this," said the Judge testily, "get in!"

Pettigrew, without further words said, got in.

Now there are certain things which in a well-conducted world simply do not occur. In a well-conducted world His Majesty's Judges of assize do not drive their own cars while on circuit. They employ the services of competent professionals supplied and paid by the county whose guests they happen to be. Further, if they do so far forget their dignity as to act as their own chauffeurs—for, after all, they are but human and may be permitted to enjoy driving as much as lesser mortals—they do not do so in the black-out, on a wet, moonless night, and after imbibing rather more than the customary allowance of old brandy. Finally, at all times and seasons, it may be taken for granted that they drive with the utmost care and circumspection. It has regretfully to be recorded that in this, as in so many other instances, the world proved to be somewhat worse conducted than it is popularly supposed to be.

The accident happened at the junction of High Street and Market Place, just after the car had taken the sharp right-hand turn necessary to bring it round the corner. Pettigrew, who was sitting alone in the back, was never able to say with precision exactly what occurred. He was first shaken out of a doze by being thrown sideways in his seat as the car swung round, then heard the squeal from the ball-bearings telling him that the corner had been taken too fast, and finally awoke to full consciousness with the realization that the back wheels were sliding over to the left in a violent skid. A moment later the car struck the nearside kerb with an impact that pitched him headlong into the back of the driver's seat. And that, as he frequently had occasion to remind himself later on, was absolutely all that he knew about it. He would be wholly useless as a witness. That was some comfort.

It was a little time before Pettigrew pulled himself together sufficiently to get out of the car and inspect the damage. When he finally scrambled out on to the wet, slippery pavement he collided with two almost invisible objects which proved to be Barber and Marshall. They were standing very close together, as though for mutual support, and even in the darkness their attitude had an appearance of helplessness. The next thing he observed was a small spot of light in the road immediately behind the car. Shaken as he was, it was a little time before he realized that this light proceeded from a policeman's lantern and that it was focused upon something—no, upon someone—lying in the middle of a pedestrian crossing close to the car's tail lamp.

"Oh Lord," Pettigrew groaned, rubbing his head. "This is a pretty kettle of fish."

He pulled himself together, and walked out into the road.

"Yes," said the constable shortly. "There's no bones broken. We might move him."

He bent down, grasped the unconscious man beneath the shoulders, Pettigrew took him by the legs, and together they carried him to the side of the road. There the constable arranged his cape to form a rough support for his head, while Marshall, who had now come forward, brought a rug from the car to put over him. There followed a pause of a few moments during which no one spoke. It suddenly occurred to Pettigrew that this was a very young officer and that he was probably racking his brains as to the next step in the road accident procedure. Obviously, the proper thing to do in normal circumstances would be for the Shaver to drive his victim to the nearest hospital, but he had not offered to do so, and Pettigrew could see several good reasons why he should not. The less publicity about this business, the better for all concerned, he reflected.

"Shall I see if I can get an ambulance?" he said aloud.

The young policeman came to life at once.

"You stay here—all of you," he commanded.

He walked a few paces away, to where in the gloom Pettigrew could now just discern a telephone box. He was only away a few moments, but it seemed quite a long time to those who waited. The Judge was still standing quite still and silent, his slightly bent form a picture of dejection. Pettigrew did not feel equal to addressing him. To Marshall he said quietly:

"Lucky there's nobody about, anyway."

"There was someone just now," Derek answered softly. "I saw him just as I got out of the car. He made off when the bobby came up, though."

"Hell!" said Pettigrew.

"I say, sir, do you think he's badly hurt?"

"M'm. 'Fraid so."

The officer returned, his steps sounding now brisk and confident.

"The ambulance will be here in a moment," he announced. His notebook came out with a flourish, and he

38

turned to Barber. "You were the driver of this vehicle, I think, sir?" he said. "Your name and address, if you please?"

"Perhaps, officer, I can explain matters," began Pettigrew smoothly.

"One at a time, if you please, sir," interrupted the constable, now evidently completely the master of himself and the proceedings. He turned to Barber once more. "Your name and address, if you please?"

Barber gave it. It was the first time he had spoken since the accident had happened, and his voice sounded even harsher than usual. The young policeman, who had begun to write automatically in his book, stopped abruptly, and his lantern wavered perceptibly for an instant. Then discipline reasserted itself and he finished his writing, breathing heavily as he did so. It was an awkward moment, and one for which no instructions are laid down in the manuals issued for the guidance of recruits to the Markhampton Constabulary.

"Er—just so, my lord," he said. "Just so. I——" he paused and gulped, but went on bravely—"I'm afraid I shall have to ask for your lordship's driving licence and insurance certificate."

"Just so," said Barber, repeating his words with what sounded like almost ironic emphasis. Going to the car, he took from it a small folder, which he handed to the constable.

"You will find them both in there," he grated.

At this point a diversion was effected by the arrival of the ambulance. In what seemed to Pettigrew an amazingly short space of time, the injured man was examined, bandaged, picked up and borne away, leaving nothing to mark his passing but the constable's cape, lying neatly folded on the pavement. It's owner took it up, shook it, and, the rain having by now stopped, rolled it up and put it under his arm. Then he resumed his study of the documents handed to him by the Judge.

In a well-conducted world—let it be repeated—all motorists without exception, but particularly Judges of the High

Court, renew their driving licences when they expire. Further, well before the due season, they take advantage of the reminders which their insurance companies are good enough to send them and provide themselves with the certificate required by the Road Traffic Acts, 1930 to 1936. The fact that from time to time they carelessly forget to do so, and thereby commit quite a number of distinct and separate offences, only goes to prove once more how far from perfectly conducted the actual world is. The fact that even Judges of the High Court are not immune from lapses of memory is perhaps an argument in favour of the proposition that in a well-conducted world they would not be allowed to drive motor-cars at all.

"I'm afraid, my lord," said the officer, "there seems to be something wrong with these here."

Barber looked at them under the lantern.

"They appear to be out of date," he remarked sadly, almost humbly.

"In that case, my lord, I must ask you——"

But Derek at this point suddenly and unexpectedly asserted himself.

"Don't you think, officer," he said, "that the best thing would be for you to report the whole matter to your superior, and then perhaps the Chief Constable could come and discuss the matter quietly with his lordship at the Lodgings? All this is—well, a little unsuitable, perhaps."

The constable, obviously relieved, jumped at the offer.

"Perhaps you're right, sir," he said. "If I can just have your name and the other gentleman's."

The notebook was flourished for the last time, and a moment or two later the incident was closed—for the time being, at least. Pettigrew, who found himself close to his hotel, walked away, while Derek, in his new-found position of authority, firmly announced that he would drive the Judge home, and got into the driver's seat without waiting for permission.

A DINNER AND ITS SEQUEL

"Damned old fool! Damned old fool!" Pettigrew found himself repeating again and again as he walked the short distance back to the County. His head was aching from the blow that it had received when the car hit the pavement, his thin soles let in the damp from the pavement, he was tired, bruised and angry. Particularly was he angry. From first to last the responsibility for his plight rested on the Shaver, but for whom he would at that moment have been snug in bed in London. In the reaction from the hilarity of the evening, he began to feel as if the mishap which had succeeded it had been deliberately planned by the Judge to cause him annoyance. The Shaver's lapse in the little matter of the driving licence and insurance certificate only served to increase his wrath. In a way, it gave him a certain grim pleasure to find his enemy in this undignified predicament, but this was more than counterbalanced by disgust that one of His Majesty's Judges should have disgraced himself in such a way. There was probably not a judge on the bench whom Pettigrew had not at one time or another criticized, lampooned or held up to ridicule in some post-prandial recitation for the benefit of the mess. As individuals, he liked not a few, admired many, but reverenced none. He knew them too well, had studied them too closely, to have any illusions about them. But for the Bench as a whole, he felt a deep unspoken respect which went to the very roots of his being. It was the symbol of what he lived by and for, and anything that would tarnish the good name of the order in the eyes of the outside world, as distinct from the little charmed circle of lawyers, affronted him deeply. As the sense of his own personal grievance wore off, the greater did the enormity of Barber's conduct appear, and by the time that he had finished his short walk, he was possessed by one thought only—that at all costs this affair must if possible be kept out of the papers.

"The City Chief Constable's a sensible man," he mused. "There won't be any criminal proceedings, anyhow. We can

41

bank on that. Let's hope he can put the fear of death into that young copper and see that he keeps his mouth shut. As for Marshall, obviously he's got his head screwed on the right way. He ought to be safe. Better have a talk to him in the morning, all the same. Lucky there weren't any outside witnesses, except one, and he wasn't there when the old idiot gave his name. Odd thing, incidentally, the way he sheered off. . . . It's always a job to stop people talking, but it might be managed. . . ."

Still pursuing his train of thought, he pushed open the swing door of his hotel and stepped into the momentarily dazzling light of the hall. His way through to the stairs led him past the inner entrance to the saloon bar, and as he passed he heard the cry of "Time, gentlemen, please!" He was astonished to find that it was no later. True, the mess had dined at its usual early hour, and, thanks to the Judge, the evening had not run its full course. But so much had happened since that he could hardly believe that the County was in fact keeping legitimate hours, and he peered in through the door to glance at the clock.

The bar was full and noisy with the mellow voices of patrons putting away their last drinks. The air was cloudy with tobacco smoke and rich with a warm, moist smell of beer and humanity. Pettigrew noted the time by the clock on the far wall and was about to withdraw when his eye was caught by an animated group beneath it. Three or four soldiers and one or two civilians were clustered round a darts board, at which a short, tubby middle-aged man in a dazzling check pullover was taking aim. Evidently the game was in its concluding stages, and excitement was running high. Evidently, also the thrower was a master of the craft. He threw, and a shout went up. "Thirty-four you want!" someone shouted. "Careful now, Corky. Go for——" But Corky evidently knew exactly what he wanted. With a look of perfect confidence he threw again. Another shout. "Double seven!" "Twenty now," said the voice. Pettigrew, who knew nothing whatever of the game felt the rising tide of emotion grip him. He became desperately anxious for Corky to do whatever was necessary, and waited breathlessly for the last throw. He need not have worried. Amid a sudden breathless silence, Corky raised his fat form on his toes with the grace of a dancer, took careful aim and loosed his last shaft. "Double ten!" The noise seemed to make every glass in the bar ring again. Sweating, but otherwise perfectly calm, the triumphant Corky suffered his hand to be wrung, his back to be thumped again and again, and retired to finish his glass, while, the barman thundered, "Time, gentlemen, *please*!"

From the moment that he had set eyes on him, Pettigrew had felt positive that Corky was no stranger; but it was not until he saw the air of quiet dignity with which he submitted to the attentions of his admirers, that he recognized him. This was the more remarkable considering that he had seen him last only that same afternoon. In view of the difference of the surroundings, however, it was not altogether surprising. Pettigrew had attended the beginning of the murder trial less for the sake of hearing Frodsham's opening address to the jury than for the sheer æsthetic amusement it gave him to listen to the modulations of Beamish. Beamish in Court, sombrely resplendent in tail-coat and striped trousers and Corky in the saloon bar, the champion of darts players, seemed about as far apart as two persons could possibly be, but that they were one and the same could not be doubted.

Pettigrew chuckled on his way up to bed. He had at least made an amusing discovery to end the evening with. "If anyone can inform my Lords the King's Justices," he said to himself, striving to recapture the opulent, over-refined tones of Beamish's court voice, "of any treasons, murders, felonies or misdemeanours done or committed by the prisoner at the bar, let him come forth and declare it, for the prisoner now stands upon his deliverance." He wondered whether any of Beamish's saloon-bar friends attended the assizes to hear him do his stuff. Perhaps he kept that side of his life as secret from them as no doubt he did his trips to the County from his employer. "Does the Shaver know he's called Corky?" Pettigrew mused.

For the moment his delight at Beamish's metamorphosis had put Barber out of his mind. Now the problem that had been worrying him returned with double force. In his estimate of the possibilities of keeping this distressing business dark he had forgotten to reckon with Beamish. Clerks always knew everything. Was Beamish reliable? After what he had seen, he did not feel so sure. Unless Beamish was able to keep Corky entirely distinct from his professional life, it was difficult to imagine secrecy and discretion flourishing in the atmosphere of the County bar. Pettigrew got into bed with a furrowed brow and a very wrinkled nose.

Chapter 4

AFTERMATH OF AN ACCIDENT

The Chief Constable of the city made an early call at the lodgings next morning. His interview with the Judge, which might well have been a difficult one, passed off smoothly enough, thanks to the fund of tact and charm which he concealed beneath his bluff buoyant manner. Nothing in terms was said about the unfortunate omission of his Lordship to provide himself with the documents which are normally essential to the legal conduct of a car on the road. Not a word was uttered which could have suggested that the affair was to be hushed up, or, indeed, that there was any affair to be hushed up. At the same time, the effect of the interview was perfectly clear. The Judge, on his side, was deeply sorry at what had occurred, and would certainly not drive his car until what had been left undone had been done. The Chief Constable, on his, guaranteed that nothing more would be heard of the matter, so far as the police were concerned. Meanwhile, without suggesting in any way that he wished his Lordship to do anything so derogatory to his dignity as to "make a statement", he contrived to extract from him a very detailed account of the whole occurrence, which Barber, on his side, was perfectly ready to give. The whole conversation, in fact, was a pleasant little comedy, played on both sides with perfectly grave faces.

When this part of the colloquy was over, the Chief Constable, with a slightly too obvious sigh of relief, blew out his cheeks, sat back in his chair, and accepted the cigarette

which the Judge offered him. He had still something further
to say, and Barber appeared to be in no hurry to be rid of
him.

"You haven't told me," said the latter, "how is the poor
fellow—what is his name, by the way?"

"Sebald-Smith," said the Chief Constable.

"Sebald-Smith," repeated the Judge. "An unusual name.
I seem to have heard it somewhere."

"Not a native of this city, my lord. He was staying with
friends. We had a little difficulty in tracing them."

"Indeed? I trust his injuries are not serious?"

"Quite light, I am glad to say, my lord. A mild concus-
sion, the doctor says, and a finger crushed. Actually the
little finger of his left hand. That is all, apart from a few
small bruises and some slight shock."

"Wounds, bruises and contusions generally, and a severe
shock to the nervous system." Barber's mind went back to
the formula with which he used to conclude the particulars
of damage in the old days when he turned out pleadings in
accident cases by the score.

"He should be out and about in a couple of days," the
Chief Constable was saying.

Barber sighed in relief. Apart from his salary, he was a
poor man. He knew—none better—the scale of damages
normally awarded to plaintiffs in such cases. This sounded
like a case that could be settled—it would have to be settled,
of course—quite cheaply. "Provided they don't have to
amputate the finger," he thought. "That always inflates the
damages in a ridiculous way." He remembered with regret
the substantial solatium that he had awarded a young
woman only the previous term for the loss of a big toe. Hilda
had said at the time that he had been influenced by the fact
that she was not only young but extremely pretty. That was
nonsense, of course, but all the same it was unfortunate. The
case had attracted some attention in the papers, too . . .
still, at the worst, it could not amount to a very large sum.

He rapidly ran over in his mind the economies he would have to make if he were called upon to find, say £200 at short notice; and was a little uneasy to discover that the majority of them would have to be at the expense of the dress and amusements of Lady Barber. On the whole, he concluded, his wife's reception of the night's adventure was going to be one of the most unpleasant sides of the whole affair.

"I am very glad to hear that it is no worse," he said. "Very glad indeed. It is a great load off my mind. Well"—he rose to his feet—"we must both be starting our day's work, I suppose. I am very much obliged to you for coming round to see me about this—this unlucky affair."

"Not at all, my lord, not at all," murmured the Chief Constable confusedly. He also stood up, but seemed somewhat loth to go.

"There is one other little matter, my lord," he said.

"Yes?"

"The anonymous letter which your lordship received yesterday. The County Chief showed it to me."

"Yes, yes! What of it?"

"Well, my lord, we have some reason to think that it may have emanated from a man named Heppenstall. Your lordship will perhaps remember the name——"

"Heppenstall! Oh, yes, quite! Heppenstall!" the Judge murmured. He was not looking at the Chief Constable as he spoke and there was a pained expression on his face that suggested extreme distaste for the name and the subject.

"We know that he was in this city the day before yesterday," the Chief Constable went on hurriedly. "He is out on ticket of leave, of course, and should have reported to the police."

"Then why can't you do something about it?" said Barber irritably. "Arrest him, or something? After all, it's your duty——"

"Quite so, my lord, I appreciate that. Unfortunately, we

47

have lost sight of him, for the time being. It is very difficult to keep touch with people in this blackout, and at the moment I have a number of men on special duty for the Assizes. But there it is. This man is at large and we can't help being a little uneasy about it."

"I should have thought I was the one to be uneasy," said the Judge with a short barking laugh.

"That is just the point, my lord—to save you from uneasiness. Now of course normally, our axiom is that people who intend crimes of violence of this kind don't advertise the fact beforehand. But this man, since his imprisonment, is not quite normal. So far as—so far as his particular grievance is concerned, if you follow me, my lord."

From Barber's expression it was plain that he followed him perfectly, and that he did not greatly enjoy the journey.

"Well?" he said.

"All that I was going to suggest, my lord, was that in the circumstances it might be advisable for us to afford you police protection—in addition, I mean, to the ordinary escort to and from the court. The Lodgings here are rather easily accessible, for instance. I should like to post a man at the door and another at the back of the house. They would be quite unobtrusive—in plain clothes, if your lordship prefers it. Then, in addition, when your lordship goes out for a walk after the court rises, it would be as well to have a man to follow, just in case——"

"I have my Marshal," the Judge objected.

The Chief Constable's face showed fairly clearly that he did not think much of Marshals.

"I should be happier in my mind if you had police protection as well," he said. "After all, it is only for a day or two, and it is my responsibility. If anything were to happen——"

"Very well, if you think it necessary. You have, of course, no proof that the ridiculous letter I received was in fact from this fellow?"

"Not the smallest, my lord. But it is a coincidence which we can't overlook. I only hope we may be wrong. Very likely we shall hear no more about him."

At this point Savage entered the room, and humbly suggested that it was time his lordship robed for Court. The Chief Constable accordingly took his leave.

Pettigrew reached the Lodgings while Barber was in conference with the Chief Constable. He asked for Marshall, and found the young man in a somewhat depressed state of mind.

"So the Judge is talking it over with the Chief, is he?" said Pettigrew cheerfully. "I suppose they're putting their heads together to keep things quiet?"

"That is the idea, I take it," answered Derek in an unexpectedly bitter tone.

"Well, isn't it everyone's?" said Pettigrew. "I imagined it was yours when you suggested it to the constable last night."

"Mine? I simply wanted to get away from the place as soon as I could. I hate hushing things up."

"But my dear fellow, it would never do to have a thing like this proclaimed from the house-tops. Surely you can see that?"

"Things oughtn't to be hushed up," said the young man obstinately. "After all, if there is such a thing as justice——"

"Good Lord! This sort of talk will never do if you mean to be a lawyer," Pettigrew reproved him. "I'm afraid you suffer from ideals."

"I am an idealist, sir, and I'm not ashamed of admitting it."

"Please don't call me 'sir', it makes me feel even older than I am. But seriously, what had you in mind? Having the Judge tried before the local beaks for offences against the Road Traffic Act?"

"Well, yes, I suppose so. I don't see why he should be treated differently, because he is a judge."

Pettigrew shook his head.

"It wouldn't do," he said. "Don't you see, the whole system depends on their being treated differently from ordinary people? It's apt to be rather bad for them as individuals, and to give the weaker brethren swollen heads, but it's good for the administration of the law as a whole, and that's why we've got to back it up for all we're worth. No," he continued, "the problem that really interests me is whether any court would be competent to try a Judge for an offence committed on circuit. You see, he's supposed to be the equivalent of the King, and all that, and the King can do no wrong, but I don't think the question has ever been tried out. Nobody's ever had the courage to prosecute in such circumstances."

"I don't suppose any Judge has ever done such a thing before," suggested the Marshal hopefully.

"For Heaven's sake don't run away with that idea! Judges in the past have done the most outrageous things on circuit. Haven't you ever heard the story of Mr. Justice——"

He launched out into a series of scabrous anecdotes, which left Derek deeply shocked, but helpless with laughter.

"And the moral of that is—hush it up!" he concluded. "None of these stories ever got out. In fact the last one I told you never has got out until this moment, because I made it up for your benefit as I went along. And in return for that kindness I want one from you. Will you keep your mouth shut about this business to all and sundry?"

"Of course I will," said Derek, somewhat hurt. "You needn't really have asked me that."

"Good! I thought there was a limit to your idealism somewhere. Well, I must be off. I'm afraid this business has been rather upsetting to everybody. I shall be surprised if it doesn't leak out somewhere, but if we all keep it under our hats and lie like troopers if necessary there shouldn't be too much harm done. The great thing is there weren't any independent witnesses of the poor Shaver's confession of his identity."

The confidence which Pettigrew had instilled into Derek's mind on this last point was not long-lived. A few minutes later, his lordship, wigged and robed, was about to leave the house, when Beamish handed him another letter. It was similar in appearance to the former one, but its substance was a good deal pithier. It consisted, in fact, of one word only: "*Murderer!*"

Barber read it and shrugged his shoulders. He did not on this occasion show it to anyone else, but crumpled it up and thrust it into his trousers pocket. With a serious expression he climbed into the Rolls Royce, and was driven to the court. There, the criminal business having been disposed of on the previous day, he sat in simple state for the trial of civil actions. The first two cases in the list were actions for damages arising out of motor accidents. Barber tried them admirably, but the damages which he awarded were perhaps rather on the small side.

Chapter 5

LADY BARBER

The Judge had intended to travel to Southington, the next circuit town, in his own car, but in the circumstances this was clearly out of the question. The guilty vehicle was left behind in a garage at Markhampton until such time as it could be moved without offence to the law, and he and his Marshal went with the rest of the ponderous machine of justice by train. It was a tiresome journey. The progress of the Southern Circuit from county to county was still along the path that had seemed good to it since the reign of Henry II. Unfortunately, the railway speculators of the Victorian age, actuated by sordidly commercial considerations, had laid down their lines with little regard for the convenience of the judiciary. Their ideas did not soar beyond the provision of a main line between Markhampton and London, and another from London to Didbury Junction, whence a branch line meandered slowly to Southington. Their soulless, urban minds, preoccupied with the problem of moving passengers and goods to and from the capital, had never entertained the idea of anybody seriously wishing to travel direct from Markhampton to Southington. At all events, perhaps because the two towns were on different railway systems, they made it as difficult as possible. The circuit, which moved with the times, but a pace or two behind them, had discovered, during the course of the nineteenth century, that travel by rail, even along this route, was somewhat quicker than by coach, and had accepted the

railwaymen's grudging facilities. Nowadays, the Southington bus, which does the journey in an hour and a half, passes
the Judge's lodgings at Markhampton three times a day,
but this development of civilization has so far escaped its
official notice.

If the journey was tiresome, involving as it did two
changes and a wait of forty minutes at Didbury Junction,
it was at least made in comfort. A first-class carriage was
reserved for the Judge and his Marshal. Another contained
the Clerk of Assize, the Clerk of Indictments, and the
Associate. Beamish and his myrmidons, as was only proper,
travelled third class, but in equal seclusion. The luggage of
the party, personal and official, absorbed the services of
several porters and almost the whole of a guard's van. The
railway authorities had raised objections to reserving carri-
ages, pleading wholly irrelevant considerations of the difficulties of wartime, but Beamish had soon put an end to
them. "I just said to them," he explained to his admiring
audience, as he dealt the hands for a quiet game of nap, "if
anyone was to get into the same carriage as one of His
Majesty's Judges——!" There was no need for him to finish
the sentence. Everybody present knew that such an event
would be enough to blow the whole British Constitution
sky-high.

The caravan reached its destination in the early afternoon. In the hour that remained before tea, Derek decided
that he ought to write a letter home. Before starting out, he
had, of course, promised his mother to tell her "all about
it"; and equally of course, had failed to keep his promise.
For one thing, he told himself in excuse, it wasn't so easy to
tell "all about it". Like many other people, Mrs. Marshall
imagined that business in the criminal courts was a succession of breath-taking thrills, that every case was a drama,
every counsel a cross-examiner of genius "who could get
anything out of you if he tried", every speech a torrent of

eloquence, every Judge a Solon. If he were to set down a day to day record of his actual experiences so far, she would be, Derek felt, extremely bored and, for she was a prudish woman, not a little disgusted. The only event of real importance that had occurred was the one which he was under an obligation not to mention. For himself, looking back on his experiences so far, he had nothing to complain of. He had learned a good deal and shed quite a number of illusions. His relations with the Judge were as friendly as could be wished, considering the disparity in their ages. At the same time, he had to admit that a prolonged *tête-à-tête* with him could become somewhat tiresome, and he was secretly rather disappointed that, whether because of the Chief Constable's precautions or not, the Markhampton Assizes had ended as tamely as they had begun. He felt himself to be in need of some diversion and wondered idly whether Lady Barber, who was to join them at Southington, would supply it. Derek had reached this point in his meditations, and the letter to his mother was still not begun, when Greene stole softly into his room and announced that tea was ready downstairs and her ladyship had arrived.

Lady Barber was small, dark, streamlined, and good-looking. She talked a good deal, in clipped, commanding tones, and was obviously accustomed to saying what she thought and to having what she said attended to. Without being aggressively smart, she contrived to make the tall, shambling figure beside her look even shabbier than usual. Derek judged her to be about twenty years younger than her husband. He was, in fact, about eight years out in his guess, but more experienced men than he might well have made the same mistake. She greeted him in a brisk, friendly manner, which just escaped being patronizing.

"How do you do, Mr. Marshall? No, I'm not going to make the obvious joke. I dislike obvious jokes and I am sure you have heard that one quite enough already. Let's have some tea at once. I'm chilled to the bone by that wretched train. You must pour out, please! Marshals always do, you know. Milk and two lumps for me, please, even if it is wartime. Now tell me, how are you enjoying this comic existence?"

Derek declared that he was enjoying it very much, and by the time that he had finished his second cup of tea was fairly convinced that he was going to enjoy it a good deal more, so long as the circuit was enlivened by Lady Barber's society. He experienced the slightly exhilarating feeling that in her hands the stately but somewhat lethargic tempo of life in Judge's lodgings would be accelerated into something brisker. She was not a particularly witty woman, nor, to Derek's mind at least, a particularly attractive one; it was simply that she had an immense fund of vitality which stimulated everybody with whom she came into contact to put his best foot foremost in thought or conversation, whether attraction or repulsion was the governing impulse. Derek reflected, after she had left the drawing-room, that he had talked more during the last half-hour than he had done during the whole of the last week; and further that he had talked with unexampled intelligence and wit. It was only later that he realized that he had given himself, his deeds, thoughts and aspirations, completely away under the spell of Lady Barber's practised "drawing out". He had, in fact, been very skilfully, relentlessly cross-examined, and without in the least realizing what was going on. Like many other ingenuous people, he prided himself on being reserved and even a trifle secretive, and the discovery was somewhat painful. Remembering his mother's belief in the capacity of cross-examiners to get "anything out of you if they tried", he told himself, somewhat ruefully, that her ladyship would certainly have made a very good lawyer. This opinion, as it happened, he shared with a number of other people—of whom Lady Barber was certainly one.

Lady Barber's husband (it was curious how easily the

embodied majesty of the law shrank in her society to "Lady Barber's husband") appeared to enjoy her presence at the lodgings as much as did his Marshal, though in a different way. At tea, he sunned himself in the light of her radiance, chuckled at her sallies, and thoroughly relished the spectacle of the young man being put through his paces. At the same time, a closer observer than Derek might have observed that behind his enjoyment lurked a certain apprehension. It would be a gross slander to say that he was afraid of his wife. Rather, he was extremely reluctant to find himself in opposition to her, and if anything had occurred which was likely to cause her annoyance he was in the habit of going to considerable lengths to prevent her knowing it. Experience had told him that as a matter of fact she sooner or later got to know anything of any importance, but at least he did all he could to postpone and so to mitigate the hour of reckoning. It followed that he had said nothing as yet about the accident to his car at Markhampton, and he still hoped against all reason to be able to avoid doing so.

The blow fell sooner than he expected. He had just finished dressing for dinner when his wife came into his room, a packet of letters in her hand.

"These came for you this morning," she said. "I wish you could persuade people to send all your correspondence to the Courts. It is such a nuisance having to forward them when you are away. They don't look particularly interesting."

They did not. Two were obviously circulars, and the rest typewritten envelopes which presumably contained bills. Barber looked at them casually, turning them over in his hand. He had to make one of those minute decisions on which important consequences sometimes depend—whether to stuff them into his pocket or to deal with them at once. He glanced at the clock. There were still five minutes to go before dinner. He decided to open them there and then. By an irony which the Judge, a lover of Hardy, would have appreciated in other circumstances the clock subsequently turned out to be five minutes slow.

He opened one letter and then another, scanning them hurriedly and dropping them into the waste-paper basket. Her ladyship meanwhile made use of his looking-glass to remove some imperceptible blemish in her make-up. He opened the third letter, just as the gong sounded from below. Unfortunately, at the same moment his wife looked up from her labours and caught sight of his expression in the glass.

"What is the matter?" she asked, turning round sharply.

"Nothing, dear, nothing," said the unhappy man in unconvincing tones.

"Nothing? You looked quite upset. Who is your letter from?"

"Oh, nobody in particular. And I'm not upset," he hastened to add. "You always will jump to conclusions, Hilda. I was only puzzled by a name that seems familiar, and I can't place it, that is all."

"What name?"

"Not one that you would know, I expect. It's a curious one—Sebald-Smith."

"Sebald-Smith? My dear, I'm not a complete Philistine. Of course I know the name. He's about the best-known pianist alive, I should think."

"A pianist? Dear me!" For all his efforts at self-control the Judge's dismay was manifest.

"What on earth is all this about?" said her ladyship pettishly and with a superbly graceful movement was across the room and had removed the letter from her husband's nerveless fingers before he was even aware of what had happened.

She read:

My Lord,

We are acting on behalf of Mr. Sebastian Sebald-Smith, who as your lordship will be aware, was injured on the evening of the 12th instant as the result of being knocked down by your lordship's motor-car in Market Place, Markhampton. Our instructions are that the accident was caused solely by the negligence of the driver of the vehicle in question. While we are unable at the moment of writing to make any estimate of the full extent of our client's injuries, it appears clear that he has suffered, among others, a serious damage to the knuckle-joint of one finger which may entail its amputation—a matter which, to a person in our client's position is, of course, one of grave consequence. We should be glad to know the name of your lordship's Insurance Company as soon as possible, and meanwhile must formally put on record our client's intention of claiming damage in respect of his injuries.

Your lordship's obedient servants
Faraday, Fothergill, Crisp & Co.

Lady Barber was some time in commenting on the letter. It was as if she were debating what attitude to take up towards her husband's latest misdemeanour. When she spoke, it was evident that she had decided upon that of one more in sorrow than in anger.

"Really, William, you are incorrigible!" she said. "You were driving the car, I suppose?"

"Yes, I was."

"And I suppose you were entirely to blame?"

"Well, as to that——"

"Of course you were!" she interrupted impatiently. "I've told you often enough that you are not fit to drive at night. It really is lamentable for anybody in your position. Thank Heaven, your name hasn't got into the papers about it. I saw a paragraph to say that Sebald-Smith had been knocked down by a car, but of course I never associated it with you. You never go to concerts, I know, but this escapade of yours is going to make a nasty hole in the musical life of London, whenever that revives again. Sebald-Smith! He's the sort of man who insures his hands for thousands of pounds."

At this reference to insurance the Judge winced.

"Don't you think we had better discuss this after dinner?" he said.

"I don't see that there is anything to discuss," said his wife, sweeping out of the room in front of him, with glorious disregard of circuit convention.

Derek, who had come down to dinner eager to resume the sparkling conversation that he had enjoyed so much at tea, had to confess himself by the end of the evening somewhat disappointed. The fault, so far as he could see, lay with the Judge. Not only had he nothing to say for himself, but his silence succeeded in throwing a gloom over the whole table. Her ladyship, indeed, seemed to be as vivacious as usual. If anything, her colour was a trifle higher, her eyes even brighter than before. But on this occasion her talkativeness seemed to be the result of a deliberate effort and not the delightfully natural ebullience that had so charmed him. Moreover, he observed that she was making no attempt to draw her husband into the conversation. She addressed herself exclusively to the Marshal and for much of the time appeared to be talking at random, with her mind elsewhere. Once or twice he suspected her of talking at the silent figure on the other side of the table. Altogether it was an uncomfortable meal. Derek, oppressed with the uneasy feeling that something was "up", found himself relapsing into tongue-tied awkwardness, and was thoroughly glad when Savage placed the port on the table and Lady Barber left the room.

The Judge drank three glasses of port. As he filled each glass, he looked towards Derek and made as though he were about to say something of importance. Each time, he balked at the fence and ended by making some trivial observation about the work of the forthcoming assize. Finally, as though surrendering to the inevitable, he threw his napkin on the table, observed, "Well, I suppose we had better join my wife," and made for the door.

In the drawing-room, the atmosphere was even more oppressive than at table. There were long periods of silence, broken only by the vicious click of her ladyship's knitting needles. She appeared to be sulky, and her husband to be nervously awaiting something to happen. For all his inexperience, it was not difficult for Derek to guess what that something was. He was waiting to be alone with his wife, and he was not looking forward with any pleasure to the experience. Derek took the hint, though he would have been hard put to it to say exactly how the hint had been conveyed. Pleading the necessity of writing his long-promised letter home, he left the drawing-room as early as he could with decency.

As the door closed behind him, Lady Barber looked up from her knitting and remarked:

"That's a nice boy. Was he with you in the car the other night?"

"Yes, he was," said the Judge, snatching eagerly at the opportunity thus presented to him. "And while we are on that subject, there were one or two matters I wanted to discuss with you, Hilda."

"If he was with you, and knows all about it," went on her ladyship, still pursuing her own line of thought, "I don't see why you had to send him out of the room beforehand."

"I did nothing of the sort, so far as I am aware."

"My dear, I never saw anything done more blatantly in my life. However, that's your affair and not mine. As I said before dinner, I don't see that there is anything to discuss about this business. Goodness knows, I'm the last person to wish to make a mountain out of this rather unfortunate little molehill."

The Judge remained silent, and she went on:

"If you give me the letter, I'll deal with it for you. There's no earthly reason why you should bother yourself about it, and you know how unpractical you always are about your own affairs. You've sent in your claim to the insurance people, I suppose? It's the Empyrean, isn't it?"

Still silence.

"Isn't it?"

The Judge cleared his throat.

"That", he croaked, "was the matter I wanted to discuss with you."

Nobody could say that Lady Barber was not quick in the uptake. She laid down her knitting, opened her fine eyes very wide, and sat up straight in her armchair.

"*William!*" she said in an ominously quiet voice, "are you trying to tell me that you are not insured at all?"

"I—I'm afraid that that is the fact, Hilda."

There was a silence during which it was only too apparent that Lady Barber was several times on the point of saying something and thought better of it each time. Finally she rose to her feet, moved to the fireplace, took a cigarette from the mantelpiece, lighted it, and stood for a moment or two with her back to her husband, looking down into the fire. When she turned round he had begun to speak but she took no notice.

"Have you considered," she asked, "exactly what this is likely to mean to you—to us?"

"Naturally," said the Judge in a somewhat peevish tone, "I have considered the matter in all its aspects. But I must admit that what you told me before dinner does put rather a different complexion on the case. I mean, the fact that this fellow is a pianist."

"Sebald-Smith!" exclaimed her ladyship, allowing her feelings to break through her self-control for the first time. "Why if you must run somebody down with a motor-car you should go and select Sebald-Smith, of all people——"

"It is unfortunate," Barber admitted. "It has—quite frankly—rather upset my calculations as to how—that is——"

61

"It means that he will want about ten times as much in the way of damages as any ordinary person would," his wife cut in.

"Precisely. I am afraid his demands for an injured finger may be somewhat exorbitant."

Neither spoke for a time, and then Lady Barber said, somewhat pointlessly:

"I cannot understand how you came to be so foolish, William!"

The Judge wisely said nothing, and her ladyship, realizing perhaps that her remark was rather beneath her usual level, tried again.

"I suppose the accident *was* your fault?" she said. "You couldn't plead contributory negligence, by any chance?"

"My dear Hilda, we need hardly consider that aspect of the case. In my position, I can't afford to fight it. That is obvious. I shall have to settle on the best terms I can."

"But, William, this may ruin us!"

"We should be very much more thoroughly ruined if by reason of this matter being litigated I had to resign my appointment."

"Resign!"

"Well, Hilda, we must face facts."

There was another rather bleak silence before Lady Barber spoke again.

"William, just how much money have you in the world, apart from your salary?" she asked.

"My dear, we went into that subject very fully only a month or two ago."

"I know we did, but then it was only a question of paying a few wretched bills of mine. This is serious."

The Judge unexpectedly uttered a loud, creaking laugh.

"You imagined that I was painting things blacker than they really were for your benefit, I suppose," he said. "That in fact I had a few thousands tucked away which I had never told you about?"

"Of course," replied her ladyship simply. "It seemed only common sense."

"Common sense or not, I was perfectly honest with you. The position is now exactly as I explained it to you then— as, indeed, I have explained it at intervals throughout our married life. For many years past we have been spending practically every penny I have earned." There was a slight emphasis on the contrasted pronouns which was not lost on his hearer. "Apart from my modest insurance policy there is nothing to fall back on. Apart from my still more modest pension—if I am permitted to earn it—there is nothing to look forward to. If anything were to happen to me——"

"Thank you, I have heard that bit before," said Lady Barber hastily. "The question is, where are you going to find the ten thousand pounds or so which Sebald-Smith will certainly expect for his finger?"

The Judge gulped. At the worst, he had not envisaged such a sum as this. It was on the tip of his tongue to remind his wife that she knew less about awarding damages than he did, but he remembered in time that she certainly knew a great deal more than he about the earning capacities of pianists.

"We shall have to cut down our scale of expenditure very drastically, I am afraid," he said.

Her ladyship looked at her elegant reflection in the glass over the mantelpiece and made a face. "It's a grim prospect," she remarked. Then, pulling herself together, she went on in a crisp, practical manner: "Well! Faraday's letter will have to be answered, I suppose, and it had better be done professionally. Shall I write to Michael and ask him to do it on your behalf? You will want him to act for you, I suppose?"

"I suppose so," said the Judge without enthusiasm. He did not greatly care for his brother-in-law, but he was un-questionably a competent solicitor.

"I shall tell him just to acknowledge the letter formally,

and then when I can find time I'll go up to London and explain the whole thing to him," she went on. "The longer we can keep Sebald-Smith hanging about, the better. People like him haven't any staying-power. After a month or two he'll be much more reasonable in his ideas than he is now, I'm sure. Besides"—she smiled a delightful unexpected smile—"it will give us time to start saving."

Shortly afterwards Judge and Lady went to bed, both in somewhat better temper than had seemed probable half an hour before. Hilda's active mind, though fully aware of the extent of the disaster that loomed over them, was almost happy in the prospect of employment in urgent practical affairs. As for the Judge, he was conscious of the relief which he always felt whenever, as so often happened, he allowed some personal problem of his own to be taken into his wife's competent hands. He felt too the virtuous pleasure which comes from confession, now that he had made a clean breast of his escapade. This latter feeling, however, was not unalloyed. It occurred to him, as he made his way upstairs, that so far he had said nothing to his wife about the threatening letters which had reached him at Markhampton. With the unquenchable optimism that always marked his behaviour in these matters, he decided that he would save trouble by saying nothing to her about the question. Barber's habit of concealing things from his wife was as instinctive as that of the dog who hides bones under a sofa cushion, and about as effective.

Chapter 6

CIVIL ACTION

Southington assizes took their normal course. The formalities of the opening day were, with a few local variations, the formalities of Markhampton. Derek, who already felt himself to be an old hand at the game, performed his part in the ceremonies with what he felt to be the proper blend of dignity and detachment. The presence of Lady Barber made little or no difference to the proceedings, he observed. She kept herself well in the background and so far as the spectators were concerned was merely an inconspicuous black-clothed figure in a back pew at the church or in a remote corner of the bench. On the second day of the assize, indeed, she did not even appear in court. Crime, she declared, bored her. She had read the depositions and there was nothing in any of the cases of the faintest legal interest. On the other hand, in the civil list that came after there were several actions which she intended to follow. One in particular, which raised for decision for the first time an obscure question of construction in a new Act of Parliament, promised to be fascinating. Hearing her utter this opinion in decided tones at dinner on the second evening in lodgings, Derek understood how the nickname "Father William" came to be attached to the Judge.

Hilda Barber, in fact, was that rare being, a woman with a real talent for law. She had been, she told Derek, called to the Bar, but had never practised. The latter statement was true in the sense that like many other women barristers she had never succeeded in acquiring a practice. Without any exceptional influence behind her she had been unable to overcome the prejudice which has kept the Bar an essentially masculine profession. But for two years she had haunted the Temple, listened to every case of importance— as distinct from cases of mere notoriety—and studied assiduously in the library of her Inn. During this period she read as a pupil in the chambers of William Barber, then at the height of his practice as a junior. It was not long after her term of pupilage expired that Barber celebrated a double event by taking silk and marrying within the same month. It was currently rumoured that both of these important steps had been taken on the initiative of the lady. Certainly, from the professional point of view, he had no cause to regret either of them.

After her marriage, Hilda Barber was seen no more in the Temple. The snowy wig and still glossy gown were put away, monuments to unrealized ambition. Thenceforward she devoted herself to the twin objects of fostering her husband's career and spending gracefully his steadily increasing earnings. It would be hard to say in which she was the more successful. She brought to Barber the social contacts which he had hitherto lacked and which he needed to put the seal upon his professional reputation. Solicitors who had fought shy of the learned Miss Hilda Matthewson, barrister at law, competed for invitations to the cocktail parties and dinners given by the smart Mrs. Barber. The evening papers which carried in one column the account of a speech by the "eminent K.C." in the fashionable cause of the day, were sure to report in another that his wife had been prominent at a first night or charity ball, in a dress which would probably be more faithfully described than her husband's argument; and each piece of publicity reacted favourably on the other.

But it would be a mistake to suppose that because she was now in a position to exercise her social talents to the full, her interest in the law had in any way diminished. Where other women in like case would have taken to charity or politics as an outlet for their superfluous energies, she remained faithful to jurisprudence. The amount of work that she did for Barber behind the scenes as a "devil" was unsuspected by anyone, except perhaps his clerk, but it was undoubtedly considerable. Barber was a man of a mental calibre that would inevitably have carried him to the bench sooner or later, but his wife was probably justified in her belief that her assistance had shortened the period by several years, while at the same time making it possible for him to cope with an enormous pressure of work which would otherwise have overwhelmed him.

Hilda was not unnaturally pleased when Barber K.C. was in due course transformed into Mr. Justice Barber. The elevation, however, was not without its drawbacks. Particularly, she discovered, as many have done before her, that a judicial salary is a poor substitute for the income of a leader in the first flight of his profession. It was agreeable to be announced at parties as "Lady Barber", but slightly less so to be compelled to greet her hostess in a frock that had already done duty for half a season. The change had another consequence which she had not foreseen, indeed, it is probable that she never became fully aware of it. Judges, if they do not exactly live in the fierce white light that beats upon a throne, are public figures, and within a limited circle there is very little about their lives that fails to become public property sooner or later. Hence it came about that whereas nobody was ever aware how much Barber K.C.'s opinions owed to the criticism and counsel of his wife, it was not long before quite a number of initiates were saying among themselves that Barber J.'s reserved judgments were written by her ladyship. On one occasion, when one of these was the subject of an appeal, the *sotto voce* question of one Lord Justice to his brother, "Is this one of Hilda's?" had unluckily reached some quick ears in counsels' seats.

Fortunately for her peace of mind, this episode was not reported to her. She had learned, however, of her husband's nickname and magnanimously professed to be mildly amused at it. So far as the public at large was concerned, however, she continued to remain well in the background and, except that she was perhaps a shade too decorative, played the role of Judge's wife to perfection.

Derek was quick to observe that Lady Barber's submissiveness in public did not extend to her private life. She soon took charge of the domestic arrangements in the Lodgings, harried Mrs. Square in a manner to which that autocratic lady was utterly unaccustomed, criticized Greene for lack of proper attention to the Marshal's top hat, trod the submissive Savage under her feet, and had more than one passage at arms with Beamish himself. Dislike between her ladyship and the clerk was mutual. Beamish had not served the Judge prior to his appointment. Barber's former clerk had, much to his master's annoyance, declined to follow him to the bench, preferring to continue to take his chance in the Temple. The new Judge had therefore to content himself with the best man he could find at short notice. Unfortunately his choice had not commended itself to Hilda, and during the period that had since elapsed she had succeeded in making her opinion only too plain.

So far as the Judge was concerned, the element of discord so introduced into his surroundings did not seem to affect him greatly. He turned a blind eye to the upheaval among his staff and firmly refused to allow Beamish to be discussed at all. Obviously, this was a sore subject of long standing on which he had wisely taken a decision and he was not to be moved from it. Apart from this, relations with his wife since his confession on the first evening at Southington were perfectly harmonious. Any reforms which she might think fit to enforce in the household were directed to increasing his comfort rather than her own, and he obviously enjoyed to the full the little attentions which she lavished upon him. The consequence was that Derek found the atmosphere of the Lodgings once more warm and friendly, besides a good deal more lively than it had been before her arrival.

Hilda galvanized the Judge into giving several dinner parties at Southington. These were merely official affairs, at which such dignitaries as the High Sheriff, the Mayor and the local County Court Judge attended with their wives, discussed local affairs and departed punctually at a quarter past ten. But they served, if nothing else, to demonstrate Hilda's admirable tact. She would manage her party with discretion, never allow the conversation to degenerate to the mere maundering of the average official gathering, and at the same time subdued her own brilliance to the level of the company. More to her taste, however, were the lunches to which the Judge invited from time to time the members of the bar engaged in the criminal cases. She was at her best with the young men. Derek observed with rueful amusement others undergoing the same process of drawing-out that he had endured. He noticed also that neither to them nor to their elders did she admit to the faintest knowledge of their trade. On one occasion she sat without moving a muscle while a very young man, holding his first brief, laboriously explained for her benefit an elementary point of procedure —and incidentally explained it wrongly.

The criminal business at Southington drew to a close and the time fixed for the hearing in which Hilda had taken such interest drew near. On the day before, she went to London. Her purpose in going, she told her husband, was to see her solicitor brother about the Sebald-Smith affair. On her return that evening, she said no more than that she had had a useful day. The Judge, to whom any reference to the Markhampton affair was acutely distasteful, asked no questions and the subject dropped. At dinner that evening, she referred once more to the case that was to be heard next day.

"I see by the pleadings that Frank Pettigrew is appearing for the defendant," she remarked. "We'll ask him to dinner. It will be a change to have somebody entertaining as a guest."

"My dear," objected Barber heavily, "I have already had Pettigrew to lunch at Markhampton. I deprecate showing favouritism among the Bar, except in very special cases, and, frankly, I do not think this is one of them."

Her ladyship pouted.

"I want to see Frank," she said. "He amuses me, and I haven't set eyes on him for ages."

"That does not altogether surprise me," retorted the Judge. "And I must say that I do not think it would be in the very best of taste——"

"My dear William, if you are going to set up as an arbiter of taste——" she began in a tone of mockery which caused him hastily to shift his ground.

"Besides," he went on, "it would be against my principles to entertain counsel on one side of a case only. Even if the arguments are concluded by to-morrow evening, as seems probable, the objection still stands."

"Then that is simple," said Hilda in decided tones. "We will ask them both. Flack is for the plaintiff, isn't he? He is quite presentable. Then we shall be able to make up a four of bridge—you play, I suppose, Mr. Marshall?"

Derek, a somewhat embarrassed auditor of the discussion, admitted that he did.

". . . And then we shan't bother you with our chatter. I've brought down some new library books for you which you will like. That's settled then."

And settled it was.

The action which had been so much canvassed in lodgings, proved, to Derek's mind at least, one of unexampled dullness. In a court completely empty save for officials and reporters, Flack, an earnest middle-aged man with a particularly ugly voice, occupied the whole morning with his opening. This consisted, so far as Derek could see, in repeating in various tones of emphasis, the words of a section of an Act of Parliament which appeared to have been composed by an illiterate with a talent for obscurity, and reading passages from judgments in other cases on other Acts which seemed to have no bearing on the matter whatever. At the conclusion of his performance, he called two formal witnesses whom Pettigrew declined to cross-examine, remarking that he was relying on a pure point of law.

What had reduced the Marshal almost to tears of boredom, had, however, apparently stimulated Lady Barber to an ecstasy. She returned with the others to lunch in the highest spirits. Indeed, she reminded Derek of nothing so much as a young girl during the entr'acte of an exciting mystery play. Presently it was revealed that part of her pleasure, at least, was due to the fact that she had, or at all events thought she had, solved the mystery.

"Flack doesn't know his job," she announced at lunch. "He hasn't cited the only case which bears on the matter at all."

The Judge looked up from his plate with interest.

"Indeed?" he asked. "What case do you mean?"

"Simpkinson and the Haltwhistle Urban District Council," replied her ladyship with her mouth full. "It's reported in 1918 Appeal Cases, and it's——"

"My dear Hilda, I know the case perfectly well. It is merely one of the line of cases on the emergency legislation of the last war. How it can help me to determine the construction of this statute I cannot imagine."

"Then you don't know the case perfectly well. It lays down a general principle which is dead in point here. The Lord Chancellor makes it quite plain."

Barber, who was listening to his wife's remarks with evident respect, permitted himself a dry laugh.

"I suppose you were getting some assistance from your brother yesterday," he remarked.

Hilda flushed.

"Certainly not!" she exclaimed. "Michael is hopeless at case law, though he's got a good enough brain. He's much too busy making wills for old ladies and helping his clients to dodge their income-tax. I simply asked him to give me the run of his library while I was in his office. I knew there was a decision that helped somewhere and it was just a matter of ferreting it out."

"I am very much obliged to you, Hilda," said the Judge. "I shall look the case up when I get back to London and see if it bears out what you say."

"You needn't bother to do that. Frank has got it with him. I was looking at the Reports on his desk this morning. He won't cite it unless you make him because it's clean against him. But there it is."

"It would be most improper for counsel, knowing that there is a reported case bearing on the matter in hand, not to bring it to the notice of the Court, whether it is in his favour or not," pronounced his lordship pompously.

"Oh, well, I only meant that I shouldn't if I was in his shoes," replied Hilda airily.

After that the conversation became merely technical and so continued until the end of the meal.

After lunch, a curious little incident occurred which, though apparently insignificant, was to have important consequences. The Judge had a passion for sweet things. After every meal he invariably ate three or four chocolates or caramels with all the gusto of a schoolboy, and a regular supply of these delicacies was a feature of the economy of the lodgings. On this particular occasion, after lunch, Savage produced a full box of chocolates with the name of a famous London firm upon the lid.

The Judge's eyes sparkled.

"Bechamel's!" he exclaimed. "This is a pleasant surprise! Where do these come from, Savage?"

"They arrived by this morning's post, my Lord."

"Indeed? Hilda, I perceive that your business in London yesterday was not entirely concerned with legal research. This was a very kind thought on your part, my dear."

"But I never ordered them," said Lady Barber in surprise. "I was never near the West End all day. They must have been sent by mistake."

"A very intelligent mistake, then. They're the kind that I always have for Christmas—with lemon centres, which you will improvidently bite, while I more delicately suck. You must try one, Marshal."

Hilda interposed.

"Not now," she said primly. "If somebody has sent us a box of Bechamel chocolates, they must be kept for this evening. A box like that gives a touch of distinction to any dinner—and goodness knows Mrs. Square's dinners need it."

"I'm sure I don't know what you have against Mrs. Square's cooking," said the Judge mildly. "But in any case, there will be plenty left for this evening if we have one or two now."

"Certainly not," said Hilda firmly. "Nothing looks more *mesquin* than a half eaten box of chocolates handed round after dinner. If you can give them a fresh box of Bechamels, your guests will feel that you have really taken some trouble for their sake, and that's half the secret of entertaining."

Derek made bold to say:

"Even if the trouble is not really of your taking, Lady Barber?"

Hilda flashed a brilliant smile at him. She was delighted to find that the young man could stand up to her.

"Especially if it is not of your taking," she said. "The effect is the only thing that matters. But in this case, I am taking considerable trouble—the trouble of persuading my husband to abstain. Put the lid back on the box, William, and tie the ribbon on again. Have one of these caramels instead."

The Judge meekly did as he was told, and shortly afterwards the party returned to Court.

Derek found the afternoon's sitting a good deal less boring than the morning had been, although nothing could have made the arid subject an interesting one. Pettigrew had a natural gift for a turn of phrase that served to make any argument attractive and even contrived to extract some humour out of the forbidding subject. Barber, whatever his failings, possessed the great, if negative, merit of not being a talkative judge. He sat quite silently and suffered Pettigrew to develop his theme without interference for three quarters of an hour, making an occasional note in the large book in front of him. He showed no sign of appreciating Pettigrew's little jokes, but it is always possible that these were also recorded in the notebook.

By the end of that time, even Pettigrew had become thoroughly dull. Having made his main submission with lucidity and force, he was as a matter of duty, referring to the authorities cited by his opponent and disposing of the contentions which had been founded on them. Then, with an apology for what he feared might be a waste of the time of the Court, he proceeded to quote one or two further cases which might possibly be of assistance. Presently, with an ill-disguised yawn:

"I ought perhaps to refer your Lordship to Simpkinson and the Haltwhistle Urban District Council," he remarked, "though perhaps your Lordship may not think it carries the matter any further."

Barber's face showed no trace of interest as he wrote down the name and reference of the case in his book. His wife, on the other hand, drew in her breath sharply and clenched her gloved hands in excitement. It may have been fancy, but

Derek thought that Pettigrew's eyes glanced in her direction at the tiny sound. Then he began to read.

Simpkinson and the Haltwhistle Urban District Council seemed to Derek exactly like all the other many cases that had been cited that day, only perhaps slightly more incomprehensible. He was just beginning to wonder what on earth all the bother had been about when the Judge opened his eyes, which up to that time had been half closed, and remarked:

"That passage you have just read seems to be against you, Mr. Pettigrew."

"My lord, I don't think so," Pettigrew said easily. "I don't think the Lord Chancellor was purporting to lay down a general rule here, and your lordship will see from what he says a little further on——"

"Very well. Go on, Mr. Pettigrew."

Pettigrew finished reading the Lord Chancellor's observations, and then put the book down.

"I don't know if the case is really of very much assistance to your lordship one way or the other," he said. "But as it seemed to be *in pari materia* to some of those cited by my friend, I thought I was bound to bring it to your lordship's attention."

"Quite," said the Judge drily. "Will you hand me the report, please?"

He took the volume in his hands, turned over the leaves, and read aloud the passage to which he had already referred. With this as his text, he proceeded to expound. He analysed it, compared it with other passages in the same judgment, linked it up with other cases already cited in argument before him, referred it to principles laid down in authorities and text-books. He made of this apparently harmless and casual paragraph a deadly instrument which, inserted delicately into the structure of Pettigrew's argument, split the defendant's case wide open. It was a brilliant performance, all the more so considering that he had had only the merest hint to go upon. What rather detracted from its merit was the obvious relish with which it was done, and the quite unnecessary brutality with which the fallacies involved in Pettigrew's submission were exposed. Barber made it only too plain that in his view counsel for the defendants had been not only wrong in law, but grossly ignorant of his trade. Needless to say, not a single discourteous word passed his lips, but the implication was there, none the less.

Pettigrew took his defeat with resignation, with apparent good humour even. He put up some semblance of a fight, but he knew when he was beaten, and it was not his habit to prolong the agony in hopeless cases. In this, perhaps, he was unwise. Clients are human, and derive much consolation from "a good fight", however vain. Not a little of his lack of success was due to his mistaken belief that other people would be as reasonable as he was himself. Accordingly, a few moments after the Judge's intervention he concluded his address, sat down, and listened to the Shaver, without calling upon Flack to reply, deliver judgement for the plaintiff.

Beneath his mask of courteous indifference, however, Pettigrew was sick with anger. He did not mind losing a case—that was all in the day's work—but he felt strongly about the manner in which he had been treated. The point on which he had failed was an obscure one, and anybody might have been forgiven for failing to appreciate it. In point of fact, his opponent, Flack, though no fool, had overlooked it entirely, while he, Pettigrew, had known of it and advised his clients that their chances of success were small upon that very ground. But would they be likely to remember that, in the face of Father William's attitude? Much more likely that they would recollect that he had lost their case and that Flack's clients had succeeded and arrange their future business accordingly. Quite probably, they would blame him for having done his duty in citing the fatal authority which would otherwise never have been brought to the attention of the Court at all. Then he recollected the slight sound that had come from the bench at the mention of the name of the case, and he began to realize how it was that the Judge had been lying in wait for him, his arguments already furnished, his poisoned arrows tipped and barbed. His sense of humour came to his rescue and he laughed aloud. Even the fact that he had probably lost a client that afternoon could not blunt his appreciation of the ludicrousness of the position. And he began to look forward to his dinner in lodgings that evening more than he had thought possible.

The party, in fact, might be accounted a success. There were no other guests at dinner and Hilda permitted herself a professional hostess's wail at the lopsidedness of her table. But this, in the event, hardly proved a drawback. The Judge and Flack had been pupils in chambers together and had many reminiscences in common which the rest could not share. Hilda contentedly allowed them to develop a duologue of their own, while she and Pettigrew talked with each other. But she knew her business far too well to leave Derek in the cold. Indeed, with Pettigrew's co-operation, she succeeded in making him feel at times that he was the focal point of the conversation. He was commiserated with on the absence of a suitable partner at table, rallied for his inattention to the important legal discussion that had taken place that day, and was made to feel thoroughly sheepish when Pettigrew appealed to him to verify a quotation from the Book of Judges—"or hadn't you time to get so far to-day?" he blandly asked. At other times, as the meal proceeded, he began to feel almost in the position of a chaperon, listening to a colloquy rich with overtones of intimacy which he could apprehend but could not share. It was obvious to him that the couple knew each other well—too well, perhaps, for either to be entirely comfortable in the presence of the other, but he was puzzled to determine the precise relationship between them. They were able to speak to some extent in shorthand. Allusions, half expressed, were taken up and answered in terms equally cryptic to the outsider. It seemed as if their minds were attuned together, so that the ordinary laborious process of explanations was unnecessary. But beneath it all the listener was conscious of a latent sense of hostility and wariness on either side. Their talk was a fencing bout between friends, in which neither desired to hurt the other—but there were no buttons on the foils.

In an oblique indirect fashion, Pettigrew let it be known that he attributed to Hilda his downfall in Court that afternoon. Derek observed that on this occasion she made no secret of her special knowledge. Indeed, she described in some detail the process of reasoning by which she had been led to seek out this particular point of law, and gave an entertaining enough account of her researches in the dusty volumes at her brother's office.

"His managing clerk thought it all most improper," she said. "Clients who look for their own law are not encouraged."

"Quite rightly. The proper place to look for law is in barrister's chambers, and on payment of a suitable fee. I expect he was wondering how he could make the service he was doing you into an appropriate item on the bill of costs. By the way, you didn't go up to your brother's office simply to find a case to floor me with, I hope?"

She shook her head.

"M'm. It was the Markhampton affair, I suppose?"

"You were in the car, too, weren't you?"

"Yes. Unfortunately I was."

"Do you know that it was Sebald-Smith?"

"*The* Sebald-Smith?" Pettigrew pursed his lips for a soundless whistle. "This is likely to be a nuisance. . . . His little finger may well prove thicker than another man's loins. First Book of Kings, Marshal—you'll hardly have time to reach that before the end of the circuit. Unless you skip the genealogies, of course. Personally, I always find them most entertaining, but I fancy I am in a minority in that respect. Haven't I met him at your house, by the way?"

"Possibly. I rather lost touch with him since my marriage, but I fancy someone brought him to a cocktail party once."

"No doubt. Sally Parsons is an old friend of yours, isn't she?"

"I haven't seen anything of her for some time," said Hilda in a manner that indicated that the friendship was decidedly a thing of the past. "Was she——?"

"She is," said Pettigrew firmly. "After much striving she has reached a position where you could hardly ask her to a party without receiving Sebald as well, and *vice versa*. A dull relationship, one would have thought—all the tedium of marriage without its respectability, but it appeals to some temperaments, and Sally, as you are no doubt aware, has several."

"Disgusting!" said her ladyship. "And to think that she and I——"

"Much better not think of it. It is a sordid subject, and I don't know how I came to introduce it. Moreover, we are shocking the Marshal. To return to the matter we were discussing, I'm afraid this may be rather serious."

He looked round the table.

"I know," she said, answering his unspoken thought. "We oughtn't to be giving dinner-parties with this sort of thing hanging over us, ought we? And this is the fourth I've had this assize. It's time I turned over a new leaf."

"Economy is the very devil when you're not used to it," he said. "I should hate to see you starting."

"I started the day William became a judge."

Pettigrew made a wry little face.

"I meant—*economy*," he said drily. "after all, even Becky Sharp didn't ask for more than a judge's salary. Do you read Thackeray, Marshal?"

"Yes," said Derek, and wished immediately that he had

had the assurance to say "Of course". "But values have changed since then, haven't they?" he added. "Not to mention taxation."

"And '*even* Becky Sharp' was not fair, Frank," her ladyship murmured.

"You are both right. They have and it was not. I spoke at random, as usual. At all events, I am relieved to find that you have decided to postpone economizing for to-night. This, for example!"

He indicated the other side of the round table, where Savage was ceremoniously handing to the Judge the still virgin box of Bechamel chocolates.

"Not an extravagance of mine," Hilda protested. "A gift from an unknown admirer."

The Judge, with a sigh of pleasure long-deferred, popped one of the round little sweetmeats into his mouth and began to suck vigorously. Savage moved round the table to Hilda, who also took one. The two elder men refused. Derek was just stretching his hand out to help himself from the box when there was a sudden disturbance at his side.

"Stop!" screamed Lady Barber at the top of her voice. "There's something—something wrong with these——"

In her hand was one half of the chocolate, it's hard core bitten clean through by her even, powerful teeth. The other half lay on the table before her, where she had spat it out. She had risen from her seat, and stood there for a moment, very pale, her free hand clutching her throat, while the four men sat gaping at her in motionless astonishment. Before anyone could move, she had leapt, rather than run, round the table to where her husband was sitting, inserted her finger into his mouth, like a nurse whose charge has swallowed an inedible toy, and neatly fished out the chocolate from between his jaws.

The Judge was the first to break the silence.

"My dear Hilda," he said, contemplating the diminished

brown sphere on his plate, "you need hardly have done that. I should have spat it out in any case."

Hilda said nothing. She grabbed the glass of water which Pettigrew had ready for her, drank it off, collapsed on the nearest chair and burst abruptly into tears.

There was, after all, no bridge after dinner that night.

Chapter 7

CHEMICAL REACTION

"Why didn't you tell me anything about this before?"

"My dear, I didn't want to worry you."

"Worry me!" Hilda's laugh was always an exceptionally pleasant and musical one, but on this occasion it seemed a little forced. "My dear William, what extraordinary ideas you have! You nearly caused us both a good deal more than worry this evening."

"I am sorry, Hilda," said the Judge humbly, "but I really could hardly have expected such a thing to follow on an ordinary anonymous letter. And, after all, it was your suggestion that we should have the chocolates for dinner."

"That is simply childish of you, William. Do you imagine that I should have dreamed of letting you or anyone else touch a box of sweets arriving in this mysterious way if I had had any idea that your life was being threatened?"

"But it wasn't a threat to my life, exactly," the Judge objected. "And after all, there's no evidence that the two were in any way connected."

"Evidence!" said her ladyship in a tone of scorn that showed that for once the woman in her had got the better of the lawyer. "It's perfectly obvious. There must have been." She switched suddenly to another line of attack. "Now is there anything else about Markhampton that you haven't told me?" she demanded.

"No, no!" Barber replied a little testily. "Really, Hilda, anyone would think I spent my life keeping secrets from you. I repeat, it was merely out of a very natural desire to save you anxiety——"

"You say the police at Markhampton arranged to give you special protection?"

"Yes."

"Then why haven't the police here in Southington done the same?"

"I understand that they were informed of the position and didn't think it necessary to do more than keep a special look out for—for the fellow."

"What fellow are you talking about?"

"Oh! Didn't I tell you? Well, the fact is, Hilda, the Chief Constable at Markhampton seemed to have an idea that this fellow, the one who wrote the letters, I mean——"

"I *knew* there was something else you were hiding!" said Hilda triumphantly. "Go on—was who?"

"It was only a theory of course, but he had a notion that it was Heppenstall. He is out, you know."

"Heppenstall! But you gave him five years."

"I know I did." The Judge's tone was sombre. "But there's always remission for good conduct and so on, you know."

Hilda was silent for a moment.

"I wish you hadn't tried the case," she said finally.

"My dear Hilda, I had no option but to try it."

She shook her head.

"It was at the Old Bailey," she reminded him. "There are four Courts there. There was no reason why it shouldn't have been tried by the Recorder. I've never mentioned this before, William, but people said you had Bob—Heppenstall's case put into your list on purpose. Was that true?"

Barber waved a deprecating hand.

"It is no good going back on these things now," he murmured.

"And I wish you hadn't given him five years."

"I did my duty," said the Judge. And seeing that this

assertion produced no response, he added, with a certain sense of bathos, "And the Court of Criminal Appeal declined to interfere with the sentence."

Her ladyship interjected a comment upon the Court of Criminal Appeal which, in deference to that august institution, may here be omitted.

"They didn't know him and you did, that's the point," she added. "Has it ever occurred to you that he may have thought he was going to get off lightly because you were trying him?"

"It would be highly improper——" Barber began.

"I know, I know," said his wife impatiently. "And that's the very reason why I wish—— But as you say, it's no good going back on things. Heppenstall is at large, and trying to kill you——"

"But I repeat, Hilda, there is no evidence——"

". . . And we must protect ourselves in every way until the police lay him by the heels. And now I'm going to bed, and so are you. You're trying the libel action to-morrow, aren't you? On the pleadings it looks to me like an undefended case. Ten to one you'll find that the defendant has paid something into Court."

"I'm inclined to agree with you, my dear. Good night."

The inquest on the Bechamel chocolates, to which this conversation formed a pendant, had been a lively, but unprofitable affair. The closest of inquiries entirely failed to clear up the mystery of their origin. Savage, Beamish and Greene were all appealed to in vain. Savage, who was sent for first, merely said that the parcel in which they were contained had been handed to him by Beamish. Beamish was summoned and somewhat sulkily reminded her ladyship that she had given him a number of packages which had arrived for her by that morning's post. He understood that they were different things which she had ordered in London the day before. He had, naturally, given them in his turn to the butler. It was not the place of the Judge's clerk, he implied, to attend to such things. One of the bones of contention between the two was that Hilda persisted in regarding him as a species of superior domestic servant and he was not sorry to remind her of the fact. Any knowledge of, or responsibility for the chocolates, he loftily repudiated. There were some parcels which had been put into his hands. No, he could not trust his memory to say how many. He had, he hinted, disembarrassed himself of them as soon as possible by passing them to the proper quarter. And now, if his lordship would excuse him, he had some rather pressing work to do. . . .

Savage gloomily took up the tale again. He had unpacked the parcels given him, he explained in an injured tone. He thought he had been doing the right thing and he was sure he had no reason to suppose there was anything wrong. In all his experience, nobody had ever suggested. . . . Reassured on this point, he went on to say that the parcels which he had opened, besides the chocolates, had contained two books from the library, a pair of gloves for her ladyship, and a bottle of preserved plums. He had disposed of all these goods in the appropriate manner. The books he had put in the drawing-room, the gloves he had handed to the maid to be bestowed in her ladyship's bedroom, the plums went into the kitchen and the chocolates into the dining-room. That was all that he could say and he humbly suggested that he had done his duty.

It was Pettigrew who had raised the next point.

"The most important evidence is the wrapping the things came in," he remarked. "Where is that?"

Savage could not say. He had done his unpacking in his pantry. He had hardly finished before it had been time to robe his lordship for Court. He had left it to Greene to clear up the mess. Perhaps Greene could help.

Greene was an expressionless manservant, who carried taciturnity to the verge of dumbness. Derek, who, with memories of Dumas, had long since privately christened him Grimaud, had been interested to see whether even such an emergency as this could induce him to utter more than two words together. As it proved, the examination of Greene rather resembled the kind of Christmas game in which questions may only be answered "Yes" or "No". Little by little, the facts were dragged from him that he had removed the wrappings from the pantry, that while some of these survived, those which had contained the chocolate box had not, that he thought he must have used them to relight the Marshal's fire which had gone out and that he could not remember what they were like, but fancied that the paper was thin and brown. He could not say whether it had a label on it or not, or whether the address was written or typed. And there the evidence ended.

"Really, Hilda," Barber had said, "I think you are properly the next witness. After all, you handled this mysterious consignment. Didn't you take any notice of it?"

"No. I saw there were three or four parcels, and as I had ordered a lot of things over the telephone in London, I thought they were them. I didn't bother to look at them at all closely. But I think I should have noticed Bechamel's name on the outside if the chocolates had come direct from them."

"Obviously they didn't," Pettigrew put in. "But weren't you surprised when you found that somebody had sent you such a welcome present?"

"More pleased than surprised. People do still send me presents sometimes, you know, Frank."

Pettigrew wrinkled his nose in acknowledgement of the thrust and the talk then turned to what action should be taken.

"Obviously, we must tell the police," said Hilda. "Put it straight into the hands of Scotland Yard, William. These country people won't be the least good."

"The first thing to do will be to get the chocolates

analysed." Flack made his first contribution to the discussion.

"Of course. The police will have that done. Then I suppose they can make inquiries at Bechamel's and try and trace the recent purchasers of these chocolates. That's all a matter for them."

"I should like to avoid bringing the police into this, if possible," said the Judge.

"My dear William, why? When an attempt is made on your life——"

"It is a little difficult to explain, but at this stage at all events, I should rather favour some private inquiry."

"But William——"

"The first thing to do is to get the chocolates analysed."

"*Dear* Mr. Flack, you have said that once already. The police will know just how that should be done."

". . . And I should very much like to perform the analysis myself."

"You perform it?"

"I am interested in chemistry in a mild way, you know, Lady Barber. In fact, I have quite a well fitted-up little laboratory at home. My 'stinks room', my wife calls it—she has a great sense of humour, I should so like you to meet her——"

"She sounds delightful," Hilda murmured with a shudder.

". . . And I should be delighted to try my hand at a piece of detective research for once. It is an opportunity one could hardly expect to recur."

In spite of his wife's obvious disapproval, Barber had eagerly accepted the offer. The evening ended with Flack departing in triumph bearing the box of chocolates and the two half-eaten ones, carefully wrapped in an envelope. He promised to call at the lodgings the next morning with what he described as his "preliminary observations".

"I can get some simple reagents in the town, I expect,"

were his parting words. "Most poisons are of a fairly ordinary character and easily detectable. I can do a little investigation in my bedroom at the hotel. Anything more elaborate will have to wait till I get back to town."

No sooner were husband and wife alone together than Hilda said challengingly:

"And now, William, perhaps you will explain why you prefer to leave things in the hands of that ridiculous creature than to call in experts?"

And from the Judge's consequent denials, evasions and confessions ensued the scene already described.

True to his promise, Flack was round at the lodgings next morning. He was early. Indeed, the Judge was still at breakfast when he was shown in, looking extremely pleased with himself.

"I must apologise for this unseasonable intrusion, Judge," he said. "But I am catching the ten o'clock train up, and I wanted to make my report at the earliest opportunity."

He produced with great solemnity a small brown paper parcel, which he handed to Barber.

"I return the exhibits," he said. "With the exception, that is, of one half chocolate, which I fear has perished in my experiment."

"But I thought you were taking them up to London with you?" the Judge said in surprise.

"That has proved to be unnecessary. The resources of my—ah!—stinks room will not have to be called upon. My investigations were completed last night before I went to bed. They proved very simple—very simple indeed," he added with a touch of disappointment.

"Indeed?" said Barber.

"Are you quite sure, Mr. Flack?" Hilda put in. "Don't you think that if the police were to send them to a proper— I mean, their laboratories must be so very well equipped, they might perhaps find something you had overlooked."

"Possibly, Lady Barber, possibly, though I do not think it very probable. In any case, the exhibits are here at the service of the police or anybody else, quite intact—subject, as I said just now, to one half chocolate, which I do not think they will grudge me. Their disposition is entirely a matter for you—and for the Judge, of course."

"Don't you think, Hilda," said Barber, swallowing the last of his coffee, "that it would save time if Mr. Flack were allowed to tell us, quite briefly, what he has discovered so quickly?"

Without waiting for her ladyship's approval, Flack proceeded to unburden himself of his views.

"Last night," he said, "in the privacy of my own apartment, I dissected one of the chocolates which you handed to me. In point of fact, I chose the very one, I think, which had been, ah! extracted from your mouth, Judge, if you will excuse my mentioning it. With the aid of a safety razor blade I removed the outer coating of chocolate, which as you may readily imagine, had already been worn to approximately one half of its original thickness (not more, I should judge, than one and a half millimetres) by the ordeal to which it had been subjected. Within this covering, I discovered a hard white substance. To this, I applied the commonest and most readily available form of reagent, namely ordinary tap-water——"

He paused for dramatic effect.

". . . With immediate, and, I may say, startling results."

Another pause, which was evidently designed to be broken by the excited ejaculations of his audience. As these, however, were not forthcoming, he went on:

"The substance hissed, sizzled and disintegrated before my eyes! A pungent and unmistakable odour arose. The application of water to the substance had produced no other than acetylene gas. In other words, the contents of this sweetmeat proved to be——"

"Carbide?" said the Judge.

Flack beamed. His audience, though less responsive than the chocolate, had at last shown signs of reaction.

"No less," he said. "Ordinary, or, as my dear wife would put it, common or garden carbide."

"But how very extraordinary," said Hilda.

"Remarkable, is it not? But naturally my researches did not stop there," Flack went on hastily, determined to finish his story. "I proceeded to examine the remaining contents of the box (taking pains, needless to say, to avoid obliterating any finger-prints there might be upon them) with a view to ascertaining (*a*) the *modus operandi* of the individual who had tampered with them in this extraordinary fashion, and (*b*) the number which had been so treated. Taking (*b*) first—if I may be excused the departure from chronological order—I found that of the three layers contained in the box the uppermost alone had apparently been touched by any hand since they left the shop. I can guarantee that you will be perfectly safe, Lady Barber, in indulging your taste for confectionery so long as you confine your attentions strictly to what I may describe as the ground and first floors."

He smacked his lips in appreciation of his own witticism and continued:

"It is in the *attics* alone that danger resides. Close examination—and this is not a matter demanding any chemical knowledge—it is perfectly visible to the unaided eye of Scotland Yard, or if you will, of a High Court Judge (which, personally, I should, if I may say so, rate far the higher of the two) close examination, I repeat, shows quite clearly— I am dealing with (*a*) now, Judge—that each of these chocolates has at some time been neatly bisected at the circumference by some sharp instrument (such as, for example, the humble but efficient razor blade which I employed myself) and that thereafter the two halves have been replaced, the resulting point of junction being secured by the application of sufficient heat at that point to make the union (or reunion, rather) binding. Do I make myself clear?"

Silence being traditionally taken to mean consent, he went on.

"When I say that the chocolate had been bisected, I must not be taken as meaning more than I literally say. I do *not* mean that the original interior—which was, I understand, of a hard and brittle nature, had also been divided. That would have been to impose upon the operator an arduous and unnecessary labour, besides entailing the risk of blunting the delicate instrument which I premise as having been employed. No! It was merely the carapace (if I may use the term, somewhat inaccurately, I admit, to describe a soft covering to a hard interior) that had in all probability been severed, thus reversing the operation of the original craftsman, who doubtless imposed upon his filling—as I believe it is termed—two hemispheres of chocolate, which, pressed together, united with each other to produce the complete article of commerce. The irresistible inference, in short, is that the malpractor in this case, having removed one half of the external covering in the way that I have described, extracted the edible core, and replaced it with the noxious substance which I have identified."

Flack mopped his brow, and bobbed to the Judge in the manner in which he invariably concluded his address in Court.

Derek was the first to break the restful silence that succeeded Flack's flow of words.

"But why carbide?" he said. "It seems an odd choice for a poisoner."

"Why indeed? Odd, my young friend, is the word. So odd indeed, that we find ourselves confronted with the problem—which, I admit, is not strictly one for me, but perhaps I may be permitted to speak in this matter as *amicus curiæ*—is this a poisoner at all? Does this not rather bear the stigmata of a rather cruel and stupid practical joke?"

"A joke?" said Hilda angrily.

"Consider," Flack went on, wagging a fat forefinger in her direction. "Consider. It is perhaps a matter for an expert toxicologist, such as I do not claim to be, to decide, but I should judge that swallowed whole, in the fashion of a pill taken medicinally, a quantity of carbide such as this might be attended with disagreeable, possibly even fatal results. I cannot say, but it is possible. I do not seek to put it higher than that. But who ever heard of anyone ingesting chocolates in this manner? The very *raison d'être* of such articles is the pleasure to the palate, which would be wholly circumvented by such a procedure. No! There are two methods only of consuming sweets. One, the procedure which I fancy you favour, Lady Barber, that of biting and *munching*—I apologise for the crudity of the phrase but I know no other way of expressing it—the other, the slower and gentler technique adopted by the Judge, namely that of *sucking* and slow absorption. Now it is clear from your own very unpleasant experience of last night (I trust you are quite recovered by the way? Forgive me for not having made the inquiry sooner) it is clear that at the very first moment of *biting*, the contact of the saliva with the carbide releases acetylene gas, the fraud is exposed and the intruder summarily ejected. On the *sucking* principle, on the other hand, discovery is slower, but none the less——" he shook his head solemnly "—none the less sure. Possibly before the moment of revelation and repudiation there would be time for a minute quantity of carbide to be absorbed into the system—enough I dare say to set up very unpleasant internal reactions, but not, I am convinced, sufficient to be a lethal dose. I repeat, as a medium for what is so strangely and inaptly termed a practical joke, carbide is all that could be desired. As a poison, it is simply not in the picture."

As though taken aback by his descent into colloquial English, Flack stopped abruptly, murmured, "I shall miss my train, I must be off," and vanished.

Chapter 8

ON TO WIMBLINGHAM

_____

"So all it amounts to is this," said the Judge placidly as he drank his tea that evening. "Somebody has chosen to play a rather ill-natured practical joke on me. Somebody else has written me a couple of abusive anonymous letters. Yet a third somebody who—who may be taken to have a grudge against me—is at large. There is not the slightest reason to suspect that any of these three facts are in any way connected. None of them, either separately or taken together, need cause the slightest alarm. I don't propose to take any notice of them."

"I think you are wrong, William," said his wife firmly.

"My dear, I have thought this matter over very carefully since Flack's exposition this morning—I know you are inclined to belittle him, but he is a sound person and I believe he knows what he is talking about—I have, I say, thought it over carefully——"

"I could see that you were thinking about something on the bench this afternoon," said Hilda tartly, "and I wondered what it was. But so far as I am concerned it is not a matter of thinking. I _know_ that all these things are not mere coincidences. It is no good arguing about it. My instinct tells me——"

"Instinct!" The Judge threw up his hands in polite mockery.

"Instinct," she repeated firmly. "I feel instinctively that from the very beginning of this circuit there has been an

93

atmosphere of danger threatening you, and I think we ought to do something to combat it."

"It's very difficult to combat an atmosphere, I should think," Barber answered. "My own instinct, if that is the right word, leads me to precisely the opposite conclusion. I believe that the circuit from now on will be perfectly peaceful and normal—unless, of course, these air attacks people talk about so much do develop, which I don't believe they will. Marshal, another cup of tea, if you please."

Derek poured out the cup, and took the occasion to suggest that the question might be left open for a little longer.

"We are going to Wimblingham to-morrow," he said. "So far, there has been a suspicious incident at each of two places. If anything happens at a third, then I think we can be fairly sure that it's not a coincidence."

The Judge was loud in his approval of the suggestion.

"By all means let us suspend judgment," he said. "And if I rejoin you after Wimblingham safe and sound we shall hope that this spell of ill luck—as I regard it—is broken."

"Very well," said Hilda. "But there is no question of rejoining you. I am coming on with you to Wimblingham."

Barber showed an astonishment which Derek did not at first understand.

"You are coming to Wimblingham?" he said. "Surely you are not serious, Hilda. Surely you know that no judge's wife ever comes there."

"I am coming to Wimblingham," she repeated. "And to every other town on the circuit. I feel that it is my duty to look after you."

"I am flattered at your concern for my safety," said her husband, "but I don't think you realize what you are letting yourself in for. The Lodgings there are really——"

"The Lodgings are lousy," said her ladyship tersely. "That is notorious. None the less, I prefer to put up with a little discomfort to taking any risks where your safety is concerned."

Barber shrugged his shoulders.

"Very well," he said, "since you insist. But don't say you haven't been warned. Mercifully, we shall only be there for a very short time. Feeling as I do that there is nothing whatever behind these different occurrences, I am only sorry that you should disarrange your plans for nothing."

"There are no plans to disarrange. It isn't as if there were any entertaining in London worth speaking of just now. J had intended to go to see Michael again, but that can wait. Which reminds me, I have had a letter from him, which I must discuss with you some time."

The hint was too broad to be disregarded, and Derek tactfully left the room shortly afterwards.

Hilda followed the Marshal's progress out of the room with her eyes, and as soon as he had gone produced a letter from her bag.

"Michael has heard from Sebald-Smith's people," she said.

"Yes?"

"He's asking for fifteen thousand pounds."

"Fifteen thousand!" The Judge started so violently that he almost fell from his chair. "But this is preposterous!"

"Obviously. The argument is, apparently, that he is maimed for life, and that his career as a pianist is at an end. Of course, Sebald's fees of recent years have been——"

"I dare say. But fifteen thousand——!"

"I shall write to Michael, of course, and tell him that it is out of all reason. He wants to know what counter offer we should suggest."

Barber rubbed the top of his head in perplexity.

"It's a very difficult situation," he said.

"I know it is, but saying so doesn't take us much further." Then, as he remained in a dejected silence, she went on impatiently, "After all, William, you must have often had to advise clients in cases like this. Try and think of it as a case brought to you for an opinion. What would you advise?"

The Judge shook his head mournfully.

"It's no good," he groaned. "There has never been a case like this—never!"

"Every litigant thinks that about his own troubles. I've often heard you say so."

"And that is perfectly true. But this case *is* different. After all, Hilda, I am a High Court Judge."

"I've heard you say, too," she went on, pursuing her own line of thought, "that nobody is competent to advise in his own case. Why shouldn't you get advice—from one of the other judges, for instance?"

"No, no!" Barber almost shouted. "Don't you understand, Hilda, that if once this matter becomes known I am lost? That is why this wretched pianist has me at his mercy. He knows that I can't possibly afford to fight the claim, and he can fix the damages at any figure he pleases. The long and the short of it is that if he can't be got to see reason, we are ruined."

"Then he *must* be made to see reason," Hilda answered. She tried hard to imagine how Sebastian Sebald-Smith would react to the present situation. She had known him well enough once, but had never had to consider him as a prospective litigant. For an artist, she believed him to be a reasonable man, and that was something. Then her mind went to Sally Parsons, that most unreasonable woman, and her heart misgave her. But she went on bravely, "Obviously this is only a bargaining figure. Even Sebald-Smith's earnings must be comparatively small during the war. Suppose we can beat him down to five thousand—a year's income——"

"Two years at least, with taxation at its present level, and it is certain to go higher."

"Well, two years if you like. We could arrange payment by instalments and"—her voice faltered—"live very simply. . . ."

The Judge shook his head.

"You don't appreciate the position, Hilda," he said. "The

moment that anything of this becomes public property, I shall be forced to resign. There will be no question of two years' income or one. Sebald-Smith has only to issue a writ to make my position intolerable. And," he added, "I have not earned my pension by ten years."

"They gave Battersby a pension, though he had only been on the bench four years," Hilda remarked.

"That was a different case. Battersby resigned merely because his health broke down."

"Why shouldn't you resign for ill health too? After all, you had some nasty colds last winter and I'm sure Dr. Fairmile would say anything if I asked him to."

"Really, Hilda! Have you no conscience?"

"Of course not, where this is concerned. And I shan't allow you to have one either. William, I think I have found the solution. I shall write to Fairmile to-morrow. It will be a hideous strain trying to live on the pension, but it will be better than nothing, and after a decent interval to get better I dare say you could get some war work, or sit as Chairman of Commissions and things. Once you are safely resigned we can bargain with Sebald-Smith on more or less equal terms. If he does get a judgment against you, he can't attach the pension, can he? I must look it up when I get home."

At this point Hilda became aware that her husband had been saying something several times over, which she had been too engrossed in her theme to attend to. As she paused to take breath he seized the opportunity to repeat it yet again.

"Stop!" said the Judge. "Stop, stop, *stop!*"

"What is the matter?"

"The matter is that your scheme is hopelessly unpractical, besides being flagrantly dishonest. Even if Fairmile were prepared to jeopardize his professional reputation by assisting in such a fraud, I am quite certain that the Treasury would not sanction the payment of a pension that had not been earned at such a time as this. It would immediately put everyone on inquiry. There would be questions asked in the House." Never having been a Member of Parliament, Barber was nervously sensitive to questions asked in the House. "And in any case," he added, "you may take it that I could not possibly be a party to such a scheme."

"Really," said Hilda, "you are most depressing. I cannot understand you, William. You make light of all these determined attempts on your life, but when it is a question of money you collapse entirely."

"That is because I see things in their proper perspective," the Judge replied. "I do not believe that there have been any attempts on my life, determined or otherwise. But this is serious, and I confess that I am perturbed at it—gravely perturbed."

And he gloomily went upstairs to dress for dinner.

Derek wondered why, when that evening he happened to mention to Greene that Lady Barber was coming to Wimblingham, the latter greeted the news with such obvious disfavour. He said nothing, it was true—it was hardly to be expected that he would—but his look was eloquent of disapproval, in which seemed blended a quite personal distress at the prospect. To probe the matter further, he tested the reactions of Savage to the same question, and found that normally gloomy individual positively sepulchral when the subject was touched upon. Beamish, however, without being approached, brought enlightenment. Rather to Derek's embarrassment Beamish had elected to make something of a confidant of the Marshal. He seemed to regard him in the nature of a go-between, through whom his views could at need be discreetly conveyed to higher authority, and nothing that Derek could say or do could persuade him that he was not prepared to take his side in any domestic row that might be going. On this particular evening he buttonholed Derek when he was on his way to bed, drew him into the comfortable little sitting-room which he occupied on the ground floor, and settled down to a chat.

"So we're leaving Southington to-morrow, Marshal," he began. "I dessay you'll not be sorry to go either. I can't say I care much for the place myself, for all the Under Sheriff is quite a decent gentleman. But things haven't been too easy on the domestic side here, as you are aware. And I was looking forward to a little peace and quiet at Wimblingham."

Derek said nothing. Beamish smoked a pipe in short angry puffs for a moment or two. Obviously he was nursing a grievance, and presently it burst out.

"And now her ladyship's coming to Wimblingham!" he exclaimed. "Well, I wish her joy of it, Marshal, that is all— I wish her joy of it. Do you know, sir, that no judge's lady has stayed at Wimblingham since nineteen nought twelve? Except Lady Fosbery, and she, of course, doesn't count."

Derek was torn between a desire to find out why Mr. Justice Fosbery's wife did not count and a feeling that it was time that he attempted the difficult task of putting Beamish in his place. Pride won by a short head.

"Really, Beamish," he said, "you can hardly expect me to discuss Lady Barber's decision with you."

"I am not discussing her ladyship," Beamish answered with some hauteur. "I am discussing the Lodgings at Wimblingham. And that's a matter that concerns us all, as you will discover to your cost. What I say is, it's not fair to the Marshal or the Judge's Clerk, let alone the domestic staff, for a judge's lady to foist herself on those Lodgings."

"I understand that they are very uncomfortable," said Derek, "but I still don't see why——"

"You heard her ladyship say that they were lousy," Beamish interrupted, "and we will let that word pass for want of a better. That's not the point—at least not the whole of the point, if you follow me. What you don't realize, Mr. Marshall, is this: there are only two decent bedrooms in those Lodgings, and one just passable."

And then the whole mystery was made plain, and with it Beamish's grievance, Savage's gloom, and Greene's mute despair. In a bachelor establishment, which had become the normal rule at Wimblingham, the larger of the two decent bedrooms was naturally appropriated to the use of the Judge. His Marshal occupied the other. The Clerk, next in the hierarchy, took the one which Beamish described as passable. The butler and marshal's man made shift in the least unattractive of the remaining rooms. Now, with the advent of a lady who would have to be accommodated in one of the two best rooms, the rest of the household would be compelled to take a step down. Derek would oust Beamish from the second-class room, Beamish in turn would have to put up with what had been barely good enough for Savage, and finally Greene would be expelled by Savage to seek some nameless dog-kennel beneath the rafters, untenanted since nineteen nought twelve. Such are the penalties involved in departing from precedent in any matter affecting the administration of justice.

The Fosbery case, Derek also learned, did not in any way impair the chain of authority which was now to be so rashly broken. The simple reason was that this affectionate couple, though well-stricken in years, had never abandoned the habit of sharing the same bed. Lady Fosbery's presence, therefore, made no difference to the billeting arrangements.

"Of course, they're old-fashioned," Beamish commented. "He doesn't even ask for a dressing-room of his own. Why, they tell me. . . ."

He launched into details of a surprisingly intimate character. Derek, somewhat against his will, was so enthralled by these that he quite forgot for the time a question that had been puzzling him ever since Beamish began his exposition.

He remembered it again just as he was getting into bed. How did Beamish know that Lady Barber had called the Lodgings "lousy"?

Nothing could be higher testimony to the power of local government in England than the accommodation provided for His Majesty's Judges in the county town of Wimbleshire. In the Lodgings there, as in all similar establishments on the circuit, a book was provided in which each visiting judge inscribed his name and was invited to add such comments as to him seemed fit upon the hospitality afforded. For upwards of thirty years judges had availed themselves of the invitation, and without exception their comments had been to the same effect. Ranging from querulous protest through bitter sarcasm to straightforward abuse, the entries made an interesting contribution to the literature of ill temper. Yet, throughout thirty years the county authorities of Wimbleshire, through sheer British determination, had succeeded in resisting the clamant demands of their exalted guests. In the spirit which had inspired the Wimbleshire Fencibles to stand fast against the Old Guard in their squares at Waterloo, they had withstood the massed assault of almost the entire strength of the King's Bench Division of the Supreme Court of Judicature. In 1938, however, their resistance seemed at an end. Authority launched its ultimate irresistible attack, and the fiat went forth that unless new accommodation for His Majesty's Judges was made available, Wimblingham should cease to be an assize town. Its ancient rank and dignity should be taken away and transferred to its hated rival, the upstart borough of Podchester. Sullenly, the County Councillors prepared to surrender. After one long last glorious debate in the Council Chamber they accepted the enemy's terms. At enormous cost a site was bought and cleared, plans were prepared by the most expensive architect who could be found, and already the foundations of the new building had been laid when, for the second time in history, the Prussians arrived upon the stricken field and the tide of battle turned once more. For the duration of the war, at least, the Lodging's book of Wimblingham was saved for a few more pages of vituperation.

That the authorities of Wimbleshire had been able to carry out their successful defence so long was largely due to the fact that the Lodgings did not constitute a separate building but formed part of a large block which held also the Council Chamber itself and the Court in which the Assizes were held. It was a picturesque pile. Resting on foundations reputed to be Roman, and with stonework in its walls that was unquestionably Norman, it had been re-modelled and patched by different hands to suit the tastes and needs of succeeding generations until, in the late seven-teenth century, somebody, whom local tradition firmly but incorrectly declared to be Wren, masked the congeries of buildings with the charming façade which now fronts the central square of the town. After that beyond the provision of a little early Victorian plumbing, no further structural alterations were ever made, and behind the orderly Renais-sance screen a labyrinth of passages and staircases gave access to offices, chambers, and halls, amongst them the suite of rooms which had been the subject of so many indig-nant memoranda.

Derek prided himself on being able to rough it when necessary, but he gave a gasp of dismay when Greene opened the door of his room and with mute eloquence displayed what lay beyond. It was a gaunt, cold apartment, far too high for its size. It was illuminated by a dormer window out of which Derek, by standing on his toes, was just able to verify the fact that the metallic clamour which filled the room proceeded from the municipal tram terminus immedi-ately beneath. The ceiling showed ominous stains of damp and the sagging wire mattress of the bed uttered a tired protesting creak when Derek incautiously tried it with his hand. Remembering that this was the room that Beamish had described as "passable", he shivered as he thought of the descending degrees of discomfort to which the staff would be subjected.

Leaving the room, Derek duly fell down the two steps

outside the door into the dark corridor beyond. He recovered himself and picked his way down three or four further steps into a broader passage, out of which the main rooms of the lodgings opened. This passage apparently served other uses as well. The first door that he tried led him straight into the public gallery of the Court, the second into what had once been the Grand Jury room and was now apparently a depository for babies' respirators. Finally, guided by the sound of voices, he reached the drawing-room. Here, in a decor that had changed little since it was originally ordered in the year of the Great Exhibition, he found Lady Barber, in surprisingly high spirits.

"Isn't this too exquisitely foul?" she said. "William and I have been trying to concoct something really stinging to put in the book. I'm sure there are rats in my room. I feel that I'm the bravest woman in England, venturing where no judge's wife has ever dared before."

"Except Lady Fosbery," said Derek. He repeated the gist of what Beamish had told him and was rewarded with a burst of laughter in which the Judge, who looked depressed and out of sorts, joined rather grudgingly.

"Divine!" said Hilda. "I shall dine out on that story for months—I mean, I should if there were any dinner-parties left to go to. Talking of dinners, I don't know what sort of food we shall get here. Mrs. Square says that the kitchen range is completely beyond control. Thank Heaven, the calendar here is very short, with no civil work, so a couple of nights will see us through. I expect you'll be glad of a day or two's rest from your duties before the next assize, won't you, Mr. Marshall? It's a mercy that next to nobody seems to commit any crimes in Wimbleshire."

"It is a singular thing," observed Barber, "but I have often observed that this county is comparatively free from serious crime."

The event was to prove that there were exceptions to this rule.

Chapter 9

A BLOW IN THE DARK

Derek turned over in bed for the twentieth time, and for the twentieth time his bed registered a tinny protest. The movement had no effect on his comfort, as owing to the deep trough in which he lay his body returned always to exactly the same spot. The knobs and protuberances which variegated the surface of the mattress went into his right side instead of his left, and that was all. Dismally comparing himself to St. Lawrence on his gridiron, Derek prepared to await the dawn.

Like most healthy people, who do not know what insomnia really is, Derek viewed the prospect of a sleepless night with horror. He would have found a book to occupy the time, but he shrank from the labour involved in replacing the cumbrous black-out curtains which he had incautiously removed before retiring. Besides, he reflected, the light was so placed as to make it impossible to read in bed without straining his eyes. There was nothing for it but to endure his fate with hardihood. It was his second night at Wimblingham, and, he was thankful to think, his last. The assize, no less grandiose and expensive than its predecessors at Markhampton and Southington, had barely filled a short working day. Three prisoners only had appeared and two of these had obligingly pleaded guilty. In the remaining case, Pettigrew, holding a brief for someone much junior to himself who was serving in the army, had skilfully jollied the jury into an acquittal in the face of determined opposition from the Bench. There had, Derek remembered, been more than a hint of personal antagonism towards Pettigrew in the summing up, and undisguised malice in the smile with which counsel had bowed to the Judge when, at the conclusion of the case, he formally asked for his client to be discharged. Why, he wondered, did the two men dislike each other so much? Had it anything to do with Hilda? (He had already reached the stage of thinking of her by her Christian name, and he vaguely wondered whether he would ever have the courage to call her by it openly.) Certainly she appeared to manage to remain on the friendliest possible terms with them both. Was there, his rambling thoughts continued, anything at all in Hilda's idea that any danger threatened the Judge? And who was this person Heppenstall whose name kept on cropping up whenever the subject was discussed? Heppenstall, in a way, had been responsible for the accident at Markhampton. At least, it was after his name had been mentioned that the Judge had started drinking all that brandy. Perhaps Beamish could explain. He seemed to have all sorts of private knowledge at his fingers' ends. But one didn't like to encourage Beamish too much. He was quite familiar enough already. Queer fish, Beamish. Can't say I like him much. Hilda can't bear the sight of him. Should like to know exactly what she has against him. Don't expect she would ever say outright, though. She's marvellous at just indicating her feelings without any direct words. Like the quotation: "Just hint a fault and indicate dislike." That's wrong—not "indicate", some other three syllable word . . . "Intimate"? No. . . . I forget. . . . Odd, what Pettigrew said to Beamish this morning, just before the Court sat. "Been playing darts much, lately?" Seemed to annoy Beamish, too. . . . Darts. . . . Beamish. . . . "Institute dislike?" Silly idea, of course not. . . . You institute proceedings, not dislike. . . . Proceedings for darts in the King's Bench Division. . . .

Derek slept.

Some time later he awoke with a start. His sleep had been a light one, and troubled with fantastic dreams, and he seemed to jump into full consciousness all at once in a manner quite different from his usual slow, reluctant morning wakening. He sat up in bed. Apart from the inevitable noise occasioned by the movement, he could hear nothing. The last Wimblingham tram had long since clanked its way to rest and the street outside was completely quiet. None the less, Derek felt certain that it was a noise that had roused him, and further, something told him that the disturbance, whatever it had been, had come, not from outside, but a good deal nearer at hand. He continued to listen for a moment or two, and had just decided to try to go to sleep again when the silence was broken quite unmistakably by a whole series of different sounds. Afterwards, Derek was annoyed to find a good deal of uncertainty in his recollection of the precise order in which these sounds occurred, but of their nature there was no doubt. Somewhere a door slammed sharply, footsteps moved hastily along the corridor —the main corridor, Derek thought, and not the little passage outside his room—there was a bump that quite certainly indicated that somebody had stumbled over one of the concealed flights of steps, and, at some point or other in the jumble of untoward noises, there was a loud, high-pitched scream. It was this last that brought Derek in a bound from his bed.

He fumbled in the dark for his dressing-gown and slippers, groped for, but failed to find, his torch, and opened the door of his room. He listened for a moment, and heard the confused hum of a household suddenly roused from sleep. Taking a step forward into the darkness he once again missed his footing on the steps so ingeniously provided immediately outside the door. This time he almost fell prone in his haste, and as he tried to right himself he was knocked into by a heavy unseen form coming from further up the side passage. Derek went down to the floor and the newcomer tripped over him, in so doing kicking him firmly in the ribs. It was, Derek felt, rather like falling on the ball in front of an advancing pack of rugger forwards.

Derek, badly winded, prepared to grapple with his unknown assailant, but at that moment an electric torch was flashed in his face and Beamish's voice said, "Oh, it's you, Mr. Marshall! You nearly gave me a nasty fall."

Derek made no reply to what he felt to be a gross understatement. "What is the matter?" he asked.

"That's what I came to find out," said Beamish. "It's a fair disgrace there being no lights in this passage. It's all skylights above, see? And the Council won't go to the expense of doing the black-out properly."

Waving his torch, Beamish preceded him down the passage into the main corridor, which was dimly lighted enough, but seemed by contrast a blaze of illumination. In it Derek recognized the other members of the household—figures familiar enough, but strangely transmogrified in their night attire. The Judge looked gaunter and gawkier than ever in an unexpectedly gaily patterned dressing-gown. Mrs. Square, was positively Dickensian in curl-papers. Savage, dishevelled but infinitely respectful, contrived still to look unmistakably a butler. Beamish, Derek now perceived, was closely buttoned into a huge check ulster which reached almost to the ground and gave him a singularly rakish appearance. A surly looking individual, whom he presumed to be a night watchman, stood rather helplessly by. All this he observed with the unreal clarity of things seen in a nightmare, before he became aware of the cause and centre of the whole uproar. When he had once seen this, however, he no longer had eyes for anything else. On the floor, her head supported by her husband's arms, lay Hilda Barber. She was very pale. One eye was half-closed and blood was trickling from a cut just beneath it. She held her hand to her throat and appeared to be breathing with difficulty. She was not unconscious, for from time to time she muttered words which Derek could not catch.

For a time that could not have been longer than a few minutes but seemed endless, everyone seemed stricken with the paralysis that sudden emergency sometimes produces. It was a paralysis, however, that did not affect their tongues. Everybody was talking at once. Mrs. Square was repeating over and over again, "Poor lady!" and "Did you ever!" The Judge said several times, "Hilda! Can you hear me?" as if he was talking on an unsatisfactory telephone. Then he added, "Fetch a doctor, someone!" and "Where are the police?" The night watchman rejoined in an aggrieved tone, "I've rung down for the police. They'll be 'ere in a minute."

Derek broke into this dialogue by boldly coming forward and seizing Lady Barber round the ankles.

"We ought to put her to bed, sir!" he fairly shouted at the bemused old man who still had hold of the other end of the patient.

"Yes, yes, of course!" said the Judge, coming suddenly to life.

Together they lifted her and carried her into her bedroom, a little further along the corridor. The spot where she lay, Derek noticed, was outside the Judge's room, next to it. As they laid her on the bed, Hilda lifted her head and said, quite distinctly, "Are you all right, William?"

"Yes, yes!" answered Barber. "Can you hear me, Hilda?"

"He hit me," she said, and then appeared to lose consciousness.

Through the open bedroom door, Derek could see that the passage had suddenly become crowded with policemen.

Ages later, as it seemed to Derek, he was sitting at breakfast with the Judge. After the turmoil of the night, which had seemed positively endless, the breakfast table, with its coffee and bacon, appeared refreshingly normal. The Judge was already seated when he came in, reading *The Times* as usual, and apparently with his appetite unimpaired. His eyes were somewhat bloodshot, but otherwise he showed no traces of what must have been a sleepless night.

Derek inquired after Lady Barber.

"As well as could be expected," was the reply. "Of course she must be kept very quiet." His eyes returned to his paper. "I don't like the look of things in Finland," he announced. "Another cup of coffee, please, Marshal. It seems to taste very peculiar, I don't know what's wrong with it. The water can't have been properly boiling when it was made." He took the cup and went on, "How did that man get in here last night, I want to know? I shall have a word or two to say to the Chief Constable when he appears." He drank a mouthful of the coffee, made a grimace into the cup, looked back at his paper and concluded, "It's a shocking business altogether."

Derek murmured agreement, although from the context he was left in some doubt whether the last words referred to the state of affairs with regard to Finland, the unsatisfactory nature of the coffee, or the adventures of the night before. He was trying to find some comment which would be equally appropriate to all three subjects when a diversion was effected by the door opening to admit Hilda.

"My dear!" cried the Judge, starting to his feet. "What does this mean?"

"I'm sorry if I startled you," said Hilda, calmly. "I know I look a hideous spectacle, but I thought you would be prepared for it. Now Mr. Marshall takes it all quite coolly."

She turned towards Derek a face disfigured by an enormous black eye. Beneath her make-up she was pale, and round her neck she wore a chiffon scarf which could not wholly conceal some ugly bruises on either side of her throat.

"But, Hilda, you ought to be in bed! The doctor said positively——"

"The doctor doesn't know what the beds in these Lodgings

are like," said Hilda, helping herself to toast and butter. "I lay there as long as I could bear it and then I decided to get up. It was all I could do to get outside my door, though. There was a great fat policeman blocking it. On the stable-door principle, I suppose."

"The Chief Constable will be here shortly," said the Judge. "He sent a message just now to ask if you would feel equal to making a statement. I told him——"

"I'm quite ready to make any statement to anybody, so long as I can get away from Wimblingham this morning and never see the place again," said Hilda firmly.

"But tell me, what actually happened?"

"My dear William, what happened was exactly what I had warned you might happen. Somebody made an attack on you last night and I got in his way, that's all. No details, please! If I've got to tell the whole story to the policeman I don't want to go all through it twice. It was quite unpleasant enough without that."

"An attack on me?"

"Certainly. You don't imagine anybody's going to take the trouble to break in here just for the fun of blacking *my* eye, do you? Besides—you'll hear all about it directly. May I have a look at *The Times*, if you've done with it?"

Barber meekly surrendered the paper.

"When I think", he observed, "of the fuss that the average woman makes about the smallest misadventure and how gladly she will seize the opportunity to tell her story twenty times over if possible, I—I am really impressed by you, Hilda."

Hilda, rustling the pages of *The Times*, looked up with what would have been, but for her disfigurement, a charming smile.

"That", she observed, "is as it should be."

Ten o'clock brought the city Chief Constable, an amiable but badly worried man. With him came a detective inspector and a doctor. The latter was professionally shocked at finding his patient out of bed, but on examining her could do no more than congratulate her on her splendid constitution. He wrote out a prescription which Hilda lightheartedly made into a spill for her cigarette as soon as his back was turned and left her to the two policemen.

Lady Barber's statement was quite short and to the point.

"I woke up in the night," she said. "No, it's no use asking me what the time was. I didn't look at my watch, and in any case it's hopelessly unreliable. I thought I heard someone moving in the passage outside, so I went along to my husband's room to investigate. It was quite dark and I was feeling my way along the wall. Just as I got to his door I bumped into someone. I said, 'Who are you?' or something like that. The next thing I knew was a torch being flashed in my face. The man, whoever he was, caught me by the throat—here"—she indicated the bruises beneath the scarf —"and then I felt a terrific blow in the eye. I think he must actually have hit me with the torch, because everything went dark. He let go of me as he struck and I fell down. Then I suppose I screamed. And that is really all I can remember."

There was a pause, and then the inspector said softly, "Why did you go to your husband's room, Lady Barber?"

"Because I suspected that there was somebody about, and I thought he might make an attempt on my husband's life —and I was right," she added triumphantly.

"Had you any reason to fear for his lordship's safety, then?"

"Certainly I had. Otherwise I shouldn't have come to Wimblingham—odious place."

The city Chief Constable blenched at this slur on his own town, of which he was oddly proud.

"Perhaps it would help us if you would tell us your reasons," he said.

Hilda nodded towards the Judge.

"You tell," she said.

Somewhat haltingly, Barber related the story of the

anonymous letters at Markhampton and the incident of the poisoned chocolates.

"I freely admit", he added, "that I did not take any of these incidents particularly seriously. But it seems that I was wrong."

The Chief Constable looked wise and said nothing. Rather diffidently, the inspector took it upon himself to speak.

"It seems a strange business," he said. "It doesn't seem to hang together, if I may say so. I mean, the person who sent the threatening letters might follow it up by sending poisoned chocolates—though it was a crude kind of poison, admittedly—or he might attempt a crime of violence, but hardly both. I mean, sir," he addressed his superior, "we don't generally find one man attempting two different classes of crimes, do we? Criminals generally tend to keep to a groove."

"That is so," said the Chief Constable. "Of course, we have no proof that the assailant in this case came here with the intention of committing an act of violence. He might have been merely a thief. Had you any articles of particular value in your room, my lord?"

The Judge shook his head.

"I had not," he said. "And frankly, what the man intended to do here is a question that does not interest me very much at the moment. What I want to know is, how was it that he got into these Lodgings and how did he get out again without being apprehended? It is a somewhat extraordinary state of affairs if the lodgings of His Majesty's Judge of Assize can be visited by a marauder with apparently complete impunity, and one which, I must say, appears to me to reflect very little credit on the police force of this city."

The Chief Constable's face bore the expression of a man who had long foreseen a blow which he could not avoid. In his distress the mask of officialdom dropped off and he became quite human.

"I can only say, my lord," he said, "that if I had had any warning at all that particular precautions were necessary—any hint of the story you have just told me, for instance—I should have stationed a constable outside your lordship's room all night. Short of that, honestly there is nothing I can do to make this place safe—nothing! I have spoken to the Clerk of the Peace about it time and again, but nothing has been done. It is hopeless!"

He went on, with an eloquence born of deep feeling, to enlarge upon the peculiarities and disadvantages of the building in which they were. It had twenty different recognized entrances and exits. Apart from these, two of its irregular sides fronted on to narrow alleys, from which it would be the simplest matter to break into one of the ill-protected ground-floor windows, and in the blacked-out streets it would be mere chance if a patrolling constable happened to catch him in the act. Once inside, there was nothing to prevent the intruder from rambling all over the building.

"There are night watchmen, of course," the Chief Constable added, "but there never were enough of them, and a good half have been taken for war service of one kind or another. Doors are locked, but there's not one in the place I wouldn't undertake to force with a hairpin."

"It would be pretty difficult for anyone to find his way about the place, though," Derek pointed out. "Unless he knew it fairly well to start with. I know I lost my way completely between here and my bedroom on the day we arrived. Don't you think that points to a man with local knowledge?"

"It ought to, but it does not," said the Chief Constable more despondently than ever. "For sixpence you can get at any bookshop in the city a local handbook with a complete plan of the building, showing all the principal rooms, including, of course, the Judge's lodgings. That's because this is an Ancient Monument. All I can say is, Ancient Monuments are all very well in their proper places, which is museums, but they have no call to put Judges in them and expect the police to guard them. If you'll excuse my saying so, my lord."

"And", the inspector put in by way of rubbing it in, "I ought to point out that it would be quite unnecessary to break into the building at all. All that anybody need do would be to come in during the day on one of a dozen pretexts—to make an inquiry about his rates, or A.R.P., or what not—and conceal himself somewhere in the place till nightfall. It's as easy as pie."

Derek had an inspiration.

"The public gallery of the Court opens out of this corridor," he said.

"Exactly. And a very likely place to choose. I'm obliged to you for the suggestion, sir."

"Well," said Barber, "this certainly reveals a very unsatisfactory state of affairs. I am not at all sure that it is not my duty to make some official representations upon the matter. But I can quite see that in view of what you tell me, my strictures upon the police force which you command, Mr. Chief Constable, may have been somewhat—ah!—more severe than was appropriate to the circumstances. Meanwhile——"

"Meanwhile," said the Chief Constable, looking a good deal more cheerful than he had been at any time since the interview began, "meanwhile, we shall of course do all we can to bring this man to justice. If he is a local man, there won't be much difficulty. By midday to-day every man in the city with a record of violence against him will have been pulled in and we shan't let any of them go until they have fully accounted for every minute of last night. I have spoken to the Chief Constable of the County and he is doing the same for his jurisdiction. If he's not a local, then it's a different matter altogether. But we'll do our utmost. You would wish the Yard to be notified, my lord?"

The Judge hesitated for a moment and then nodded.

"Yes," he said, "I think that that will be necessary."

The Chief Constable rose and was about to leave the room when his subordinate murmured something in his ear which caused him to turn back.

"There is one further possibility, my lord," he said, "which you may think very far-fetched, but I feel bound to mention it. Do you consider that this assault could have been committed by someone *inside* the lodgings, a member of the household, I mean, and not an intruder at all?"

There was a moment's stupefaction and then the Judge laughed.

"Apart from ourselves, there are only four persons who were sleeping here last night," he said, "and one of them is a woman. I think I can safely say that from what I know of them you can discard that theory."

"Thank you, my lord. That is as I expected but I thought I ought to mention it."

Later that morning the party left for London. Hilda had contrived a rakish veil which fell over one side of her hat and completely concealed her black eye while looking exceedingly becoming. She need hardly have bothered, however, so far as any spectators at Wimblingham station were concerned, for an impressive body of police kept nearly half the platform free until they were safely in their carriage. Evidently the Chief Constable was taking no chance. Looking out of the window, Derek could see his broad chest heave with a sigh of relief as the train steamed out.

"Shut the window, Marshal," said Barber.

As he tugged at the strap, Derek was conscious of a sharp pain in his side. He realized that he was still sore from his encounter with Beamish of the night before. How hard he had kicked him! You wouldn't have thought bedroom slippers could hurt so much. He put his hand to his ribs and winced. Could they have been bedroom slippers? And if they were not, why not? He tried to recollect Beamish's appearance. There had been a big ulster which had hidden everything else. He had been too busy to look at his feet. . . . A fantastic notion, born of the Chief Constable's last words, floated into his mind, and refused to be dislodged.

"Mr. Marshall, you look quite distraught," said Hilda kindly. "Have one of the Judge's caramels. They're quite safe. I bought them myself."

Chapter 10

TEA AND THEORY

━━━━━━

"Will you come to tea with me to-morrow?" Hilda said abruptly to Derek, just before they parted at the station.

It was more than an invitation, Derek felt. A command? Not exactly. An appeal then? Something between the two, perhaps. In any case, without knowing exactly why, he accepted, simply because he felt that he had no option in the matter. It was not in the least what he wanted to do. He was going home to his mother in Hampshire that evening and he did not at all enjoy the prospect of breaking into his short holiday. But when a hostess of Lady Barber's calibre looks a young man firmly in the eyes—even though she may happen to have only one eye of her own available at the moment—it takes a very determined young man to refuse her proferred hospitality.

As it turned out, he found himself next day only too glad to have the excuse to return to London. Since he had been away, he had to some extent forgotten the maddening feeling of uselessness which had oppressed him ever since a medical officer had told him brutally that he was hopelessly unfit for active service. At home once more, it returned to him in full measure. All his friends in the village had disappeared into some form of war work or another. His mother was spending all her days at an A.R.P. centre, waiting patiently at the telephone for warnings of air raids which never seemed to come, and had no time for him. Moreover, the two spare rooms of the small house were now occupied by a couple of London mothers and their small children, with whom with the best will in the world he could not get upon speaking, let alone upon friendly terms. He had been accustomed to leading the rather spoiled life of the only son of a widowed mother and the contrast was somewhat painful.

Derek spent his evening composing yet another letter to somebody who he hoped might be able to find him a job in the ranks of the temporary Civil Service and in filling up yet another form supplied by that disheartening institution, the Central Registry of the Ministry of Labour. Next day he took an unnecessarily early train to London.

Hilda had appointed the meeting at her club. Derek went there vaguely expecting something in the nature of a party. He found his hostess by herself, in a small room which she appeared to have secured for her exclusive use, to judge by the fact that while they were together only two other members intruded and straightway tiptoed out again with muffled apologies. She greeted him in her usual friendly fashion and rang for tea. While this was being brought she chattered away amusingly enough but to little purpose. Derek began to wonder whether her seclusion was merely due to her disfigurement, as to which she made various more or less facetious allusions. But as soon as tea had been brought in and the waitress had withdrawn, her manner changed to one of seriousness, almost of solemnity.

"I asked you to come here," she said, "because I wanted to talk to you without being disturbed."

She did not say by whom she was afraid of being disturbed, but it was obvious to whom she was referring. Indeed, her next words showed in what direction her thoughts were running.

"Derek," she went on earnestly, "this is serious. William does not appear to me in the least to realize how serious it is."

Derek was so impressed by being addressed by his Christian name that for the moment he paid little attention to what she was saying, and during that moment looked, for him, uncommonly stupid. Hilda instantly noted his lack of attention and apparently guessed the meaning of it, for she coloured slightly and then continued, frowning in the effort to concentrate upon her subject.

"He doesn't—he never has—pay any regard to his personal safety," she said. "For that matter, in his own affairs he has always been quite childishly careless. You've had some experience of that already. And it puts a very heavy responsibility on you."

Derek shifted rather uncomfortably in his chair under her purposeful gaze. Nobody had hitherto indicated to him that the position of Judge's Marshal entailed any particular responsibility, apart from wearing a top hat and pouring out tea, and he had some difficulty in adjusting his mind to the idea.

Hilda, as usual, seemed to divine what was going on in his thoughts. "Do you know what the Marshal originally was?" she said. "A bodyguard for the Judge. In the old days it was part of his duty to sleep across the door of the Judge's room to protect him from any intruders."

Derek was moved to say that he could hardly have slept worse at Wimblingham if he had followed the old custom, but his levity was not well received.

"A bodyguard," Lady Barber repeated. "That is what the Judge needs, and that is what you and I together have got to supply during the rest of this circuit."

"Then you really think there is still danger of some attack on him?" Derek asked.

"I have not the smallest doubt of it. Has anybody? It isn't only that from the very beginning of the circuit things have been happening, it is that they have been getting more and more serious each time. Just consider. First we have an anonymous letter. Then comes the motor accident——"

"But that surely can't have had anything to do with it," Derek objected.

"Followed immediately by another letter," Hilda went on triumphantly. "That means at least that whoever is planning all this knew about the accident and means to use it for his own purposes. As for the accident itself—even there I am not sure. You may think it absurd of me but I have a very strong feeling that all these things hang together in some way, and that means that we have to deal with a very subtle, dangerous person. Then come the poisoned chocolates, and finally this assault on me, which of course was intended for him. What is coming next? For that something will come, I am absolutely certain, and we have got to be on our guard against it."

"Of course I am ready to do anything I can," Derek said, "but I should have thought a Judge on circuit was about as well guarded as anyone could be. And isn't this a job for the police, in the first place?"

Hilda smiled.

"I haven't forgotten the police," she said. "You may have wondered why I have come out alone to-day instead of keeping an eye on him while he is in London. Well, the answer is that he has been followed all day by a plain-clothes man from Scotland Yard. He's probably waiting for him outside the Athenaeum at this moment. William doesn't know anything about it. I arranged it myself. One of the Assistant Commissioners happens to be a friend of mine, you see. And that reminds me——" She looked at her watch. "I am expecting someone here directly, whom I want you to see. He should be here by now. And meanwhile"—she smiled her most winning smile— "will you help me—Derek? It means a lot to me, you know."

Somehow or another, Derek found her hand in his. In a voice suddenly gone very husky, he grated:

"I'll do my best—Hilda."

The brief moment of emotion passed as suddenly as it had arisen. An instant later Hilda was sitting back in her chair, talking in a business-like fashion about the precautions which would have to be taken to safeguard the Judge during the rest of the circuit.

"We don't know where the next attack may come from," she said. "And after my experience at Wimblingham I feel that we have got to be prepared for anything. The only safe way will be for us to agree that at any time, day or night, he should be under the protection of one or the other of us. We should take it in turns, of course, like sentries, and there's no reason why, if we do it properly, he should even know that there is anything unusual going on. Perhaps you think all this rather absurd?"

Derek protested that he did not.

"Very well then. I will work out a little scheme between now and Monday, and——"

There was a knock on the door, and a servant appeared.

"A gentleman has called to see you, my lady," she said.

A mountain of a man appeared behind her.

The newcomer stood quite silent in the middle of the little room, which his great bulk made to appear even smaller than it was, until the servant had withdrawn, taking with her the tea things. When the door had closed behind her, he said in a quiet voice, "Detective Inspector Mallett, of the Metropolitan Police."

At Hilda's invitation he brought forward a chair and sat down. Derek noticed that for all his size he moved as lightly as a cat. He found himself looking into a pair of very bright grey eyes, set in a large red face the geniality of which was oddly contradicted by a fierce, pointed military moustache. It was a brief scrutiny, friendly but appraising, and at the end of it Derek felt that he had been sized up, noted, described and docketed for future reference. A good many people had reason to remember—and to fear—that quick, purposeful glance.

"Have you had tea, Inspector?" Hilda asked.

"I have, thank you, my lady," said Mallett in a polite

voice, in which a keen ear might nevertheless have detected a tinge of regret.

He cleared his throat, and became at once the official.

"On the instructions of the Assistant Commissioner," he said, "I made certain inquiries this morning in Bond Street, at the shop occupied by Messrs. Bechamel's."

He pronounced the name unashamedly, "Beechammle". In the rather stiff, police tone which he had adopted, any but a purely British pronunciation would, one felt, have been ridiculous.

"I was directed to report the result of my inquiries to you," he went on, "and to take your further instructions in the matter—as to which I am at the moment very largely in the dark. Perhaps it will be most convenient if I make my report in the first place. You will then be able to judge to what extent it affects the other matters on which police assistance is required."

He took from his pocket a regulation police notebook, carefully found his place in it, and then laid it down on the table beside him. Somewhat ostentatiously, he never glanced at it again during the course of his recital. Mallett was pardonably vain of his powers of memory and the presence of the notebook might be explained as a sort of vestigial survival from an earlier stage in his evolution as a detective.

"At eleven a.m. to-day I visited Messrs. Beechammle's shop in New Bond Street," he said. "I had with me a one-pound box of chocolates handed to me that morning by the Assistant Commissioner, with the information that he had received it from Lady Barber in the same state in which it was given to me. At the shop I saw the manageress, a Mademoiselle Dupont. I informed her that I was a police officer and that I was making inquiries concerning the box which I then produced to her. I explained that there was reason to suppose that the contents had been tampered with and that it was required to ascertain if possible the date on which the box had been sold and the person to whom the

sale had been effected. Mademoiselle Dupont informed me
that chocolates of the type in question, known by the name
of *Bouchées Princesses* were made and sold by the firm in
comparatively small quantities only, approximately fifty
pounds a week. Of these about half went to restaurants and
other customers who gave regular orders. A list of these was
furnished to me. So far as the date of purchase was concerned, she was in the position to say that the box in question had been packed in the factory on or after the 2nd
instant. She was able to establish this from the paper wrapping of the individual chocolates. Due to difficulties of
supply following on war conditions, paper of a slightly
inferior quality was employed on and after that date.
Chocolates are normally on sale in the shop on the day
following the packing of the box in the factory. It follows
therefore that the box in question must have been purchased
between the 3rd instant and the day on which they arrived
at Southington, namely the 7th."

"Unless they had been repacked," said Hilda sharply.

"I invited Mademoiselle Dupont to deal with that possibility," Mallett went on smoothly. "She informed me that
so far as the upper layer of chocolate was concerned, they
had undoubtedly been repacked, though in paper identical
with, or similar to, the original. The lower layer, however,
with two exceptions, was to all appearances untouched, and
she expressed the view that nobody other than an expert in
the firm's own factory could have arranged the packing in
the state in which it then was. I then inquired as to the sales
of chocolates of this type during the period in question. I
was supplied with a list of firms and individuals to whom
boxes of one pound capacity had been sent by post on those
days. I have it here. Perhaps you will tell me whether any
of these convey anything to you?"

He handed to Hilda a slip of paper with a short list of
names and addresses on it. She examined it briefly and
shook her head.

"So far as cash sales over the counter were concerned," Mallett went on, taking back the list, "no record was kept of the names of the purchasers, naturally, and the assistants were unable to supply me with the description of any of them. I was, however, able to ascertain the numbers of boxes sold on the different days. They are as follows: on the 3rd, three boxes; on the 4th, one; on the 5th, being Sunday, there were of course, no sales; on the 6th, four boxes; and on the 7th, two."

"That makes ten boxes altogether," said Hilda. "And you say there is no means of saying who bought any one of them?"

"That is so."

"Then I don't see that your inquiries have been very much use."

"I wouldn't go so far as to say that," Mallett replied politely. "We have been lucky enough to narrow down the date on which this box was bought to one of four days. That cuts both ways. It means that we can eliminate from our reckoning any suspect who could not have been in Bond Street during that time, and it means further that we know exactly to which period we must confine our attention when we come to investigate the movements of any particular person. And that, believe me, is a good deal more than the police have to go upon in the great majority of their inquiries. I ought to add," he went on after a pause, "that we have had the contents of the box examined in our laboratory, and the results entirely confirm the analysis which I understand has already been made privately."

"Oh!" said Hilda in a somewhat disappointed voice. That the odious Mr. Flack should have been proved to be correct was evidently not entirely to her taste.

"I think that that concludes the matter of the chocolates," said the Inspector, putting away his notebook. "We shall, of course, continue our inquiries, but it does not look as if we shall be able to go much further at the moment.

Now we come to the other matter on which I am told you wished to give instructions."

"As I was explaining to Mr. Marshall just now, I think it is all part and parcel of the same matter," said Hilda.

The Inspector looked somewhat doubtful.

"Indeed?" he said. "We have received a report from the police at Wimblingham on the occurrence there, and at first sight there would not seem to be any connection between them."

"But you haven't heard the whole story yet," Hilda objected.

"That is so, of course," said Mallett, and he sat back patiently in his chair, while Hilda related once more the whole catalogue of misfortunes that had marked the progress of the circuit.

When she had finished her story, the Inspector said: "And have you any suggestions to make as to who is responsible for all this—supposing that one person is responsible?"

"I should have thought that there was one perfectly obvious suspect," Lady Barber said.

"You mean Heppenstall?"

"Yes. Once lay your hands on Heppenstall——"

"But we have done so. That is to say, he has been interviewed. I saw him myself this morning."

"Do you mean to say that he has not been arrested?"

"Unfortunately, my lady, there was no charge on which we could arrest him."

"But he is a convict on licence——"

"Exactly, and even in such a case our powers are very limited. They are laid down by Act of Parliament."

"I know," said Hilda quickly. "The Prevention of Crimes Act, 1871."

Mallett looked at her with respect.

"Precisely," he said. "All that is required by that Act is for a man in Heppenstall's position to notify the authorities of his address and to report once a month. This he has done. He admits that he went to Markhampton at the time of the Assizes there, and he gave me what appeared to me genuine reasons for his visit. He denies being in or near Wimblingham at any time and I am not in a position to disprove it. I am checking up on his statements, of course, but that is as far as I can go."

"Do you mean that this man is at liberty to murder my husband whenever he pleases, and you don't propose to do anything whatever about it?"

"Oh, no." Mallett smiled indulgently. "I don't mean that exactly. All I said was that we have no evidence on which we can arrest Heppenstall. But that doesn't mean that we shall not continue to keep him under observation."

"Then you can guarantee my husband's safety?"

"So far as any danger from Heppenstall is concerned, I think I can, for the present."

"You mean that you think that there is danger from some other source?"

Mallett shrugged his shoulders.

"I am not satisfied," he said simply. "You see, we have here three distinct things to be considered. First, there are the anonymous letters. Second, the chocolates. Third, the assault on you. Either all three are part of a concerted plan or they are not. If they are, and Heppenstall is at the back of them, then we can eliminate the probability of another attempt being successful—but only if both these suppositions are correct. I don't like to give any guarantee based on a double supposition like that. Now, let us consider the probabilities. Heppenstall may have written the anonymous letters—it seems to me quite in keeping with what I know of his character. I can't exclude the possibility of his having been at Wimblingham. On the other hand, the case of the chocolates seems to me to be quite apart, and I don't personally believe that he had a hand in it. None of the assistants in the shop could recognize his photograph when I

showed it to them this morning, though that is of course far
from conclusive. He may have bought them through an
intermediary. But would he have had the necessary knowledge that this particular brand was likely to appeal to the
Judge?"

"If he had an exceptionally good memory—yes," Hilda
put in.

Mallett raised his eyebrows, but did not put the surprise
which he evidently felt into words.

"Even so," he went on, "I do not think that the man who
committed the violent assault at Wimblingham last week
would be likely to have preceded it by what was really not
much more than a very stupid practical joke. I may be
wrong, but the two things just don't seem to me to hang
together."

"And I think you are wrong," said Lady Barber firmly.
"I feel convinced that all these things do hang together, as
you put it, and that my husband is being subjected to an
organized persecution."

"Well, let's look at it from that point of view," said the
Inspector good-humouredly. "Leaving Heppenstall out of
it, I mean. Is there any common feature in the three cases
—or rather in the four, for we must remember that there
were two letters? Was there any one person who could
physically have been responsible for all four occurrences?"

There was a pause and then Derek said:

"Let me see. To start at the beginning, the first letter was
left at the Markhampton Lodgings while we were having
lunch."

"Who was we?"

"The Judge, myself, the High Sheriff and his wife, the
chaplain, and Mr. Pettigrew."

"The staff was also in the house at the time, I suppose?"

"Yes, that is, Beamish, the clerk, the butler, the Marshal's
man, and Mrs. Square, the cook."

"Nobody actually saw the letter delivered, I think?"

"No."

"So it is possible—we are only testing possibilities—that it might have been introduced into the house—or prepared in the house itself by any of these people?"

"Yes. I suppose so."

"And the same applies to the second letter?"

"I think Beamish found it in the letter-box—or perhaps Savage did. I forget."

"And had anybody been to the house that morning before the letter arrived?"

"Only the Chief Constable and Mr. Pettigrew. The Under Sheriff came a little later to take the Judge to Court."

"One other point about that second letter. It seemed to refer to a rather unfortunate incident of the night before. Who knew of what had occurred?"

"Well, nobody, except the police and the three of us who were in the car. There was, too, the man I saw in the street just afterwards who made off."

"We mustn't forget him. The three of you in the car were the Judge, yourself and——?"

"Mr. Pettigrew."

"Really——" said Hilda, but Mallett with less than his usual good manners brushed her on one side.

"Coming now to Southington," he went on. "We are on rather different grounds there. The chocolates came by post, did they not?"

"Beamish said they did, but the wrapping of the parcel was destroyed and both he and the other servants seemed very vague about it."

"At any rate, they came from London, and had been bought not more than a few days previously. Who was there at Southington who had been in London just before?"

"Lady Barber."

"Anyone else?"

"Nobody else in the Lodgings."

"That excludes all the people we have been considering in the Markhampton case, with the exception of——"

Hilda would be denied no longer.

"Inspector Mallett," she said, "I can't listen to this nonsense any longer. It is utterly absurd to suppose that Mr. Pettigrew could possibly have had anything to do with this! You are simply wasting our time."

"I hope not, my lady," said Mallett with great urbanity. "All that I am trying to do is to test your theory that these matters are in some way connected and see what the possibilities are. If they lead us on to an absurd conclusion, so much the worse for the theory. Just to follow it out for the moment, was Mr. Pettigrew at Wimblingham, by any chance?"

"Yes," Hilda admitted. "He was. But that doesn't prove——"

"Oh, we're a long way from proof yet. Now suppose we eliminate the chocolates, can we extend the possibilities at all?"

"I don't want to eliminate the chocolates," said Hilda obstinately. "You said yourself just now that they could have been bought through an intermediary. Surely that means that anybody in the lodgings could have arranged for them to have been sent there?"

"Certainly. Anybody in or outside the lodgings, for that matter. But if we are to confine ourselves to the people who had the opportunity also of being concerned in the affairs at the other two towns, that means only Mr. Marshall and the members of the staff. Is there any particular individual whom you suspect?"

"There is one whom I certainly distrust," said Hilda at once. "And that one is Beamish."

"His lordship's clerk?" said Mallett in surprise. "Surely his bread and butter depends on his master remaining alive and on the bench?"

"That may be so, but I distrust him all the same. He is a thoroughly unreliable, dangerous man."

"What precisely led you to form that opinion of him?"

But Hilda would not, or could not, be precise in the matter at all. She could only repeat in general terms that she was sure that if a potential murderer was among the circuit household, it could be no other than Beamish.

"And it is no good suggesting that he could not have written the second letter," she concluded. "I am sure he knew all about the accident as soon as it happened. The lawyer isn't born who could keep a secret from his clerk."

Mallett did not attempt to dispute this piece of legal lore, but continued to press for concrete facts.

"Can you recall any occasion at the period of these incidents in which Beamish's behaviour struck you as suspicious or unusual in any way?" he asked.

"I can," said Derek. "The night of the business at Wimblingham."

He went on to describe his painful encounter with Beamish in the passage and his reasons for thinking that the clerk had not in fact been in bed and asleep when the household was roused.

"I can still feel the place in my ribs where he kicked me," he concluded.

"There you are!" said Hilda, triumphantly, turning to the Inspector. "I always knew there was something fishy about that man, and now we've proved it!"

"It certainly sounds strange," said Mallett doubtfully. "But you say, Mr. Marshall, that apart from the long ulster you mention you can't say how he was dressed?"

"No. I took no notice at the time. It was only next day that I began to try to think things out."

"I think I can help you there," Hilda said. "I remember next day the Judge saying to me how comic Beamish looked with a pair of green pyjama trouser legs showing underneath his overcoat. Oh!" she added, in a disappointed tone. "That's rather against our case, isn't it?"

"Not necessarily," said Mallett. "It is just what one would

expect in the case of a man, fully dressed, who wants to look as if he has just got out of bed. He pulls on his pyjamas over his outdoor clothes and then puts an overcoat on top to hide what he doesn't want to show."

"That's all right, then," said Hilda.

"What troubles me," the Inspector continued, "is the very fact that originally started Mr. Marshall's suspicions. I mean the boots, or shoes, which did the damage. If a man is going to creep about the house in which he is sleeping to commit a crime one would not expect him to wear outdoor footgear. He would be much more likely to put on soft, rubber-soled shoes, if he had them, and if not, to go about in his stockinged feet. No, I'm afraid that Beamish's clothes tell against the theory of his being the person who assaulted you, Lady Barber."

"Then what was he doing being dressed at all at that hour in the morning?" Lady Barber demanded.

"That is another question altogether, which may have all sorts of interesting answers. All I am saying is that it is not an argument in favour of his having committed this particular crime."

"Really!" said Hilda pettishly. "I thought that you were coming here to help us, Inspector. Instead, you seem to do nothing but raise difficulties all the time."

"I am sorry you should think that, my lady. As I said, all that I have been doing is to test the probabilities of different theories, and I am afraid that that is bound to give the impression of raising difficulties, as you put it. You see"— here the Inspector rose to his feet and began to pace the room with long strides—"you see, this isn't an ordinary case, by any means. In the general way, we are called in when a crime has already been committed and it is our job simply to identify the person who is guilty of the crime. Sometimes we have reason to think that someone is contemplating a crime and we have to keep an eye on him and see that he doesn't put his design into execution. But here is something more indefinite—a great deal more indefinite. What are we being asked to do? To prevent someone, unknown, from doing something, we don't know what. It isn't easy, you know. But we'll do our best."

And then, almost before they were aware of it, this big, substantial man had melted away, leaving Hilda and Derek alone in the room.

Derek left the club about ten minutes later. The ten minutes were occupied by a good deal of somewhat inconsequent conversation, during which the same ground was covered again and again without any tangible progress being made. Before he left, Hilda once more exacted and he reiterated his promise to help her in guarding the Judge from all the perils which might beset him. But he found it impossible to recapture any of the emotion which had accompanied the first giving of the promise. In the dry light of Inspector Mallett's reasoning, the whole affair seemed to have dwindled to a rather tiresome problem to which the Inspector might find the key but which was obviously insoluble to him. As he came out of the club into the growing darkness of Piccadilly Derek's thoughts were mainly occupied with the reflection that he was going to earn his daily two guineas more hardly than he had been led to understand when he consented to become Marshal to Mr. Justice Barber.

Chapter 11

WHISKY AND REMINISCENCE

Derek bumped into somebody on the pavement as he turned from saying good-bye to Lady Barber. Automatically he murmured an apology and passed on, but he had not taken two steps before he felt his arm gripped, and a voice said quietly in his ear, "Not a word! We may be observed!"

Looking round Derek saw that it was Pettigrew. He held one finger to his lips in the manner of a stage conspirator. Then he glanced over his shoulder, still keeping his hold on Derek's arm, and went on in his natural voice,

"It's all right! She's getting into a taxi. Now we can go and have a drink."

"It's awfully kind of you," said Derek in some confusion, "but I'm afraid I can't. I've got to get to Waterloo to catch a train."

"Nonsense! There are plenty of trains from Waterloo, and it can't be of any consequence to you which you catch. You will be travelling in the black-out in any case, so it won't make a ha'p'orth of difference. Is your presence very urgently required at wherever it is?"

Derek, the memory of his disappointing holiday strong within him, felt impelled to answer, "No."

"Very good. Well, your presence is urgently required by me. Because I am going to have a drink. Several drinks. In fact, by the end of the evening I should not be surprised if I were verging on the blotto, in a quite gentlemanly way, of course, but definitely verging."

"But——" said Derek.

"I know what you are going to say. As a purist, not to say an idealist, you object that a verge cannot be definite. And you are, of course, perfectly right. Nothing could be less definite than this particular verge. I have often tried myself to distinguish the precise moment when one goes over it, but in vain. At one moment you are depressingly, stupidly sober, at the next you are gloriously, happily tight. But where exactly the transformation takes place, I never can determine. And goodness knows, I have tried often enough.

"However," Pettigrew continued, hurrying Derek along and completely disregarding his attempts to protest, "I am not asking you to accompany me as far as the verge. For one thing, a young man of your obvious attainments will almost certainly have a very good head for liquor, and it would be much too expensive. For another, the spectacle of their seniors upon the verge or—who knows what the evening may bring?—actually over it, is not good for persons of your age. All that I require from you is your company on the first stage of the journey. I always find", he said, turning a corner, going up a flight of steps and pushing open a door, "that the first few drinks of the evening are cold and unsatisfying affairs unless one has a friend to share them. Later—put your hat and coat over there—a man is his own best company, perhaps. That depends on the man of course. I can only speak for myself, and even then without much assurance. I am having a double whisky. What about you?"

Derek found himself in a comfortable arm-chair in the smoking-room of what was evidently Pettigrew's club—a shabby little place about as different from the smart establishment which he had just left as could well be imagined. While the drinks were being brought, he had for the first time the opportunity of seeing clearly the face of his host. Pettigrew's flow of words had come to an abrupt end. He looked tired, Derek thought, and wore an expression of discouragement which he had not seen before. He sat silently, staring into the fire, as if he had forgotten the existence of the guest upon whom he had forced himself a moment or two ago.

The appearance of the whisky recalled Pettigrew to his surroundings.

"Your health!" he said, taking a long drink. "And how are the ideals? Still as rampant as ever?"

"I haven't lost them yet, anyhow," said Derek.

"Quite right. I had them too at your age. Ideals and ambitions and oh! lots of things. They don't last, though. Have you seen the evening paper, by any chance?"

"No. Is there anything about ideals in it?"

"Not exactly. About ambitions, though. I don't mean your ambitions, of course. I expect they are front page stuff with headlines. This is very small beer—merely a small paragraph in a corner somewhere."

He took another drink.

"They've gone and made Jefferson a County Court Judge," he said.

Derek tried to look intelligent.

"Jefferson!" Pettigrew repeated in a tone of contempt.

"Was that a job you—I mean, had you expected——?" Derek began diffidently.

"Had I applied for the job? is what you are trying to say. Certainly I had. It's an ingrained habit of mine. To be accurate, it is the fifth County Court Judgeship which I have applied for. The fifth and last."

Pettigrew put down an empty glass.

"Oh, well," Derek said, "I don't see why it should be the last. It's rotten luck, of course, but next time——"

"No!" said Pettigrew in an irritated tone. "My young and unlearned friend, you miss the entire point. (Just touch the bell beside you, will you?) It is not the fact that I haven't got the job that distresses me and causes me to drink, but the fact that Jefferson has. Now do you see?"

"Not knowing Jefferson, I can't say that I do."

"Quite right. In not knowing Jefferson you have a very decided advantage over me. (Two more double whiskies, please, waiter.) But I don't want to prejudice you against him. After all, you are thinking of coming to the Bar and may have to appear before him. The essential odiousness of Jefferson—and he is odious—is not the point. Neither is the fact that the public has been presented with a thundering bad judge when it might have had an average good one. The point is that nobody, not even the rummiest Lord Chancellor, is ever going to make me a County Court Judge after Jefferson. D'you see? If he and I are on a list of possibles together and they choose him, with all his imperfections on his wig and five years my junior, well, it simply means that next time I'm not a possible at all. If only because, as you will have occasion to observe one day, one does not grow any younger. It was bound to happen sooner or later, I suppose, but I had rather it was anybody than Jefferson. (Thank you, waiter.) Well, let's forget about him."

He raised his second glass to his lips.

Derek did not often drink two whiskies so close together, and he found that their effect, at first at any rate, was to produce an unusual clarity of mind. He was not particularly interested in Jefferson, but he was interested in Pettigrew and in a good many things with which Pettigrew was in some way connected; and this seemed to be a good opportunity for improving his knowledge of them. His host's next words gave him the opening he sought.

"Well," he said, "and how is her ladyship? Have you been enjoying an afternoon's poodle-faking?"

"She is quite well," said Derek. "But rather badly worried."

"That I can quite believe. A black eye is a very worrying thing for a good-looking woman."

"How did you know about that?" Derek asked in surprise. The events at Wimblingham had, at the Judge's particular request, not been made public in any way.

Pettigrew grinned.

"Things do get about you know," he said. "Besides, I was at Wimblingham myself."

"I know," said Derek rather uncomfortably. "But of course it isn't only the black eye that is worrying Lady Barber."

"No. One way and another Father William has been having a fairly uncomfortable circuit. What does Hilda think about it all?"

"She thinks that there is someone behind it all."

"All?"

"Yes—the letters, the chocolates, her black eye. She thinks that one person is responsible for them."

"M-m." Pettigrew wrinkled his nose. The second half of his whisky remained forgotten at his elbow. "Well, that's always possible, of course. And who does she think this one person is?"

"Well, the first name she suggested to the detective was Heppenstall."

"The detective? So this wasn't a *tête-à-tête*? Scotland Yard was represented too?"

"Yes. A fellow called Mallett came along."

"Oho! That looks as if somebody was really worried. And what did Mallett think about Heppenstall?"

"Not very much. In fact, he didn't seem to be very much impressed by the whole theory. But I found it all very difficult to follow, I'm so much in the dark. I wish you'd tell me who this Heppenstall is. His name seems to keep on cropping up and I don't know what it's all about."

Pettigrew emptied his glass and leaned back in his chair, his legs stretched out, looking at the fire. He seemed to be seeing something there and to be intent on what he saw.

"Just ring the bell again," he said. "This confounded

waiter never seems to be about when you want him. Thanks. Heppenstall? Oh, he was just a solicitor who went wrong. He misappropriated some of his client's money, came up before Father William at the Old Bailey, and got a pretty stiff sentence. That's all."

"Oh," said Derek in a disappointed tone.

"Yes. Oh, here you are, waiter. Will you have another? Well, perhaps you are wise. One more double, then, please. What were we talking about? Oh, yes, Heppenstall. A sad case, as these cases always are."

Nothing further was said until the fresh whisky had been brought. Pettigrew put into it the smallest possible dash of soda, drank it off at a gulp, set down the glass and said violently, "*No!*"

Derek looked at him in surprise and began to wonder whether the "verge" had been reached. But Pettigrew was now talking as collectedly as ever, though, if possible, with even greater fluency.

"There is something about the third glass of whisky," he said, "which makes it quite impossible to tell a lie, even by implication. For me, at any rate, the third glass is the third degree. The last barriers go down and I come clean— or dirty, as the case may be, but at least I come true. I told you a thumping lie, just now."

"About Heppenstall?"

"Yes. He *was* a solicitor and he *was* sentenced by the Shaver for pinching his client's money. But that's not all, by a very long chalk. If it were, nobody would be bothering about him. I don't see why I shouldn't tell you about it. If I don't somebody else will, and I can do it very much better than anyone who is likely to talk about it. And since you are more or less mixed up in his affairs, I'm not at all sure that it's not my duty to tell you."

Pettigrew lit a cigarette.

"Heppenstall was a client of mine in my early days," he said, idly watching the smoke curl upwards. "I rather liked

him. He was smart—in both senses of the word—clever at
his profession and by way of being a man about town, both
the City and the West End. He put quite a lot of work in
my way. It was mostly small stuff, but Heppenstall was a
small man then. I was in the same chambers as the Shaver.
The head of them was—but that wouldn't interest you. The
Shaver was senior to me and a cut above the kind of stuff
Heppenstall was handing out then. Well, the war came,
and of course I went. It was while I was away that his
practice really began to grow."

"Whose practice do you mean?" asked Derek. "Heppenstall's or Barber's?"

"Both. Simultaneously and conjointly. Heppenstall began
to get into a really big class of business. He acquired some
important City clients, and at the same time managed to
collect some flashy society litigation of the kind that makes
a splash in the newspapers. And my clerk—who was also,
of course, the Shaver's clerk—saw to it that he remained
faithful to the chambers. Not that he wanted much persuading, I fancy, after the first two or three briefs had been
dealt with. The Shaver did him well—and Heppenstall did
the Shaver well. It's not too much to say that Heppenstall
made him. He came along at just the critical moment, you
see, when the Shaver was too senior to be seen messing
about with the small stuff which I had been only too glad to
do, but hadn't properly established himself among the
heavy-weight juniors. It was Heppenstall who just gave him
the push that put him where he belonged, among the people
who counted. And when the big boom in litigation developed immediately after the war, the pair of them were
right in the thick of it, and Heppenstall must have put
thousands of pounds into the Shaver's pockets while it
lasted."

He yawned and threw his cigarette into the fire.

"I was back from the war by then, of course," he said.
"Naturally I went back into the old chambers—of which

the Shaver was the head by then—but I didn't stay there
long. I—I didn't find it altogether agreeable, so I took
myself off elsewhere. I never had another brief from
Heppenstall again. I can't blame him—he was very well off
where he was. And when the Shaver took silk, there was
another perfectly competent junior in the same stable to
carry on. However, that is neither here nor there. This isn't
my history, but Heppenstall's. After the Shaver went into
the front row, he continued to brief him. He dined and
wined with him, he held Hilda's hand after dinner, discussing, no doubt, the Rule in Shelley's Case and other
subjects dear to the heart of that learned lady——"

"And all the time he was stealing his client's money?"
said Derek, horrified.

"My dear idealist, these things happen, you know. As a
matter of fact, it was not until 1931 that Heppenstall began
to be a little unconventional in his treatment of other
people's funds. He had been speculating a good deal—the
man about the City working overtime to keep up the
appearance of the man about the West End, I suppose—
and the slump caught him short. He borrowed a little from
one account to put himself right, helped himself out of
another to get the first account straight, and so it went on.
Then just when the Law Society was beginning to interest
itself in the *affaire* Heppenstall, the Shaver went on to the
Bench, and the pair of them met again at the Old Bailey.
Comprenez?"

"Yes. It must have been a pretty dreadful moment for
them both."

"If you think that, you miss the whole point of the story.
It was dreadful enough for Heppenstall, no doubt. He
pleaded guilty, of course, and somebody or other put up
the usual palaver in mitigation. But the Shaver—who, if he
had had any bowels, would never have allowed himself to
try the case at all—he positively gloated over the wretched
man. It wasn't only the sentence he gave him, though that

was stiff enough in all conscience, but the way in which he behaved. I wasn't there myself—thank goodness; but I have talked to people who were, and I read the reports in the papers afterwards, and I tell you it was beastly—beastly—*beastly*!"

Whisky had made Derek bold.

"Is that the reason why you dislike him so much?" he asked.

Pettigrew seemed to shrink into himself.

"I said just now that this isn't my story but Heppenstall's," he answered stiffly. "But I'll go this far—that if Heppenstall is giving him a few bad nights, I shan't be sorry, and I don't think I'm the only person to feel that way, either. Can you wonder?" He looked at the clock. "What about your train?" he added.

Derek saw that he was dismissed, and rose to his feet.

"I must be going," he said. "But I ought to mention that the Inspector didn't take very kindly to the notion that Heppenstall was responsible for everything that has happened."

"So you've said already. Did he suggest anybody who was?"

Derek began now to regret that he had spoken, but it was too late to draw back.

"Well," he said. "He went through all the possibilities in a methodical sort of way, and he seemed to think that if one person was at the back of everything—which he didn't altogether believe——"

"Yes?"

"The one person must be you."

For the life of him, Derek could not say whether Pettigrew was amused or not. Certainly his lips twitched at the corners as though he were about to laugh, but his eyes remained grave and his voice, when he finally spoke, was quiet and serious.

"Thanks," he said. "I'll remember that."

"But please don't think that I——" Derek stammered in confusion.

"My dear chap——!"

"It was only just a suggestion of the Inspector's. I don't think he meant it seriously. And Hilda wouldn't hear of it for a moment. She fairly snapped his head off."

"Oh, Hilda did, did she? That was kind of her. You might thank her for me. No, on second thoughts, better not. By the way, have there been any more developments in that unfortunate affair with the car at Markhampton?"

"None that I know of. I think the Judge has had some letters about it, but of course I haven't been told any-thing——"

"H'm. For what it's worth, I have a notion that that's a good deal the most serious thing threatening the Shaver at the present moment. In his position, a writ can do more damage than a dozen poisoned chocolates. Well, good night, and thank you for your company. I've enjoyed our talk. In fact, I've enjoyed it so much that I don't somehow think I shall want now to get anywhere nearer the verge than I am at this moment, and that's a long way off. So if any-body asks you why you're so late home to-night, you can explain that you've been occupied in saving an old gentle-man from a nasty headache to-morrow morning. Good night!"

Derek travelled home on a slow train in utter darkness. He felt that he had spent an interesting day. His one regret was that it was to be followed by another day of boredom and stagnation at home. Never was regret less justified. For on the next morning, chance brought him into contact with Sheila Bartram, and his whole world was instantly trans-formed.

Chapter 12

SOMEONE HAS TALKED

———

Sheila Bartram was tall and fair, with large, rather pro-
tuberant, grey eyes and a pale complexion which some
would have classified as anaemic but which others found
"interesting". She was nineteen and was occupied in trying
to qualify as a Red Cross nurse. Her father was the managing director of an important manufacturing firm and spent
most of his time travelling about the country from one
branch to another superintending its different Government
contracts. Sheila and her mother meanwhile had been
evacuated from London to the house of an aunt in the
neighbourhood. All this, and a great deal more Derek
learned within the first half hour of their acquaintance. He
had been with difficulty induced to drive his mother over
to the next village for a committee meeting which was to
deal with comforts for the forces, he had been left hanging
about for most of the morning and had there encountered
Sheila, who was in much the same case. Before either of
them knew what had happened, the morning's boredom
had become an enchantment, and Derek drove his mother
home and Sheila returned to her hospital, each in a condition utterly besotted, entirely natural but completely inex-
plicable, to be envied or pitied by the rest of the world
according to the rest of the world's taste or experience.

That was on a Saturday. Derek was due to rejoin the
Judge at the station on Monday afternoon when the circuit
would resume its travels. He contrived to spend almost the

whole of Sunday in Sheila's company and the hours when he was not actually with her in meditating on her perfection and marvelling at his good fortune in meeting her. How Sheila spent the same hours can only be judged by her surprising and disastrous failure to pass her examination a few days later. On Monday, after a leave-taking as intense in its affection as if Derek had been *en route* for the Western Front, the lover reluctantly returned to London.

Seeing Hilda, elegant and slim, chatting to an obsequious guard at the door of the reserved carriage, Derek felt a slight but unmistakable qualm. It was a qualm which he instantly suppressed, but the memory of it lingered, and with the memory a faint sense of guilt. For in the state of mind in which he then was (if indeed his mind could be said to have anything to do with his condition) it was inevitable that the sight of Hilda, or any other woman, necessarily provoked a comparison with his adored. And the first fruits of comparison, in this instance, were something very near to disloyalty to Sheila—or rather, to the idea of Sheila which he had been occupied in building up during the last two days. He had forgotten quite how attractive Hilda was. Of course, she was a much older woman—positively elderly, in fact. There was no true comparison possible. At the same time, judged by the touchstone of Hilda's poise and tact, her cool assurance in any surroundings, was there not something a little too naïve about Sheila, was not her delightful ingenuousness just the least bit lacking in savour?

The suspicion disappeared almost as soon as it had arisen and long before Derek's conscious mind had acknowledged its existence. Five minutes later he would have conscientiously taken his oath that it had never been. But its passage was not after all without its effect. Deeply embedded beyond the reach of memory it remained thenceforth as a minute source of irritation, while over it the compensating forces of imagination laid layer after·layer of glamorous fancy, producing in the end a pearl of inhuman perfection —an ideal Sheila, whom the flesh and blood article would in time discover to be her most dangerous competitor.

Meanwhile, the source of all this disturbance was not without troubles of her own. If to Derek's eyes she appeared at this moment calm and serene, it was a greater tribute to her self control than he imagined. She had, indeed, spent an agitating weekend. She had returned home from her club, feeling a good deal more reassured by the placid stolidity of Mallett than she had thought fit to acknowledge at the time, only to find the Judge, just back from the Athenæum, sunk in utter dejection. A letter from his brother-in-law, in which he expressed the gloomiest views on the prospect of negotiations with Sebald-Smith's solicitors, was open before him; but he soon made it clear that this, though serious enough, was the least of his anxieties. What really preyed upon his mind was an incident which had occurred that afternoon within the quiet precincts of the club itself. Over the tea-cups, he had been engaged in conversation by a brother Judge, Barber's senior by several years, a man whose immense fund of learning he openly admired and whose caustic tongue he secretly feared. In the course of a few casual words, which to any third party would have conveyed nothing beyond a friendly interest in the doings of the Southern Circuit, the hapless Barber had been given quite clearly to understand that the speaker was perfectly familiar with all that had passed at Markhampton. Having instilled the poison in the mild and paternal manner for which he was famous, the torturer had callously lighted a cigar and departed, leaving behind him an infuriated and badly frightened man.

"Someone has talked!" Barber groaned, as he recounted this to his wife. "After all our precautions, someone has talked!"

"Well, that seems obvious," said Hilda, rapidly making

up her mind that an air of brisk efficiency on her part would be the best antidote to her husband's collapsed condition. "After all, that was to be expected, wasn't it? Things like this are certain to get round sooner or later."

"Who could it have been?" Barber went on. "I could have sworn that that boy was reliable. And Pettigrew went out of his way to insist on his anxiety to keep the thing quiet. . . . Of course, the police officer was very young and inexperienced, but still. . . . You don't think Pettigrew could have let me down, do you, Hilda? After all, we are such old friends. . . ."

Hilda's lips tightened.

"No," she said. "I don't think he would have let you down. In my opinion since the affair has come out, it doesn't seem to me to matter in the least who was responsible for it. But if it is of any interest to you, William, I should have thought the answer was fairly obvious."

The Judge looked at her in surprise.

"You seem entirely to have forgotten that there are two parties to an accident," she said impatiently. "And of the two, it is the person who is knocked over and his friends who are the most likely to do the talking. Sally Parsons has a pretty large acquaintance and I have no doubt that she has let them all know about it."

Barber threw up his hands in despair.

"It will be all over the Temple by now," he moaned. "All over the Temple!"

"William! You must really pull yourself together! If it is all over the Temple, what substantial difference is it going to make? You can be quite certain that if this can be settled without an action, it will never get into the papers, and that is the only thing that matters. Really, you are behaving like a child!"

Under her chiding, Barber recovered some of his dignity.

"There are things that matter quite as much to a man in my position as an open accusation in the newspapers," he said. "Don't you understand, Hilda, what an intolerable situation it will be for me, with this thing a subject of common gossip among my brother judges? How far it has gone yet I don't know, but at any moment now I may have the Lord Chief Justice sending for me and suggesting——"

"Suggesting what?"

"Suggesting that I should resign."

"Resign?" said Hilda in spirited tones. "Nonsense! He can't make you resign. Nobody can. Nothing can."

"Except a resolution by both Houses of Parliament."

"Well, there you are."

But the Judge refused to be comforted.

"I could never face that," he said. "It would only want a question in the House to make my position untenable. And not only myself, but the whole judiciary would suffer. . . ."

He shuddered at the prospect.

"All that this amounts to," said Hilda crisply, "is that we have got to settle Sebald-Smith's action, and we knew that already. Once that is out of the way, neither the Lord Chief Justice nor anybody else will want to rake up any scandal. And people's memories are very short for this kind of thing, as you know yourself—particularly now they have the war to think about. Let me have a look at Michael's letter."

The letter was certainly not calculated to give any comfort. The injured man's solicitors, it reported, were not showing any signs of abating their demands. A letter from them demanding an early reply was enclosed. A consultation had been held between medical men nominated by both sides, and the report submitted by the doctor who had examined the patient on the Judge's behalf was, if anything, worse than had been feared. Besides the amputation of the little finger, there was present damage to the muscles of the hand which would for the time being seriously restrict its use and might prove permanent. In any event, remedial treatment would be prolonged and expensive. An opinion from a distinguished musician had reinforced the plaintiff's contention that the absence of one finger would almost certainly reduce his earning powers as a pianist to zero. There was more to the same effect. The letter concluded by asking for instructions.

Hilda put down the letter with a sinking heart. She stood up and smoked a cigarette half through before coming to a decision. Then she said:

"I think I shall have to go and see him."

"Perhaps that would be best," her husband replied. "But in view of his letter I am afraid that there is little more that he can do for us."

"Who? Michael? I didn't mean him, though I shall probably see him in any case. I mean to go and see Sebald-Smith."

"Hilda! You are not serious?"

"Of course I am serious."

"But it is out of the question. You—you can't do a thing like that."

"Why not?"

"Why, to begin with, you know as well as I do that when matters have passed into the hands of legal advisers it is most improper for a party to the case to go behind their backs and——"

"I don't care what the proprieties are. Something must be done and this seems to me the only thing to do. And if you insist upon technicalities, I am not a party to the case."

"Hilda, I implore you to think twice about what you are doing. An intervention of this kind can do no good—may, indeed, do irreparable harm. What do you imagine would be the reaction of a complete stranger——"

"He's not a complete stranger."

"I grant you that he has been to this house once or twice though I personally was unaware of the fact, but for all practical purposes he is a stranger."

"I used to know Sebald-Smith pretty well," said Hilda slowly. "In fact, at one time, very well indeed."

The Judge looked at her in surprise, a shocked suspicion dawning in his face.

"Oh, no! Not as well as all that!" Hilda protested with a laugh, and kissed the top of his head. Then she sat down on a footstool beside his arm-chair and said coaxingly, "So we can consider that settled, shall we?"

"If you go," the Judge protested feebly, "it is entirely without my sanction."

"And you can repudiate me if necessary. Very well, that will have to do. Now the next point to settle is, what terms can we offer him?"

From this point on the tone of the discussion degenerated, as the tone of discussions is apt to do when money becomes their subject. From a consideration of the Judge's present financial position it passed to the grisly subject of possible economies in the future. Hilda was unexpectedly resigned on this point where her personal expenditure was concerned, though pertinacious in what her husband thought unreasonable demands as to his own. But the colloquy became positively acrimonious, and Hilda increasingly vocal, when it drifted, as it did inevitably, to the utterly sterile region of the past. What had become of the huge fees which he had earned in his last years at the Bar, when income-tax and surtax were less than they were to-day, and as nothing compared with what they might be to-morrow? Hilda, her nerves unstrung by an agitating afternoon, lost her usual self-control when she found old accusations of extravagance being raked up afresh. Instead of letting these pass, she began angrily to justify the cost of frocks worn out years ago and dinners long since digested. She became first indignant, then shrill in her self-defence. Every penny that she had spent had been to his honour and glory, had assisted in the furtherance of his career to which she had devoted—her astonished ears heard herself uttering the cliché—the best years of her life. Had it not been for her wise outlay, as he very well knew, he would never have been in the position he was now, a position which his criminal carelessness had put in jeopardy. And if it came to extravagance—Here it was Barber's turn to repel an attack which, truth to say, was not very well-founded, for his own tastes had always been simple enough.

The injustice of it stung him to make some retorts which were in their turn wholly unjustified and brought the sorry scene to a climax with Hilda in floods of angry tears, the Judge stammering apologies and the original subject of debate wholly forgotten.

By next morning, peace had been restored, but the problem from which the dispute had developed was no nearer solution. If Sebald-Smith did not abate his demands, Barber was financially a ruined man. If the demands could not be met, and an action resulted, he was ruined not only financially but professionally. The only hope appeared to be that the plaintiff, or his advisers, would realize in time that it was not to his interest to push matters to extremities and that a judge of the High Court, drawing his salary and paying a reasonable sum by instalments, was a better debtor than a broken man without income or prospects. And, as Barber eventually agreed with reluctance, a direct approach by Hilda was perhaps the best chance of inducing him to see reason.

Hilda put her plan into execution without delay; but she met with a check at once. Sebald-Smith, she had ascertained, was staying at his country cottage, and she put a telephone call through that day. But she did not speak to Sebald-Smith. The voice that answered the call was the voice of Sally Parsons, and Hilda put down the receiver at once without disclosing who she was. Not for anything would ـhe speak to, or risk a meeting with, that woman. The memory of certain social snubs which she had had occasion to administer to her came clearly to her mind—

and she could be perfectly certain that Sally Parsons had not forgotten them either. The thought made her shiver slightly. If the attitude of Sebald-Smith, as reflected in his solicitor's letters, was a vindictive one, was her influence the cause? But all was not lost. If she could but get at him alone, she might displace that influence long enough to snatch a victory. His cottage was close to Rampleford, the next town on the circuit, and Sally Parsons could never bear the country for more than a day or two at a time. She would surely be able to find an opportunity to slip over there—that is, if it were safe to leave the Judge unprotected. . . .

The recollection of the other dark and more mysterious danger that threatened them returned with added force for having been temporarily forgotten. She threw it off with an effort, and went back to the telephone. This time she spoke to her brother's office and made an appointment to see him on Monday morning.

Michael was younger than his sister, though he looked several years older. Like her, he was short and dark, but unlike her, he had allowed himself to run to fat. He had a subtle, intelligent mind and was capable of great charm and tact, which he knew how to vary from time to time with brutal frankness. On this occasion, he chose to be frank.

"Your worthy husband is on a spot, Hilda," he said. "They've got us by the short hairs and they know it."

"You needn't show quite so much relish about it," his sister complained. "Even if you don't like William."

Michael let the remark pass without comment.

"Something has got to be done, you know," he said. "People are beginning to gossip already."

"I know."

"Well, what does he propose to do about it?"

"I propose to go and have a talk to Sebald-Smith," Hilda replied, with a slight emphasis on the pronoun.

"The direct approach, eh? I expect that shocks him a bit, but I'm not sure it's not the best thing to do. When will that be?"

"In the next few days, I hope."

"There's not much time to lose. Meanwhile, this last letter of theirs has to be answered. Otherwise they are quite capable of issuing a writ straight away."

"I've thought of that," said Hilda. "I think the best thing to do will be simply to tell them that the Judge is on circuit and that you will communicate with them as soon as you can get instructions."

"Well, let's hope that will keep them quiet for a bit. Luckily they're a fairly sleepy firm and may not tumble to the fact that he's had some days off in which he could have given all the instructions he liked. In fact, it's damned lucky for us that they aren't really wide awake. If I'd been handling this case for the other side, I'd have dropped a few hints into the ear of the Markhampton Police."

"Why?"

"Why? I'd have only had to suggest that they were suppressing proceedings for an undoubted breach of the law and they'd have been compelled to prosecute. That would have turned the screw with a vengeance. Mind you, they may do it yet. There's always a risk."

"Let me see," said Hilda. "Under the Act, proceedings for dangerous driving have to be begun within fourteen days, unless there is a warning at the time that they are being contemplated—and in this case there wasn't. So we're safe so far as that goes, anyway. It is still open to them to prosecute for driving an uninsured car, though. They have six months for that, and more in some circumstances."

Michael grinned.

"Good old Hilda," he said. "You always were the best lawyer of any of us. I'd quite forgotten that, and I should have had to look it up to make sure, anyway. But I'll accept it from you."

"I think you can," said Hilda primly. "Limitation of actions was always a subject that interested me and I made particular study of it."

"You would. What an inhuman brute you always were, Hilda."

"I don't see that there is anything inhuman about being a lawyer."

"There is—for a woman, at all events. Tell me, was that what you married William for—so as to become a successful lawyer by proxy?"

"Are you always as rude as that to your clients, Michael?"

"Good Lord! Of course not!"

"Well, I am consulting you as a solicitor at this moment, and that's not a question I should expect my solicitor to ask unless I was wanting a divorce, which I am not."

"You win," said Michael good humouredly. "Well, I'll do my best for you, and for William. I'll send a letter on the lines you suggest, and meanwhile you will let me know if you have any luck with Sebald-Smith. God bless you."

Hilda caught Derek's eye as he advanced along the platform and waved to him with a smile. Her black eye was by now completely cured, or at all events masked under an efficient make-up. She was looking as carefree and sure of herself as a woman of good looks and assured position has a right to be. A moment later, Derek climbed into the carriage and was greeted with a handshake that was the least trifle more warm than politeness demanded—sufficiently so to remind him of the friendly conspiracy that had been sealed between them, and no more. Five minutes later, the plain clothes man on the platform turned upon his heel as the train steamed out, bearing the strangely assorted group of human beings who composed the Judge's party, and with them a yet stranger medley of hopes and fears, ambitions and anxieties.

Chapter 13

CAT AND MOUSE

———

It is unnecessary to describe Rampleford. The place is in all the guide-books. A thriving city in the seventeenth century, a decaying and corrupt corporation in the eighteenth, it began to acquire merit as a quaint survival in the nineteenth, until the dawn of the great tourist industry set it on a new career of prosperity. The fortunate discovery that one of the signatories of the Declaration of Independence was born in the city and the still more fortunate, if not quite fortuitous, identification of his birthplace with the most picturesque house in the High Street, put Rampleford in the very first class in this important branch of commerce. There were some who declared that in a good season Rampleford's turnover of picture postcards exceeded Stratford's. This, no doubt, was an exaggeration, but the very fact that the claim could be seriously made was sufficient indication of the city's standing in the trade.

Rampleford in wartime, on the other hand, was a depressed and depressing place. Its only overseas visitors now were bored Canadian soldiers, quartered, to the city's disgust, in the best hotels, who knew not Jonathan Pennycuick, founder of the Constitution, and were openly critical of the olde worlde tea-shops which lined the High Street. A heartless government having chosen to build a vast munitions works two miles away, the district could not even replace its vanished tourists with evacuees from target areas. Grimly facing the worst, the shopkeepers of the stricken city put away their stocks of souvenirs and memorial china and prepared to face the siege until better times came.

No economic distress, however, could affect the real beauty of Rampleford Cathedral or the charm of the Close in which it stood. By ancient custom, the Judge was lodged in the house of one of the minor Canons. Derek was enchanted with his surroundings. For a young man in love, it would be difficult to find a place more congenial. In the morning he would be awakened by the clatter of jackdaws in the Cathedral spire from a sleep which the chimes of the belfry never seemed to disturb. At night, when the gates of the Close had been shut, and the great bulk of the Cathedral loomed black against the stars over the darkened town, he could imagine himself back in the Middle Ages. Such conditions are apt to be productive of bad poetry, and at Rampleford Derek contrived to write a good deal.

Hilda was quick to notice that the situation of the lodgings had other advantages besides their romantic appeal. The Close gates were shut and barred at sunset, and anybody seeking entry after that time had to pass the scrutiny of the doorkeeper who had for the duration of the assizes been reinforced by a plain clothes policeman. In addition, a constable in uniform was continually on duty at the door of the lodgings. At night, Derek could hear his measured footfall on the gravel outside. Obviously, no risks were being taken with the Judge's safety. Nevertheless, Hilda did not allow herself to be content with official precautions. On the evening of their arrival at Rampleford, she outlined to Derek a system which she had prepared by which one of them should be continuously on guard over the Judge by day and night—particularly by night. A year later, when fire-watching had become commonplace, Derek could recall with amusement the hardship which this proposal seemed to him at the time. He hinted that this was a duty which should be shared by Beamish or Savage, but Hilda rejected the suggestion with contempt. They were not to be trusted. Nobody could be trusted. The work devolved on them alone.

In the result, on alternate nights thereafter Derek kept watch over his lordship's slumbers from eleven till three, and from three till seven. Contrary to his expectations, it did not turn out so irksome after all; but for this some credit is due to his state of mind at the time. To sit up for a few hours, writing yet another interminable letter to Sheila, or trying to coax into rhyme sentiments which if not exactly original were at least sincere, was no very heavy task, even though it had to be varied every half hour or so by creeping stealthily down the corridor and listening to the reassuring vigour of the Judge's snores.

By day, the matter was simple enough. The weather was cold and the Judge showed no disposition to take any form of exercise. It was simply a question of accompanying him to the Courts and back again. Whether from new-found motives of economy or not, he invited no guests to the lodgings, and apart from the Sheriff or his Chaplain (who did not look as though they were disposed to perpetrate a criminal assault on the Judge) no outsider penetrated into the lodgings. Within the Court itself, one glance at the ranks of policemen at every conceivable point of vantage made it clear that any amateur bodyguard was quite unnecessary.

In short, Rampleford assizes proved to be not only quite uneventful but intolerably dull. Indeed, if it had not been for the distraction afforded by Sheila's letters—and these, though fairly frequent, were somewhat disappointingly short and uncommunicative—Derek would have been more thoroughly bored than at any time on the circuit. Even Hilda's vivacity, he noticed, had flagged a little. She was often listless and silent for long periods at a time. Inaction rather than the sleepless nights which she had imposed on herself, obviously preyed on her. As for the Judge, the realization of the peril in which his professional career stood had produced a curious reaction. As though determined in any event to go down with his colours flying, he assumed a manner that was an exaggeration—almost a caricature— of his every-day self. Never had he been so dignified, so pompous, so loftily condescending to the junior Bar, so icily critical of the leaders. His allocutions to convicted prisoners were longer than ever and, as the prisoners found to their cost, were followed by sentences proportionately long. The whole system of English justice depends upon the immunity and security of those who administer it. A psychologist would have observed with interest the effects of threatening one of these with loss of his position. Perhaps the only person with knowledge of the facts who could thoroughly have appreciated the position was Pettigrew, and he, to Derek's regret, did not attend the assize.

After the first week Hilda considered the position at Rampleford to be sufficiently secure to justify her in leaving her husband for the day. She did not say where she was going; she simply hired a car and had herself driven from the lodgings. Barber displayed an almost ostentatious lack of interest in her movements, but it might have been observed that his manner on the bench that morning was even more pontifical than usual. It was as though he strove to project the sense of his power and importance beyond the narrow confines of his court, to influence in some fashion the drama that was being played out ten miles away, on which his fate depended.

Hilda had chosen her time well. She had seen advertised for that day a concert at the National Gallery which she knew Sally Parsons would be bound to attend, and an examination of the railway guide had assured her that she would be well on her way to London by the time of her arrival. She left her car at the gate of Sebald-Smith's house (which was in effect a huge music room with a minute cottage attached) and walked boldly in. The maid who opened the door to her had obviously had instructions to admit no visitors, but took one frightened glance at Hilda's determined face and surrendered at discretion. Hurriedly she flung open the door of the music room, mumbled, "Lady Parker, sir!" and fled back to the kitchen.

Sebastian Sebald-Smith was lying on a sofa in the centre of the great, bare room. His left arm was in a sling and with his free hand he was turning the pages of a music score. He raised his head as Hilda entered and looked up at her with his disturbing, yellow-brown eyes.

"Hello, Hilda!" he said with no trace of surprise or embarrassment in his voice. "I'm just looking at this new suite of Katzenburg's. Have you heard about it?"

"No," said Hilda. She remembered how absentminded Sebastian could be when he was absorbed in anything that interested him, and realized that he was for the moment quite unaware of anything unusual or unexpected in her presence. "No," she repeated. "Do you like it?"

"M-m, I'm not sure yet. I'm pretty sure the Great British Public won't. I've been asked to conduct it at Bristol in January, if I'm fit enough."

"Mitigation of damages!" was Hilda's instant mental reaction. Aloud she said, "That sounds splendid, Sebastian! It's quite a new departure for you, isn't it? I'm sure you'll be a tremendous success as a conductor."

"I'm sure I should be, if I knew the first thing about the orchestra, which I don't. I can only imagine the B.B.C. thought of me because I played in Katzenburg's piano quintet the first time they did it over here. But one must do something."

"Of course, of course," Hilda cooed. Then in an anguished tone she went on, "Sebastian, you can't think how *miserable* this dreadful accident has made me!"

"It's bloody, bloody, bloody!" exclaimed Sebald-Smith with sudden violence, banging his fist upon the open pages beside him. "God! when I think what this swine has done

to me—— I say, Hilda! I'm sorry, I clean forgot! You——
I——"

"Go on!" said Hilda in tragic tones. "You needn't mince
your words so far as I am concerned. We deserve it. If saying
anything would help——"

She went through the motions popularly known as
wringing one's hands. Her hands were long and beautifully
shaped, and the effect was very attractive.

There was a moment's silence. Sebald-Smith, sitting up
on the sofa, was looking at her with close attention.

"It's awfully good of you to come and see me, considering
everything," he said at last, in a somewhat embarrassed
tone.

"It was the least I could do."

The pale eyes narrowed.

"But I don't quite see what you have come for," he went
on, with a perceptible hardening of his voice.

"Come for? But Sebastian, I *had* to come. Ever since I
heard about this awful affair, I've been thinking of you,
lying here, eating your heart out——"

"It won't do, Hilda! We'd much better not beat
about the bush. You've come here for a purpose. Hadn't
you better tell me what it is?"

Hilda dropped her hands to her sides and raised her head.

"You are perfectly right," she said steadily. "It was silly
of me to try and pretend to you. I have come for a purpose.
Can't you guess what it is?"

"If it is to ask me to let your husband off, you had better
think again."

Hilda's manner underwent yet another change. This
time she became the business woman, brisk and sensible.

"Sebastian," she said. "We are grown-up people. Can't
we discuss this reasonably, without indulging in schoolboy
talk about 'letting people off'? I simply want to see what
can best be done in everybody's interests."

"'Everybody's interests' is good. Your interests aren't mine..

In fact they are the exact opposite. Your husband has sent you here, to see how cheaply he can get out of this mess."

"That isn't true, Sebastian. As a matter of fact, I didn't even tell him I was coming to-day. I wanted to put the position squarely before you as it affects William."

"Why should I be interested in how this affects him? It's myself I'm thinking about."

"I'll show you why in a moment. If you insist on the demands your lawyers have been making, William will be ruined."

"I am sorry, Hilda," said Sebald-Smith coldly, "but much as I like you—very much as I used to like you—nothing would give me greater pleasure than to ruin your husband."

"And ruin me?"

"Aha! Now we are getting to the point!"

"No, we are not. It's a side issue, really. I only asked out of curiosity."

"Very well, then. Personally, I should be sorry to see you deprived of the flesh-pots you always longed after." Hilda thought she could detect a significant emphasis on the "personally". She knew only too well that there was another member of the household who would wish to see nothing better; and it was against her unseen influence that she was striving. "But one can't make an omelette without breaking eggs, and you, my pretty egg, will have to go the same way as that precious bad egg, your husband. So the answer is— Yes, and ruin you!"

"And ruin yourself?"

"My good woman, I am ruined already—and for life, I may remind you. All I want to do now is to get what compensation I can for it."

"Which is precisely what you won't get if you go on the way you are now," snapped Hilda. "Let's leave sentiment out of this, and discuss it as a pure matter of business. Everybody knows that you are the standing example of an artist who is a good business man too."

Sebald-Smith, who had dissipated most of his very large earnings in the wildest speculations, swallowed this gross untruth with gusto.

"Very well," he said. "Let's talk business, by all means. But I warn you, I set a pretty high value on this hand of mine."

"It's not a question of how much it is worth, but how much there is to give you. A bankrupt debtor is no use to anyone. Now listen. Either you force my husband off the Bench or you let him stay there, earning his salary. I'm going to tell you just how much you can expect in either event, and your solicitors can satisfy themselves that I am speaking the truth."

Hilda had her case cut and dried. Into the pianist's ears she poured an endless stream of figures and calculations, entering into every detail of the Judge's past, present and future financial position, providing for every possible contingency. The gist of her argument was, of course, the impossibility of the Judge's being able to provide immediately any sum remotely approaching adequate damages for the injury he had inflicted, and the folly of taking action which would deprive him of the only source of income from which future payments could be made.

Sebald-Smith listened, at first incredulously and rather resentfully, then with interest and finally with resignation as the flood of words poured over him. It was obvious to Hilda that what she said was taking effect. He was evidently beginning to look upon the matter in a new light. For the time being, at any rate, he had laid aside the crude ideas of revenge which had at first obsessed him, and was considering the question from a purely financial aspect. To give their due to the solicitors acting for either side, very much the same arguments had already been quietly suggested by Michael to Messrs. Faraday, Fothergill, Crisp & Co., and they had in their turn passed these on to their client. The fact remained that Sebald-Smith had been impervious to words of reason when expressed by his advisers and a good

deal more prepared to attend to them when spoken by
Hilda. Hilda, while giving herself due credit for her charm
and persuasiveness, knew quite well what was the main
reason for her success. She was able to develop her argument unopposed. The lawyers' letters, on the other hand,
were read by somebody else besides the man to whom they
were addressed—a somebody who could be relied upon to
garnish them with a spiteful commentary of her own; a
somebody, moreover, who would certainly be even far more
interested in humiliating Hilda through her husband than
in securing damages for Sebald-Smith. It was Hilda's one
hope that she could succeed in so far convincing Sebastian
of the good sense of what she was now saying that he would
stand up to the pressure which Sally Parsons was certain
to put upon him as soon as she returned.

In all, Hilda's interview with Sebald-Smith lasted for the
best part of an hour. When she left, it was with the feeling
that she had succeeded in her mission. Sebastian had been
brought to agree in principle that it would be futile in his
own interests to make public property of the Judge's fall
from grace. He had promised to write to his solicitors
instructing them to settle the matter on the best terms
possible. He was naturally unwilling to take on trust the
figures with which Hilda had plied him (a neatly written
copy of which she was careful to leave with him) but she
assured him that Faraday and Co., would be given the
fullest opportunity to verify them at their leisure. She had
been unable to extract a final decision from him, but this
was more than she had ever allowed herself to hope for.
He had promised to consider the question afresh in the light
of her arguments and to take proper advice upon it, and
with this she was well content.

Hilda thought it wise to refuse Sebastian's invitation to
stay to lunch, but she accepted a glass of sherry, and they
parted good friends. His parting words to her stuck in her
mind.

"You have certainly fought the good fight for that husband of yours," he said. "I'm glad to think you find him worth all the trouble. Or is it only your own flesh-pots you are fighting to preserve?"

It was the second time in a few days that someone had suggested to her that the bond between her and the Judge was essentially only one of common interest.

"At any rate," she reflected with pride, "nobody has ever suggested that I haven't been faithful to him."

The party at the lodgings that evening was more cheerful than it had been for some time. It was as though a dark shadow had been lifted from the household. Hilda, on her return, had said two words in private to the Judge which had caused his frozen dignity to thaw into something approaching common humanity. He was unusually talkative at dinner and alluded more than once to the fact that Derek was Marshall by name and Marshal by occupation. As for Derek, he had his own sources of contentment. He had successfully completed a sonnet which embodied two new and highly effective similes, and he had received an exceptionally long letter from Sheila. True, the letter was chiefly remarkable for an exhaustive account of an embittered dispute between the Sister at the hospital and the Red Cross Commandant concerning some missing Thomas's splints, which to an unprejudiced mind would not have seemed of any great or general interest; but Derek's mind was highly prejudiced, and he was happy. The general atmosphere of relaxation affected even Savage, who served the port with an air of cringing geniality. Whether it extended to Beamish was known only to the contestants at a dartboard near by, whither he had repaired very early in the evening.

That night it was Derek's turn for the second watch. Consequently he was awake when the rest of the household was beginning to stir. It naturally followed that he was shaved, bathed and dressed by the time that the postman made his early morning delivery. It was, of course, pure coincidence that he happened to be standing in the hall at the moment when the letters were pushed through the slit in the front door. A man of mature years does not hang about waiting for the post in that way, even if he does happen to be in love. At the same time, he felt that it was a very fortunate coincidence indeed when the first thing that he saw, lying face upwards on the mat, proved to be a deliciously fat envelope addressed to him in Sheila's straggly hand. He picked it up and then glanced cursorily at the rest of the post. There was nothing else for him, but he observed with interest a very small, untidy brown paper packet, addressed to the Judge in roughly printed capitals. He examined it with interest. After the episode of the chocolates, anything coming through the post for the Judge was, he felt, a proper object of suspicion, and this, for some reason or other, seemed to him particularly suspicious. He was trying to decipher the postmark when he heard footsteps approaching.

One does not want to be found at an unreasonably early hour investigating postal matter addressed to somebody else. Acting on the spur of the moment, Derek slipped the little parcel into his pocket and was half-way up the stairs before the approaching servant had reached the hall. Once in his room he naturally enough turned his attention first to his letter.

It is, perhaps, always a mistake to read letters on an empty stomach unless one is quite sure that their contents will be agreeable. Derek had every reason for expecting nothing but the purest pleasure from this particular letter, but by the time he had finished reading it he had no appetite for breakfast left. It was not that it was lacking in affection. On the contrary. It began with the words, "Derek *darling*," the adjective being underlined twice. But it continued ominously, "We are in *awful* trouble!" and this time the adjective received three underlinings. Derek's natural disquiet at this introduction was not allayed by the fact that when he had finished the letter he was still entirely in the dark as to what the nature of the trouble was. It related to Daddy—hitherto a dim figure on the horizon, whom he had never met and to whom he had given little thought—so much was clear. But what Daddy's trouble was, and why it should affect Sheila and apparently Derek himself, even a second and third re-reading of the letter failed to determine. It was, according to Sheila, "too Dreadful", apparently too dreadful to be put into precise words. She asserted several times that so far as she was concerned it would make No Difference to her feelings for him but at the same time she gloomily contemplated the possibility of never being able to look him in the Face again. If on his side, he never wanted to have anything more to do with her she would absolutely Understand. Which was considerably more than her correspondent did.

The only conclusion that Derek could come to was that in some unspecified way Daddy had succeeded in bringing disgrace upon his family. He tried to fortify himself with the reflection that, as Sheila said of herself, it would make no difference to him. At the same time, he would have felt a good deal more confident even on that point, if he had known what it was that was to make no difference. It is somewhat difficult to disregard with lofty chivalry a blot on the family scutcheon unless you can see the blot. Daddy might merely have run off with somebody else's wife. On the other hand he might have been arrested for murder, or, worse still, have been discovered to be a fifth columnist in disguise. It was all most unsettling.

Gloomily Derek descended for breakfast, gloomily he toyed with his food and gloomily accompanied the Judge to Court. It was not until, sitting in his place on the bench, he put his hand in his pocket to take out and read once more the mystifying letter, that he found the parcel which he had put there some hours before. Until that moment he had entirely forgotten its existence.

Having found it, he was rather at a loss to know what to do with it. Obviously, he had no right to have it in his possession at all, and the morning's spirit of suspiciousness which had induced him to examine it in the first place had long since evaporated. If he were to be found waylaying what was probably a perfectly normal and innocent package intended for the Judge, his position would be, to say the least of it, awkward. Meanwhile, what the devil was he to do with the thing?

He took it out of his pocket, and under cover of the ledge in front of him stole a look at it. He noticed that the string, which was loosely tied, had nearly slipped off one corner. It would obviously be perfectly easy to take it off without even untying the knot. Well, since he had already gone so far, he might as well go the whole hog. After all, there was always a chance. . . .

He left the bench quietly and went into the stuffy little apartment at the back which was his lordship's retiring room. There was the inevitable policeman at the door, but luckily the authorities had not gone so far as to station one inside. As Derek expected, the string slipped easily off the brown paper. Inside the paper was a cardboard soap-box. Inside the box was the corpse of a mouse. Attached to its neck by a piece of string was a label on which, written in the same crude capitals as the address, Derek read:

"WHEN THE CAT'S AWAY——"

"Anyhow," Derek said to himself a few minutes later, as he listened to one of Flack's most florid speeches, "I bet I'm the only man who ever sat on the bench of a Court of Justice with a dead mouse in his pocket."

Chapter 14

REFLECTIONS AND REACTIONS

———

It was the interval between tea and dinner. Barber, who had declared his intention of preparing a reserved judgment, was (as a stealthy reconnaissance proved) slumbering in an arm-chair in the smoking-room. Derek judged this to be a good opportunity to show the parcel and its contents to Hilda. She examined it with the greatest interest and, he was glad to note, seemed to think that he had acted quite properly in waylaying it on suspicion. It was clear that she attached a certain significance to the unpleasant little incident, which to Derek was as pointless as it was disgusting; but she seemed unwilling to tell him what it was.

Hilda looked first at the legend on the label (which Derek had at her request removed from the mouse before she would consent to touch anything) and, having read it, said significantly, "Ah!"

Derek waited for something more enlightening, but in vain.

Next she examined the brown paper wrapping. This time she observed, "Addressed to him and not to me. Typical!"

Derek was more and more puzzled.

Hilda then turned her attention to the rather smudged postmark. "Can you make it out?" she asked.

"I'm not sure," said Derek, but it looks like 'Rampleford'."

"Yes. I believe you're right. And the time is—what?"

"Something 45 p.m. It looks like a six to me."

"Six or eight," said Hilda doubtfully. "We can find out what the time of the last collection is from the post-office here."

"Perhaps the police would do that for us," Derek suggested.

"I don't think this is a matter we need trouble the police about. If it is what I think it is, I am sure we needn't."

"Then you don't think——?"

"Would you be very kind, Derek, and fetch me a Bradshaw? Beamish has got one in his room, I know. And do dispose of that horrible object somewhere. It makes me quite sick to look at it."

Derek incinerated the mouse in the dining-room fire and duly fetched the Bradshaw. When he had brought it, Hilda thanked him prettily, begged him quite unnecessarily not to mention the affair to the Judge or anybody else, and retired with it and the exhibits in the case to her own room, leaving Derek gloomily wondering why females always had such a passion for secretiveness.

Hilda had decided in her own mind at her first sight of the message attached to the mouse that Sally Parsons had sent it. It remained to see whether or not it was physically possible for her to have done so. If not, she concluded, so much the worse for possibility. But fortunately for her faith in her own instinct Bradshaw appeared to bear her out. She found that by leaving Trafalgar Square punctually at 2.15, Sally could have caught a fast train which would bring her in to Rampleford at 4.35. Supposing that she was met at the station, she would be home by five o'clock. Allow her half an hour in which to extract from Sebald-Smith an account of his visit from Hilda that morning, another half-hour in which to decide on a suitable retort and to prepare the parcel, she would be left with just sufficient time to make her way back to Rampleford in the dark and to reach the head post-office before 6.45.

None the less, though the scheme seemed possible in theory, Hilda was doubtful whether it could have been accomplished in practice. For one thing, it allowed hardly any time for catching the mouse—unless, indeed, the charming creature kept a store of them all ready for distribution among her friends. More important, perhaps, was the obvious fact that however anxious Sally was to show her opinion of Hilda's interference, and however nimble in devising her retort, she would be most unlikely to do anything about it until she had had some tea. After all, she had probably eaten nothing for lunch beyond a hasty snack at the National Gallery canteen; and Bradshaw did not credit the train with a restaurant car. Everything, therefore, depended on whether Derek was right in reading the postmark as 6.45. Until that could be determined the matter was still uncertain.

Carefully locking away the label, box and paper, she went back to the drawing-room. There Derek looked up from the evening paper to inform her with an air of sulky martyrdom (which was completely lost on her) that he had rung up the post-office and discovered that the last collection for local delivery was, in fact, at 8.45. This put the matter beyond any doubt in Hilda's mind. She received the news with such complacency that Derek, who had firmly determined not to oblige her ladyship by showing any curiosity at all, was provoked into asking further questions.

"Do you think you know where this parcel came from?" he asked.

"Yes. I am quite sure."

"And you still don't want to tell the police about it?"

"No, I don't. Because, Derek, knowing what I know, I am certain that it has nothing to do with the threats against the Judge which we have been watching. This is just a nasty piece of vulgarity, directed against me, really—and I'm afraid that's all I can tell you about it now."

"I must say I should have thought there wasn't a great

deal of difference between sending a dead mouse to a person and sending him a box of chocolates stuffed with carbide. But I dare say you know best."

And thereupon, somewhat moodily, Derek went upstairs to dress for dinner.

Hilda had been so pleased at her own perspicacity in detecting the identity of the sender of the mouse (though, candidly, this was obvious enough, and obvious also that the sender had intended it to be so) that she had not yet seriously considered its implications. Now that she began to do so, however, she found some course for disquiet. In the first place, Derek's comparison of this parcel with the other one which had caused so much trouble at Southington was clearly a justifiable one. There was an obvious difference between them. The first had been a carefully disguised form of attack, though not perhaps a very serious one; the second was an open piece of bravado. But none the less it certainly looked probable enough that one mind had conceived the two. And if so, that mind was the mind of Sally Parsons.

From this it followed (Hilda's thoughts ran on) that Inspector Mallett was right and she was wrong. Her theory that everything untoward which had happened during the course of the circuit must be traced to one source would not stand. Obviously, Sally Parsons was not responsible for an anonymous letter sent before the motor accident; and Hilda doubted whether she was likely to have procured someone to come to Wimblingham to give her a black eye. It was sufficiently galling to have to admit that her instinct had played her false. The fact also that there were now at least two enemies in the field gave her the uneasy sensation of being compassed about with dangers.

But it was when she began to consider the significance of the message in the parcel itself that she really felt unhappy. Obviously, it was a message of defiance. But was it not also one of triumph? Hilda had been positive, when she returned from her visit to Sebald-Smith, that she had been successful in persuading him to come to a reasonable compromise in his claim for damages. Now she was not so sure. Her enemy's impudent gesture seemed to suggest that she had already won back the vacillating Sebald-Smith and that Hilda's arguments of reason and interest alike would be forgotten under her influence. And if that were so, the outlook for herself and her husband was black indeed. She was under no illusions as to the intensity of Sally Parson's dislike for her. If she had been, this latest manifestation of it would have opened her eyes. Moreover, the fact that she had addressed her disgusting communication to the Judge made it clear that she was anxious to lower Hilda in the eyes of her husband and add domestic unpleasantness to all their other troubles. Thank Heaven, that part of the scheme at least had miscarried. Meanwhile—and to Hilda's active nature this was the hardest part to bear—there was nothing to be done except to await events. She had the night before written to Michael, telling him of what she then believed to be the success of her negotiations, and asking him to put forward a proposal to the solicitors on the other side. She could do nothing now until their reply was received, although she was only too sure in her own mind what it would be.

Fortunately for her peace of mind, dinner that evening provided Hilda with some distraction, and distraction of the kind which she most enjoyed. Her husband, having slumbered away the time which he had intended to devote to his judgment, made up for his neglect by discussing the points at issue during the meal. Hilda, more to keep her mind off other subjects than for any better reason, debated each turn in the argument with vigour and the result was that Derek was treated to a first-rate exposition, by experts, of, among other things, the liabilities of innkeepers at Common Law and the precise meaning and effect of trespass *ab initio*. It is to be feared, however, that his private preoccupations prevented him from profiting as he should have done from what should have been a valuable contribution to his legal education.

By the end of dinner, the case in all its aspects, both of law and fact, had been thoroughly debated, the Judge had stated what his decision would be, her ladyship had been good enough to concur with him, and there, it might have been imagined, the matter would have ended. But just as Pettigrew drank whisky to try to forget the fact that Jefferson had been preferred to him as a Judge of the County Court, so Hilda plunged into legal argument in an endeavour to dull her mind to the fact that Sally Parsons had got the better of her. It was the distraction from disagreeable reality to which she instinctively turned, just as more ordinarily constituted people turn to the cinema, the pub, or the lending library. Her means of escape certainly was more intellectual than the normal ones. On the other hand, it had the disadvantage that, given time, it became extremely boring to anyone else who happened to be in her company.

The Judge displayed exemplary patience for some time while Hilda continued to hold forth on a subject which had long since lost its interest. Sitting back in his chair, he was content to utter monosyllabic words of agreement in the intervals of eating chocolate caramels. Finally, however, he evidently thought it time to create a diversion.

"I think, my dear, since you are so interested, that you ought to refresh your memory of the original authorities," he said. "Marshal, you will find some books on my desk. Would you mind bringing them here?"

From that moment, silence reigned in the drawing-room. Hilda buried her head in the heavy volumes of the Law Reports as though they had been the most enthralling of adventure stories. Presently Barber went upstairs to bed, and presumably also to write his judgment, for it was duly delivered next morning. Not long afterwards Derek followed him. His last sight was of Hilda, still preoccupied in her reading, and apparently forgetful of the fact that according to their agreement she was to be called at three o'clock for her turn of duty. She was sitting with a volume of the King's Bench Reports on her knee. Apparently she had strayed beyond the subject which had originally brought it there, for she was turning its pages, reading here and there as a lover of poetry might dip into first one and then another of the contents of an anthology. It was an odd spectacle, he thought at the time, and one that he had reason to call to mind long afterwards.

Chapter 15

INSIDE OR OUTSIDE?

———

Rampleford Assizes lasted for another week. To Derek, at least, it was one of the dullest weeks of his life. The long night watches, which Hilda continued to insist upon, although there did not seem to be the smallest purpose in them, had become a weariness to the flesh. His anxiety over Sheila had not been relieved by any message from her, and he spent the hours of watching in a state of gloomy impatience. By day, matters were not much better. The Judge was so aloof and Olympian as to be scarcely human, and since the incident of the dead mouse Hilda had become quite unsociable, preoccupied with thoughts and calculations which she did not choose to share.

Indeed, the only member of the household who seemed to be perfectly contented with his lot was Beamish. Rampleford, he confided to Derek, suited him. In fact it suited him Right Down to the Ground. Apart from the fact that the High Sheriff was a Decent Gentleman, he did not say in what the peculiar suitability of the town consisted; but Derek observed that he had formed the habit of slipping out of the lodgings soon after the party returned from court each day and coming back sometimes quite late in the evening in an unusually genial state. More from boredom than from any other motive, Derek found himself beginning to cultivate the clerk, or rather to allow himself to be cultivated by him. Against his will, he had to admit that he was quite an entertaining companion. He had a store of anecdotes connected with judges and counsel, which were a kind of servant's hall edition of Pettigrew's stories on the same themes. But what struck Derek chiefly about them was the underlying malice which seemed to characterize them all. Beamish's pig-like little eyes never seemed to gleam with such pleasure as when he was recounting the story of someone's discomfiture or humiliation. There was, Derek felt, a strong vein of cruelty somewhere in his conceited, self-centred little character.

One evening, after the Judge and Hilda had gone to bed, Derek, whose turn it was to take the first watch, was in the hall about to go upstairs when Beamish let himself in at the front door. He greeted him in the tone of mellow friendliness which Derek had learned to associate with his evening expeditions. It occurred to Derek that he was on this occasion slightly more mellow than usual. As a matter of fact, this had been a somewhat notable evening for Beamish. After a period of comparative failure, he had suddenly run into irresistible form at the darts' board, and his defeat of the champion of the local Canadian forces had just been celebrated as it deserved.

"Come into my room a minute, won't you, Marshal?" said Beamish. "Have a quiet chat and a pipe."

"No, thank you very much," said Derek. "It's rather late, and I was just going up."

Dominion hospitality had loosened Beamish's normally well guarded tongue.

"Going up, eh?" he repeated. "Don't tell me you're going to bed, though. It's your turn on, isn't it?"

"What do you know about that?" said Derek in surprise.

Beamish chuckled.

"Good Lord!" he said. "D'you think I don't know all about it? I wasn't born yesterday, you know."

So saying, he made his way to his sitting-room. After a little hesitation, Derek followed him.

"I should have been a pretty poor sort of clerk if I hadn't

spotted it, with all the goings on there've been this circuit,"
Beamish went on, throwing himself into an arm-chair and
filling his pipe as he spoke. "It's a clerk's job to know things,
Marshal, don't forget. I dare say I could tell *you* a thing or
two you don't know."

Derek was always somewhat irritated when Beamish
addressed him as "Marshal". True, he had been careful to
explain before that in doing so he was calling him by the
title of his office and not by his surname, and that no dis-
respect was intended, but it continued to jar on Derek's
ear. So his reply was in somewhat sulky tones.

"I suppose everybody in the house knows all about it,"
he said.

"Well, I wouldn't answer for Mrs. Square," said the clerk.
"She not interested in anything much outside her kitchen.
And as for the two resident maids here, they wouldn't notice
anything if it wasn't right under their noses. And they don't
even notice that, if it happens to be something that wants
dusting. If her ladyship was in anything like her usual form
she'd have been at them long ago."

He gave up the attempt to light his pipe and closed his
eyes.

"Where was I?" he went on suddenly, sitting up with a
jerk. "Oh yes! Savage knows all about it, Marshal, you may
be sure, and Greene too. Not that *I've* gossiped with 'em.
I know my place, and I've taught them theirs. But in a
small commun-community like ours, things get about,
y'know."

Derek said nothing. He was trying to think out the implications of this surprising news when Beamish began to speak
again.

"Personally, I think you're wasting your time," he said.
"And I'm sorry to see a young gentleman like yourself losing
your beauty sleep for nothing. Not but what you may not
have other things to keep you awake o' nights, for all I
know." There was a knowing leer in his face as he said this

that brought the blood to Derek's cheeks. "Y'see," he went on, "it's like this, Marshal. Either this is an outside job, or it's an inside one—if it's a job at all and not just a hallu-hallucination. If it's an outside job, what are the police for? They're all on the Kee Veev—the Close is stiff with 'em this minute. And if it's an inside job, well there's only me and Greene and Savage to do it, and what any of us would want to lose our position for, I don't know. However, if it amuses her ladyship, I suppose it's all right. And if she was to get another black eye one of these nights, as the result, I for one wouldn't grieve."

He shut his eyes again and Derek began to think that he had gone to sleep. But presently he added, with his eyes still closed: "And in any case, Marshal, I could've told you in advance that nothing would happen this assize. There's one great diff'rence between thisassize and any other so far. Great diff'rence."

"What difference?" Derek asked impatiently.

Beamish opened one rather bleary eye.

"Can't you guess?" he said thickly. "The diff'rence in the comp-composition of the Bar. Pettigrew isn't here. Thatsall."

"What the devil do you mean?" Derek shouted at him angrily.

"Y'needn't make s'much noise, Marshal. I'm just making a nobservation, thatsall. There's Bad Blood between those two—always has been. Known it a long time. Clerks know —everything. Their business, know everything. Bad Blood. . . ."

This time Beamish was certainly asleep.

Neither on the next day, nor on any subsequent days did Beamish by word or sign allude to this discreditable episode. Derek, for his part, was only too glad that it should be for-gotten—which meant, of course, that it remained in his memory, along with that brief instant at the railway station, as something that refused to be altogether forgotten. To

Hilda, naturally enough, he said nothing at all; except, indeed, to suggest diffidently that the watchkeeping system might be relaxed—a suggestion which was promptly turned down.

At all events, Beamish proved right, so far as Rampleford Assizes were concerned. Nothing whatever occurred to vary the monotonous course of Justice. Nothing, that is, except for two incidents, the one so trivial that in normal circumstances it would have escaped notice, the other so late in time as barely to belong to the assize at all.

Two days after Beamish's alcoholic confidences, and the day before the assizes were due to end, the Under Sheriff called as usual to escort the Judge to court. Criminal business being at an end, he came alone, but apart from this the procedure was exactly the same as it had been on every previous day. Punctually at ten o'clock, the Under Sheriff would arrive, be received by Greene and shown into a small room on the first floor which was used apparently for this purpose only. Here he would be engaged in conversation which, as the days went on, became more and more desultory, by Derek and, if she chose to appear, by Hilda. Savage, meanwhile, would be in his lordship's room, arraying him in wig, bands, gown and that odd, transverse piece of material known to initiates as "the gun-case". After the proper interval of time, the Judge, in the full panoply of his office would descend to his expectant acolytes. The Lodgings being built on several levels, the corridor in which Barber's room was situated communicated directly with the waiting-room, by a short flight of steep stairs. Down these it was the Shaver's custom to descend with slow and solemn gait and a ceremonious expression on his face as though to emphasize the fact that whereas at breakfast a short hour ago he had been merely a rather peevish elderly gentleman, he was just now His Majesty's Judge of Assize. It was evident that the little ceremony gave him a good deal of harmless pleasure.

What happened on this particular occasion can be very briefly told. The Judge was about four steps from the bottom in his progress, one hand clasping his white kid gloves, the other delicately hitching up the skirts of his robe when Hilda, who happened to be present, gave a sudden cry of alarm and dashed forward just as he lost his footing and pitched head first into the room. For a moment it looked as if there was going to be quite a nasty accident, but his wife's presence of mind prevented what would have been an ugly fall for a heavy, stiff-jointed man. As it was, she was in time to receive his weight on her shoulder, and the pair of them tumbled ignominiously but unhurt to the floor.

The Marshal and the Under Sheriff helped them to their feet, the Judge's wig was recovered from the floor and restored to his head, his gown was hastily brushed down, and the usual ejaculations were made by those present that are commonly made on occasions of minor disasters. Hilda, however, did not ejaculate. After assuring herself that her husband was unharmed and having answered rather petulantly to inquiries that she was all right but her dress wasn't, she cut short the flow of commiseration and congratulation by saying firmly, "What I want to know is, how did this happen?"

She was answered from the head of the stairs, where Savage had all this time been a spectator of the mishap.

"I think a stair rod has come away, my lady."

"But why on earth should a stair rod come away?" she asked, going to the foot of the steps to see for herself.

Nobody was in a position to answer this.

"Dangerous things, stair rods," observed the Under Sheriff, "I remember——"

"Mr. Under Sheriff, if you are ready, I think we ought to be going," said Barber, who was in no mood to listen to reminiscences of other people's accidents.

"I don't think I shall come to court this morning," said Hilda.

"As you please, my dear. I dare say you would like to lie down for a little. You must have been rather shaken, I'm afraid."

"No, I'm perfectly all right, as I've said already. I've just changed my mind, that's all."

As the party left the room, Hilda caught Derek's eye and gave him what is generally described as a meaning look. Derek had no difficulty in recognizing it as such, but unfortunately he was not able to determine for himself exactly what it meant. She certainly looked very purposeful, and somewhat excited, but what about? Surely she could not have got into her head that this accident had anything to do with the supposed conspiracy against the Judge?

But this, it appeared, was exactly what Hilda had got into her head. That evening, she took him aside.

"Derek, I want to talk to you," she said seriously. "I looked at the stair rods very carefully this morning. They were all perfectly firm. They were quite difficult to move. This one had been deliberately pulled right out."

"But that's not possible," Derek objected. "Who on earth could have wanted to do such a thing?"

"That is what I am asking myself," said Hilda solemnly.

"Well, I can only suppose it must have been the housemaid. They have to take these things out to clean them, don't they?"

"I have spoken to the housemaid. She is quite positive that she has not touched the stair rods since we have been here."

Derek, remembering Beamish's comments on the servants in the Lodgings, had to admit to himself that this sounded probable enough. He tried to reckon up the possibilities, supposing that Hilda's astounding suspicion was well founded. The last person to use those stairs had, presumably, been Savage. Would he not have noticed the missing rod? Not necessarily, perhaps, if he was going up them. He certainly looked astonished enough when he witnessed the

Judge's fall from above. Or was it really astonishment that he had shown? It was hard to remember a man's expression afterwards. Perhaps there had been something peculiar about it. . . .

"Now do you see why I feel that we must always be on our guard?" Hilda was saying. "We know now that we must be prepared to meet danger from within as well as without. It's a horrible situation, and I don't know whom I can trust."

Again Beamish's remarks came back to Derek's mind. "An inside job" or "an outside job?" And if "an inside job", then why not Savage as well as another? But why Savage any more than anyone else? What did he really know of these people with whom he had been leading a peripatetic existence during the past few weeks? What really lay behind Greene's taciturnity, Savage's humility, Beamish's familiarity? Or was the whole affair, to borrow Beamish's expression again, a hallu—hallucination? Certainly it seemed too absurd to be true, the incidents too unrelated to each other, the theory too unrelated to ordinary life. The one undoubted fact was that her ladyship was in a highly nervous condition. A little more of this and he felt that he would be not much better himself.

Derek was heartily glad to leave Rampleford. His last day there had been distinguished, if not greatly cheered, by a letter from Sheila, in which she told him that she found it Too Difficult to explain in a letter, but if they could only Meet Soon, she would be able to tell him Everything. The move was at least a stage on the road towards that desirable, if anxious moment, and not even the fact that Beamish tersely described Whitsea, their next stopping place, as "fierce", prevented him from looking forward to it with impatience. It was therefore with genuine relief that he found himself once more in the reserved carriage, watching through the window the inevitable guard of police and the

Under Sheriff dutifully making conversation against a background of Canadian soldiers who seemed to find the whole spectacle a source of great amusement.

The whistle had been blown and the last of the unprivileged many had been stowed somewhere in the overcrowded train when a police officer appeared running on the platform. He saluted the Chief Constable hastily, handed something to him and said a few inaudible words. The Chief Constable in his turn hammered on the Judge's window which Derek had just shut.

"This has just come from the lodgings, my lord," he said, when the window had at length been persuaded to open again. "It must have arrived after you left. I hope it is nothing important."

Through the window he handed a letter. The Judge took it, opened it, and glanced at its contents.

"Here!" he cried angrily. "How did this. . . ?"

He was too late. The train had started. The Chief Constable, his hand at the salute, a fixed grin on his face, had glided backwards behind them. The Under Sheriff, thankfully replacing his topper on his head, was already almost out of sight. And on the Judge's knees lay a little typewritten slip of paper, and an envelope without a stamp.

Hilda picked up the paper. It did not take long to read. It ran:

"*You're not going to get off as easy as this again, you know.*"

Once more Hilda gave Derek a meaning look. This time it was quite simple to see what it meant.

Chapter 16

GAS

━━━━━━

Whitsea was, as Beamish had foretold, "fierce". A greater contrast to the serene and self-conscious beauty of Rampleford it would have been hard to imagine than that grim, unlovely and, in wartime, desperately hard-working seaport. In place of the monastic seclusion of the Canon's house in the Close, the Judge's household was lodged in a gaunt Victorian mansion, with vast ill-furnished rooms which contrived to be at once chill and stuffy, whose huge plate-glass windows gave on to a wilderness of smoky chimneys by day and raised perpetual difficulties over the black-out at night.

Blackness, indeed, was Derek's principal impression of Whitsea. By now the days were short. Work at the assizes was heavy, and in consequence the hours of sitting were long. Barber, who seemed to have become all the more conscientious with the threat to his position, sat late each day in an endeavour to finish his list, and never rose until long after sunset. It seemed to Derek that the only daylight which he saw was through the windows of the High Sheriff's car at lunch-time, driving to and from the murky court where yet murkier crimes were investigated. He found himself envying Beamish, trudging through the rain which fell unceasingly—for, to cap everything, was not the Sheriff a Mean Bastard?—almost as much as that harassed man undoubtedly envied him.

By now, he was heartily sick of the circuit and all that

appertained to it. He was sick of the top hat which he had
to lug about everywhere with him, sick of the tail-coat
which never had room in its pockets for anything that he
wanted. The ceremonies and formalities which had amused
him so much at first became stale with repetition. He knew
now just where the Clerk of Assize would lose his way in
the reading of the Commission, every modulation in Beamish's Court voice. He knew almost to a phrase the admoni-
tion which the Judge would address to the first offender
about to be bound over to keep the peace, the biting scorn
which he reserved for the swindler, the mournful severity
with which he would send the habitual thief down for his
tenth term of hopeless imprisonment. Even the criminals
and their offences began to wear an air of sameness. The
varieties of wrong-doing are limited, and older and wiser
men than he have sat longer in Courts of Justice without
realizing that the varieties of human nature are not.

The only cases from which he derived any enjoyment
were those in which Pettigrew was engaged. He, at least,
could always be relied upon for some fresh turn of phrase,
some unexpected quip to relieve the monotony. And
Whitsea Assizes, fortunately, were the sheet anchor of
Pettigrew's practice. Here he had first begun to make his
mark, and here several clients remained faithful to him.
Not so long ago, indeed, he had confidently hoped for the
Recordership of Whitsea. But when the vacancy occurred,
the wrong Home Secretary happened to be in office, and
this prize, like so many others, had eluded him.

Within the Lodgings, life was almost as drab as it was
outside them. The social jollities which Hilda had introduced to the circuit at Southington were past and over.
Almost the first letter to reach her on her arrival at Whitsea
was one from her brother, indicating only too clearly that
her mission to Sebald-Smith had been a failure. No arrangement now would be acceptable at any but a ruinous figure,
and his solicitors were becoming more and more pressing

for a speedy settlement. "Luckily," Michael wrote, "they are an old-fashioned and respectable firm, and I think they are rather awed at the prospect of suing a High Court Judge. If it were not for that we should have had a writ before now. But I have the definite impression that they are being pushed by their client and it can only be a question of time before their respect for his lordship gives way." Hilda, knowing only too well who was pushing the client, began despairingly on a course of rigid economy. She attempted the impossible, the unheard of thing, to live within, even to make money out of, the lodging allowance granted by the State to Judges of Assize. To Mrs. Square's horror, the standard of meals was reduced to a level which in her eyes was barely above starvation. Hilda was unfortunate in that her necessity arose some six months before the country's, and what a little later would have been the highest patriotism, looked now very like cheese-paring.

One traditional piece of entertaining which could not be avoided was the dinner which custom enjoined the Judge to give the Mayor of Whitsea. What Hilda endured on that evening was known only to herself. She had a double reputation to keep up—that of the Bench for hospitality, and her own, of which she was acutely conscious, as a hostess of charm and brilliance. To scintillate as a woman of London society should among the provincial dignitaries, to be witty, tactful and agreeable all at once, and at the same time to grudge her guests every morsel they ate and every drop they sipped, to sit in the drawing-room inwardly praying that her husband would not think it necessary to order another bottle of port to be decanted, was a strain which even her resilient spirit could hardly bear. When it was all over, and the company had gone, she confessed to an overpowering headache.

The sentry system was, of course, still in full vigour. It was, as it happened, her turn to watch for the first period. Derek, moved to pity by her wan cheeks, took advantage of an opportunity when the Judge was out of the room to propose that he should make himself responsible for the entire night. He was not, he declared, suppressing a yawn, at all sleepy. But Hilda shook her head.

"I shall be all right," she said, "if I can only lie down for a few hours. Do you mind, Derek, if you take first go again to-night? Just knock at my door and wake me at——"

"I shan't wake you at all," Derek protested chivalrously.

"That's sweet of you," Hilda smiled. "Then I shall wake myself. It's become second nature to me now. But if I should be half an hour late or so, you *will* understand, won't you?"

And Derek, his heart beating warm with altruism beneath his white waistcoat, said he would understand perfectly.

In point of fact, she was not half an hour late, but almost exactly an hour and a quarter. By that time Derek, if not by the strictest standards sound asleep, was sufficiently so to be quite unconscious of anything taking place within more than a very few yards of him. The second bottle of port had been ordered up that evening, when it had become apparent from the Mayor's glazed expression that the reputation of the whole Judiciary was at stake, and Derek had taken his full share. This contributed to make the long, still hours a grim struggle against sleep in which sleep was very nearly the victor. In the early part of his vigil he was watchful enough. For the first time since this nightly task had been imposed upon him, he was conscious of a feeling of apprehension. Since the arrival of the last anonymous letter, he had reluctantly begun to believe in the bogeys that haunted Hilda. It was no longer to his mind a question as to whether anything would happen at Whitsea, but when it would happen, and what. And on this particular evening, for no definite reason, he felt that danger in some form or another was very near. But if and when the danger arose, would he be in a condition either to recognize or to combat it?

Just when he was beginning to wonder how much longer he could keep awake, he was startled by the ringing of a bell and a loud hammering at the door. Going downstairs, he found outside a deferential but determined constable. A light was showing at the back of the house, and would he remedy it at once, please?

Derek went outside with the officer and after some difficulty found the small chink of light which was the course of the trouble. It came from one of the few rooms which had hitherto given no anxiety—a little-used library which was provided with heavy outside shutters. The high wind which was blowing at the time had evidently broken the fastenings of these, so that they gaped in the middle. The door of the room, which opened on to the hall, having been left open, some light was reflected from the upstairs landing, where Derek was keeping his watch. This having been established, the trouble was simply rectified for the time being by going back into the house and shutting the library door.

After bidding the constable good night, Derek returned to his post. This little episode, he told himself, was just what he needed. Now he would have no difficulty in keeping awake. No difficulty at all. He never felt less like sleep in his life. . . .

At the moment when Hilda's near approach roused him, he was sitting slumped in a chair outside his own bedroom door, a position from which (when his eyes were open) he had an excellent view of the door of Barber's room. Hoping that his drowsiness would not be perceived, he struggled hastily to his feet.

"Here I am at last!" she said softly. She seemed to be quite recovered. Her cheeks indeed were flushed rather than pale, and she looked undeniably handsome in a garment which, though technically known as a négligée, had nothing negligent whatever about it, either in its design or the manner in which it was put on.

"It was good of you to let me sleep," she went on. "You must be dreadfully tired. Is everything all right?"

"Oh, yes," said Derek. "Nothing's happened at all."

"That's good. I don't know why, but I felt particularly nervous to-night."

She went towards the Judge's room, while Derek followed, reflecting as he did so that at all events her nerves had not prevented her from sleeping pretty well. From some distance he could hear quite distinctly Barber's heavy breathing, even louder and deeper than usual, he thought. No occasion for alarm there!

He was just about to say good night and return at long last to his own bed, when he saw that Hilda had stopped outside her husband's door, a peculiar expression on her face.

"Come here a moment, Derek," she said in an uncertain voice. "Do you smell anything?"

Derek sniffed. His senses were rather muzzy, whether from sleepiness or from the effects of the port, and he could not be positive.

"I—I don't think so," he mumbled.

But Hilda by now was down on the floor, her nose to the bottom of the door.

"Gas!" she exclaimed, scrambling to her feet. "I was certain I smelt something! Quick!"

She flung open the door and Derek followed her into the room, which was in complete darkness.

"He always *will* sleep with his windows shut!" she said crossly, and indeed the room, besides being dark, was distinctly frowsty. But Derek was now conscious also of a quite unmistakable heavy odour, and through the stertorous breathing from the bed he could hear a continuous, quiet hiss which came from the opposite side of the room.

The two of them fell over one another in the blackness as they fumbled for the tap of the gas fire. Eventually, after what seemed a maddening delay, Hilda found it, and the

snake-like hissing sound ceased. Then Derek went to the
window, pulled back the heavy curtains and flung it wide
open. A fresh cold wind blew into the room, bringing with
it a spatter of rain. Hilda meanwhile had gone to the bed,
and was vigorously shaking the still sleeping man.

"William!" she called urgently. "William! Are you all
right?"

The snores stopped, and after a pause Derek heard a
sleepy voice say. "What is it? What the devil's the matter?"
Then the bed creaked as the Judge sat up. "What have you
opened my windows for?" he asked peevishly.

Hilda drew a deep sigh of relief.

"There was an escape of gas," she said. "You might have
been killed."

"Oh?" said the sleepy voice. "Silly of me. I thought I
turned it off all right. All right now? Thanks, Hilda."

There was another creak, as he sank back into bed. In
a moment or two the snores were resumed.

Derek and Hilda tiptoed out of the room with unnecessary caution. Outside she turned to him, her eyes very
bright, her breath coming fast.

"Thank God!" she said. "We were just in time."

"Yes," said Derek. "It was lucky you noticed that smell."
He spoke at random, his mind preoccupied with the
thought that if he had been keeping his watch properly this
danger would never have been incurred.

"Will he be all right, do you think?" Hilda asked anxiously. "Ought we to get a doctor?"

By this time Derek's mind was beginning to function
properly.

"I don't think so," he said. "There wasn't much gas in
the room, really, or we should have been affected. And by
the time we came out, the air was perfectly clear. I think
he may wake up with a bit of a headache, but apart from
that I'm sure he won't be any the worse. It's odd," he went
on, his brain beginning to assume the unnatural clarity

that sometimes comes to the fatigued, "that there wasn't much more gas. The tap must have been only a very little on."

"I didn't notice," Hilda said. "I just turned it as far as it would go until the noise stopped."

"I don't know much about these things," Derek went on, "but he's been in bed now for well over five hours. I should have thought that if he had simply not turned the fire off properly when he got into bed, the whole place would have been reeking of gas by now, even if it was quite a small escape. But there was a distinct hiss when we went into the room."

"That means that it must have been turned on quite a short time before," said Hilda.

"It looks like it, doesn't it?"

"That somebody got into the room and did this"—her voice rose ominously—"while you were supposed to be watching—while you were asleep——"

"I wasn't asleep," Derek objected.

"I could have come right up to you without your knowing, if I had cared to walk quietly just now. Anybody could have gone in and out of the room and you would have been none the wiser."

This accusation was, as Derek knew, not far from the truth, but coming from her in the circumstances in which it did, it seemed to him grossly unfair. This led him to say something which he afterwards was to regret.

"I don't think anyone could possibly have done that," he said. "After all, the fact that it wasn't an accident doesn't mean that he didn't do it himself."

He did not need to look at Hilda's face to know that she was mortally offended. After a frozen silence, she said simply, "I think you had better go to bed now. We can discuss this better in the morning when—when you are more yourself."

Without another word said, Derek went to his room, but

it was some time before he slept. The whole episode troubled him very much—far more, indeed, than anything that had gone before in the troubled history of the circuit. Here, for the first time, was something that could not be dismissed as a mere threat, or a vulgar joke. It could only be explained as a deliberate attempt on the Judge's life. If Hilda had not come on the scene when she did and detected the smell of escaping gas, he would have been asphixiated. Derek had always been reluctant to believe in the possibility of genuine danger, and this feeling, as well as his wish to excuse his undoubted slackness as a guard, had led him to make his rash suggestion of attempted suicide—a suggestion in which he did not really believe himself.

But if this was indeed an attempt to kill Barber, the fact had to be faced that it had been made by some member of the household. The lodgings were well guarded, and the chances of an outsider penetrating in were very small. He passed in review once more the men of whom he had seen so much and knew so little. To connect any one of them with a crime which, to say no more, would bring on all of them immediate loss of particularly snug and comfortable jobs seemed on the face of it absurd. He remembered, too, that Beamish (Suspect No. 1, as he felt sure his favourite detective novelist would christen him) knew quite well of the watching system in vogue. Was it likely that in that case he would incur the risk of being caught in the act, when he must in the ordinary course of his work have innumerable opportunities far better suited for an intending murderer?

An odd theory floated into Derek's head at this point. Suppose Beamish had crept into Barber's room and turned on the gas, not with any murderous intention, but simply as a crude joke, to show up the inefficiency of the Marshal's guard, with the intention of coming back later to turn it off and to have the laugh of the sleepy sentinel? Fantastic as it was, the notion seemed in accord with what Derek had learned of his malicious sense of humour. If that were so, then the joke had been spoiled by Hilda's unexpected appearance. He made up his mind to watch Beamish carefully next day to see if he betrayed any knowledge of the night's events.

He passed to a fresh consideration of Savage and Greene and was annoyed to find that their characters as potential assassins still remained as blank as ever in his mind. He decided that he should henceforth cultivate them, and make a study of them as individuals; but how to set about it he had not the least idea. Mrs. Square, he felt, might immediately be dismissed from the reckoning. One had only to look at her to see that she was not the woman to leave her bed at three o'clock in the morning in order to murder anyone, or for any other reason, except under dire compulsion. And the only other possible suspect was—Hilda herself. Here another even more far-fetched idea occurred to him—that she had turned on the gas in her husband's room merely to have the satisfaction of "discovering" the danger and averting it. Apart from the pleasure of demonstrating the necessity of keeping a watch at night, he could not imagine the object in such behaviour, but he was quite prepared to credit her with motives beyond his comprehension. Perhaps she was slightly mad, and her madness had taken the form of inventing the whole story of a plot against the Judge and the concoction of incidents to support it. After all, persecution mania was a recognized aberration and this might be merely an unusual form of it. Derek toyed with the idea for some time and for a moment almost believed that he had the clue to the whole mystery. But he soon saw that it would not do. He had seen Hilda's face at the moment when she tasted the poisoned chocolate, and he had seen her immediately after the assault at Wimblingham. She had not invented either of those two misfortunes. Of that he felt quite positive.

Derek gave it up. As he finally drifted off to sleep, he thought of something else. If an outsider, Inspector Mallett, for example, were to investigate the case of the attempted gas poisoning of Mr. Justice Barber, his list of suspects would contain one name additional to those he had been considering—the name of Derek Marshall. And this, oddly enough, seemed to Derek the most fantastic notion of all.

Chapter 17

REFLECTIONS

Hilda did not fulfil her promise, or threat, to discuss the events of the night next morning. Indeed, it was a curious aftermath of the affair that none of the three persons involved showed any disposition to refer to it. Whether or not Derek was right in prophesying a headache for the Judge could not be determined from his demeanour. Certainly he was rather glum at breakfast, but scarcely more so than usual. It was equally impossible to say if he had any recollection whatever of having been roused in the night to be told that he was in danger of gas poisoning. The consequence was that the breakfast table was the scene of an odd little conspiracy of silence, with two of the conspirators wondering whether the third member of the party was really a fellow conspirator or not.

During a particularly dull day on the bench, however, Derek (in the intervals of dipping into the First Book of Samuel) had leisure to ponder further on the whole matter, and as a result made up his mind to speak to Hilda that afternoon. He began somewhat awkwardly, remembering the terms on which they had broken off the discussion in the small hours of the morning.

"There was something I meant to tell you about last night," he said. "I'm very sorry I——"

"I'm very sorry I——" said Hilda at the same moment. They both laughed, and the ice was effectually broken.

It was impossible, Derek felt, to be angry with Hilda for

long. And he felt, too, quite childishly glad that she was no longer angry with him.

"Something happened before you came which I didn't mention," he went on. "It didn't seem important at the time, but thinking it over, I feel that it may be."

He went on to recount the visit of the constable and his discovery of the defective shutter in the library. Hilda was puzzled.

"Very annoying," she commented. "We shall have to see that the shutter is put right, of course. But I don't see what this can have to do with what happened in the Judge's room. You don't think anybody could have got into the house that way, do you? If so, how did he get up the stairs without your seeing him?"

"No," said Derek, "I'm pretty sure nobody came in that way. The library windows were shut and the bolt wasn't disturbed. But what was to prevent anyone coming in by the front door, while I was round at the back with the policeman? I had to leave it open, you see, because I hadn't a key with me."

"I see," Hilda reflected doubtfully.

"Suppose someone was hanging about on the offchance of getting in, he might quite well have jumped at the opportunity."

"I suppose it is just possible," said Hilda, plainly unconvinced. She thought for a moment, and then her puzzled expression suddenly cleared. "No!" she said abruptly. "I have a much better idea than that. It was an outside shutter, wasn't it? Isn't it far more likely that this man deliberately broke the fastening so as to produce the light? He would know that that would draw the constable away from the front door and give him his chance."

"And I made the chance a certainty by going outside and leaving the door open for him. You're right, Hilda. He would have plenty of time to go upstairs and be down again and away before I came back. You see what this means?

I've been worrying for hours, wondering who in the house could have done such a thing. Now it's obvious that this need not have been an inside job, after all."

"And someone outside is still at large, trying to kill my husband," said Hilda bitterly. "So much for Scotland Yard! All the same, it is a weight off my mind, in one way. It's not very pleasant to be driven to believe that someone in the house *must* be either a criminal or a maniac. But I'm not going to let your theory run away with me, Derek. After all, there is absolutely no proof this was done in the way you suggest. We still have to be on our guard in every direction, and more so than ever now."

"In the meantime," Derek said, "I suppose you will want to put this matter into the hands of the police."

Hilda shook her head.

"No," she said. "I can see that this means more work and more anxiety for us, but that's just what we can't do."

"But surely," Derek objected, "if there really is, as you say, somebody at large trying to kill the Judge, we ought to do all we can to protect him."

"I know," said Hilda. "But I've been thinking over this, as well as you. There's one great objection to telling the police about this particular business which you don't realize. If we did, what do you think their first action would be?"

Derek had by now read sufficient depositions of witnesses to have some idea of how the police go to work.

"I suppose they would begin by taking statements from all the witnesses," he said.

"Exactly. And who would be the first person they would approach for a statement?"

"The Judge, I suppose."

"Exactly."

"Of course," said Derek, still rather fogged, "we don't know whether he could say anything about it. Unless, perhaps, he has told you——?"

"No. He has told me nothing. Very likely, he remembers absolutely nothing of what happened last night."

"I see. And naturally, you don't want to give him anxiety by telling him."

"Yes," said Hilda slowly. "There is that, of course. But there is another reason why I don't want the police to come round taking statements about this. Suppose after all, he *does* remember—all about it?"

"I don't quite understand," said Derek.

"Don't you? I wish you did, Derek, it would make it a bit easier for me. You see—last night you made a suggestion as to how this might have happened. I was rather rude to you about it, I'm afraid. But suppose—just suppose that you were right—that he really meant to—oh! Derek, I needn't say it outright, need I?"

She was very near to tears. Derek, made terribly uncomfortable by the spectacle, blundered hastily in to comfort her.

"But look here," he said. "I didn't really mean what I said last night. It was only that I was annoyed at your saying I had been asleep—and so I had been, as near as anything. Please don't take it seriously. I never really thought that the Judge was trying to kill himself. After all, there's not the smallest reason to suppose that he should do such a thing."

"Thank you, Derek," said Hilda, wiping her eyes. "It's sweet of you to say that. But I'm afraid it's not so easily got over as that. You see, you don't know my husband as well as I do." She contrived a wan smile. "That's not very surprising, is it? Really, it is an odd situation. We have only known each other a few weeks, and now I find myself having to talk about things that I never thought I should discuss with anyone. Well, there's no good beating about the bush. What it comes to is this: I do think that my husband is a man who might in some circumstances want to kill himself."

Derek was about to speak, but Hilda stopped him with a gesture.

"Now that I have started you must let me go on," she said. "You see, he is, as you must have seen for yourself, a very proud man, intensely proud of himself and his position. You know the danger that he is in of losing that position because of what happened at Markhampton—or perhaps you don't, but the danger is there, and a very real one. He has been terribly worried by it, though he has not shown it openly. And that, added to the anxieties which this other matter must have given him, might drive him to—I don't know. It's fearfully difficult to guess what really goes on in his mind. He is in many ways a very reserved man. I said just now that you didn't know him as well as I did. But when I come to consider, I begin to wonder whether I have ever known him properly myself."

To Derek, with his small experience in the ways of the world, it came as something of a shock to realize that it was possible for two persons to live together for years and still to be in all essentials ignorant of each other's true natures. Unbidden, the image of the ideal Sheila floated into his mind. How different, he felt, the perfect communion of mind and soul that marriage to her would be!

"Well, so there you are!" Hilda concluded, with a sudden air of brightness that did not quite convince. "I've said my say, and it had to be said, but you needn't take it too much to heart. And now we must both fly, if we are not to be late for dinner."

Derek studied the Judge with interest that evening. Indeed, it might be said that he really looked at him for the first time. At the end of his scrutiny he had to admit that he found nothing in his appearance suggestive of a disposition to commit suicide. True he had equally to admit that he had no very clear idea of what an intending suicide normally looked like. So far as he could judge, however, there was nothing remarkable about him at all, unless it was that the moroseness which had become habitual with him was perhaps a shade deeper than usual.

Hilda, however, who might be presumed to be the better judge in this matter, evidently thought otherwise. Her anxiety manifested itself in a determined attempt, which ultimately proved successful, to cheer his lordship up. It was the first time for many weeks that Derek had seen her exercising her social talents on her husband, and he found it an enthralling spectacle. Putting into the task every ounce of tact and charm that she possessed, little by little she contrived to dissipate the gloom that enveloped him. By the end of the meal Barber, to his own obvious surprise, had become talkative and almost cheerful. Derek, who had been carried along by Hilda's stream of gossip, comment and allusion, so that almost without knowing it he had contributed not a little to the success of the attempt, realized suddenly that he too was actually enjoying his evening. Really, he thought, as he drank his coffee after dinner and listened to a judicial anecdote which, though technical, was not unamusing, if every evening on circuit were like this he would have no reason to complain. Savage came in to remove the coffee tray and before doing so, piled the fireplace high with the Whitsea Corporation's coal. A mellow glow began to spread even through the chilly acres of the drawing-room. The Judge produced a cigar and began to discuss with enthusiasm the impregnability of the Maginot Line. Hilda, her purpose accomplished, had fallen silent. From the corner of his eye, Derek could see that she looked tired but content. He fancied that she was holding her husband's hand. It was a moment of peace and comfort.

Looking at them now, it seemed to Derek impossible that only a short time before he had been seriously discussing with one of the pair the probability of the other's committing suicide. After all, whatever Hilda might say, people positively did not commit suicide. People, that is, whom one knew. But if suicide seemed a ridiculous notion, sitting there amid the Victorian splendours of Whitsea Lodgings, it seemed even more absurd to think that this lank long man, pulling at his cigar on the other side of the fireplace, could conceivably be in danger of being murdered. After all, murder was one of those things that simply did not happen, except in books and newspapers. The fact that since the Circuit began he had heard three or four trials for murder did not shake this conviction in the least. People in the dock were not real, that is, ordinary people—else why should they be there? And as for their unfortunate victims, photographs of whose mangled remains the police exhibited with such relish—fortunately for Derek's peace of mind they remained photographs.

The improvement in the Judge's spirits, obtained at the cost of such exertion, did not last long. For the rest of the Assize he was once more remote, pontifical and irritable. On the very last day of work at Whitsea he indulged in a quite gratuitous and somewhat painful altercation with Pettigrew during the hearing of an undefended petition for divorce. Derek never wholly comprehended what it was about (except that it involved one of those wholly artificial rules of evidence which are the very breath of the nostrils of the true lawyer), but from a mild difference of opinion it developed into what the local press next day inevitably described as a Scene. For once Pettigrew lost altogether his usual air of ironic deference. He raised his voice, went rather pink in the face, interrupted his lordship without ceremony, and, when the decision had been given against him, slammed his brief upon the desk and strode out of court without the slightest pretence of a bow towards the Bench. He was not without excuse, for he had been treated with the grossest discourtesy, but it was a surprising outburst for a man of his usually restrained temperament.

Apart from this unhappy incident, there was little of moment to record of the concluding days at Whitsea. The shutter of the library was mended, and there were no further complaints from the police. The nocturnal watchers added to their routine an occasional sniff under the Judge's door, without ever again succeeding in detecting the least trace of escaping gas. No further hint of danger appeared to vary the monotony of the days and nights of the household.

One effect of the events which had followed the dinner to the Mayor and Corporation, for which Derek was grateful, was to bring him and Hilda more closely together. Although the subject of their talk on that occasion was never alluded to again, the fact that a confidence had been given and received remained as bond between them. He found himself talking to her quite freely on all sorts of subjects and almost on equal terms, an experience which was quite new to him. He no longer felt in awe of her greater knowledge of the world. Quite abruptly, he realized that at long last he had grown up. But although he found himself in this new position of confidence with her, it remained, in diplomatic jargon, a unilateral confidence. Never once did he feel in the least inclined to unbosom himself as to his own romance. With a new-born faculty of insight, he saw quite clearly that while Hilda had a wide range of interests there were some things that did not interest her at all, and that among these things other women were included.

Derek had all the more leisure to cultivate his friendship with Hilda in that he was no longer subjected to any of Beamish's less welcome familiarities. For some reason or another, Beamish's attitude towards him and the rest of their little world had undergone a distinct change. Hitherto, whatever his failings, he had been consistently cheerful, or at all events serene, as though buoyed up against all difficulties by a sense of his own importance. But as Whitsea Assizes were on, it was noticeable that he had become careworn and haggard to an extent which was not to be explained merely by the indignities put upon him by the Sheriff. He became unusually taciturn and spent long hours alone in his room. Derek suspected that he drank a good deal, but if so, it had not the mellowing effect upon him that he had observed before. Indeed, his temper had deteriorated badly. He lost no opportunity to snap the heads off Savage and Greene and he went out of his way to have several acrimonious little disputes with the Clerk of Assize. Derek had never liked him when he had been ostentatiously friendly and condescending. In his new guise, however, he found himself unexpectedly sorry for the man. It was so plain that his ill-temper was due to some hidden cause of unhappiness and anxiety that Derek almost wished that he was in a position to console him, or at least to talk over his troubles with him. The glimpse that he had had into the frustration and dissatisfaction that underlay Hilda's marriage had produced in him a general feeling of charity towards the world at large, and it positively hurt him to see this bumptious, assured little man so obviously the prey to wretchedness.

Naturally enough, Hilda was also not unaware of the change in Beamish's manner. But her attitude towards it was very different from Derek's. To her, Beamish was merely an objectionable person who had now added to his other offences an extremely bad temper. This lack of charity on her part gave Derek a somewhat priggish but none the less satisfying sense of superiority. All in all, a growing sense of the little drama of human relationships within the lodgings kept Derek more interested and amused than he had ever expected, and the last week of Whitsea Assizes was for him by no means the least entertaining of the Circuit. None the less did he look forward to the return to London and the end of his servitude with all the enthusiasm of a schoolboy towards his holidays.

Chapter 18

REX v. OCKENHURST

———

By working hard himself, and exacting hard work from everybody around him, Barber contrived to finish the Assizes at Whitsea just before those at Eastbury were due to begin. In so doing, he found it necessary to break into the "travelling day", which should have been consecrated to the task of conveying the paraphernalia of justice from one county to another. This, it appeared from the comments of the Circuit officials, was a breach of tradition barely to be excused even by the exigencies of war. The two towns lay less than twenty miles apart and upon the same main railway line. It was not, therefore, an altogether impossible proposition to finish work at Whitsea on one day and start again at Eastbury on the next. None the less, everybody, from Clerk of Assize to Marshal's Man, agreed that as a matter of principle an attack on the travelling day was an attack on the very soul of English Justice. Derek, listening to these opinions very firmly expressed by persons of experience, could only conclude that there were good reasons behind them, but he did not pretend to understand what they were.

Eastbury is an unpretentious market town, the centre of a small and sleepy county. Its criminal calendar is usually equally unpretentious. Coming at the end of the circuit, the Assizes there are in the nature of a light savoury to supplement the heavy and often indigestible judicial fare provided by Rampleford and Whitsea. It is at once inconvenient and unusual to conclude a circuit with the town where the least work may be expected. The Southern Circuit is naturally extremely proud of the fact that it does things differently from any other, and has firmly resisted any attempt to alter the arrangement.

On this occasion however, the calendar at Eastbury, though as short as usual, was anything but unpretentious. It consisted of three cases only, but of these one sufficed to prolong the period of the Assizes to the unprecedented length of four days. They were four days of intense interest to those who were present, and of equally intense discomfort. The Court, as though designed to match the volume of work which was to be anticipated, was minute. Bench, jury-box, dock and witness-box were huddled together on the four sides of a tiny hollow square within which counsel jostled with solicitors and one another, and manœuvred purposefully for the one corner from which it was possible to examine a witness without turning one's back on the jury. On the outer fringes of the square, the rest of those whom duty or inclination compelled to attend sat in varying degrees of misery—mostly upon hard, backless benches.

It was in this setting that for three and a half days John Ockenhurst was tried for the murder of his wife's lover. The case never attracted very much attention. Possibly if the accommodation for the gentlemen of the press had been less exiguous, or if Ockenhurst had been of better social standing, it would have been more widely reported, even in the middle of a war. But to the people of Eastbury and its neighbourhood it was of passionate interest and the little Court was packed to suffocation from start to finish of the trial. In the village where the prisoner laboured as a blacksmith, indeed, the interest has survived both the trial and its subject; and it will be many years before a visitor cannot rely on producing a stormy discussion in the bar of its inn by raising the question whether Ockenhurst was properly hanged or not.

REX v. OCKENHURST

The story which Sir Henry Babbington K.C. rose to open for the Crown in the afternoon of the first day of the Assizes, was at once simple and melodramatic. Sir Henry, who had a leaning towards melodrama himself, recounted it with impressive power. In that small arena every modulation of his beautifully resonant voice, every fleeting expression on his mobile countenance was given full value. Any who listening to him could so far resist the spell as to glance from him to Pettigrew, sitting in the corner, his wig tip-tilted till it almost touched his wrinkling nose, must have felt a certain sympathy for the man who had to cross swords with such an opponent, and who had to meet a case so overwhelmingly strong.

Pettigrew, indeed, had reason to be anxious. He was not in the least afraid of Babbington, whom he knew and liked, and whose weaknesses he had often explored. But he was very much afraid of the line which the defence was compelled to take, all the more so because he more than half believed in it himself. "On the whole," a sarcastic senior had observed to him when he was newly called to the Bar, "it is sometimes not a bad thing for a young man to believe in his client's innocence." Pettigrew was no longer young, and he felt that this was decidedly one of those times when he would have been happier if he could be fairly certain that his client deserved to be convicted. A better judge of a case than most, he knew that the odds were against him, and he strongly disliked the feeling that here there was a possibility of an innocent man being found guilty.

"To conclude, members of the jury," Babbington was saying, "the prosecution will prove to you that the victim of this crime had over a long period of time indulged in an unlawful passion for the prisoner's wife; that this was, if not known to, at least strongly suspected by the prisoner; that he had threatened the deceased on more than one occasion; and that on the night in question the deceased was found outside the back door of the prisoner's cottage, stabbed in the back with a weapon actually manufactured by the prisoner in his own smithy. You will hear the evidence, which I need not now recapitulate, of the sounds and voices heard by the neighbours on the day of the tragedy. You will consider, and weigh carefully, the statements made by the prisoner to the police officers charged with the investigation of this crime—statements, I am bound to suggest to you, at once ambiguous and self-contradictory. And taking that and all the other matters into consideration, it will be for you to say, when all the evidence on both sides has been given, whether or not the prosecution has discharged the burden of satisfying you that this grave accusation has been made out.

"And now, with the assistance of my learned friend, I shall call the evidence."

"I think," said Barber, glancing at the clock, "that this would be a convenient moment to adjourn."

"As your lordship pleases."

Pettigrew had expected nothing else, but none the less he swore quietly under his breath while the Judge explained to the jury that although under the system introduced by reason of the war they were permitted to return to their homes during the course of the trial, they were in honour bound not to discuss the case with anyone. He knew, none better, the anodyne effect, when counsel's opening was concluded, of calling the two or three formal witnesses who always came first and how the matter of fact discussion of photographs and plans would have instantly lowered the emotional atmosphere engendered by Babbington's fine phrases. If Father William had consented to sit for another twenty minutes the jury would have gone away with a vague feeling of anticlimax, and a sense that the case before them, though concerned with life and death, was, like most of life itself, essentially humdrum. As it was, they would leave the court with the echo of that beautiful voice ringing in their ears, and return to it next morning with their view of the case firmly, and, perhaps, irrevocably fixed. "And don't you know it, you old brute!" said Pettigrew under his breath, as he bowed respectfully to Barber's retreating figure. Wherein he did him an injustice. The Judge was thinking only of his tea.

Anybody who wishes to read a full report of the case of *Rex v. Ockenhurst* must search for it in the files of the *Eastbury Gazette and Advertiser*, where alone it is set out verbatim. It is sufficient here to say that the evidence for the Crown bore out all that Sir Henry had said in his opening address, and —since he well knew the value of understatement—a good deal that he had left unsaid, or only lightly touched upon. Young Fred Palmer, to whom Alice Ockenhurst had turned when tired out by her husband's continual ill-treatment and infidelities, had undoubtedly been murdered. The weapon used was a peculiar one—the blade of an old knife, skilfully enough fitted into an iron handle to make an effective little dagger; and there was not lacking evidence that this work had been done by Ockenhurst at his forge. There was evidence, too, of a bitter quarrel between the prisoner and his wife, overheard by neighbours on the afternoon preceding the night of Palmer's death. So bitter was it, alleged the prosecution, that she fled the house for her own safety, and it was while she was absent that Palmer, coming there at the hour when Ockenhurst was normally at the public house, met instead of his mistress the husband, madly jealous and armed with the home-made dagger.

"You know," Pettigrew had said in conference to the solicitor who instructed him, "this doesn't ring quite true to me. I know our client's a bad hat, and I wouldn't put it past him to kill anybody. But what's a blacksmith doing with a stiletto, as if he was an Italian bravo? Why didn't he use one of his hammers, or something more in keeping?"

"It does seem odd," was the reply. "But we can't get over the fact that he made the thing. And his explanation for that is desperately thin."

"So thin that I'm half inclined to believe it. He says he saw a dagger hanging up in an old curiosity shop priced ten pounds, and being hard up, with little work coming in at the forge, he thought he could make something like it and pass it off as a genuine antique. It's the sort of imbecile thing a fat-head like that would think of! But what on earth will a jury make of it?"

"From what I know of juries in this county," the solicitor had said, "I'm afraid they'll say: 'If Jack Ockenhurst didn't kill Fred Palmer with that there knife, perhaps you'll tell me who did?'"

By the time that Alice Ockenhurst, pale, handsome and unexpectedly distinguished in appearance, had finished her evidence in chief, the moment had arrived for Pettigrew to answer that unspoken question. And the answer, as conveyed by a cross-examination as suave as it was pertinacious, provided the real sensation of the trial. At first the drift of the questions was not altogether clear. The jury were plainly puzzled, as it was intended that they should be. They realized, as question succeeded question, that Mrs. Ockenhurst was not quite so white as she had been painted, that she had treated her husband badly, and perhaps Fred Palmer too. Indeed, if all that was being suggested to her was true, she had been playing fast and loose with Palmer. The gentleman was making out that she was a light woman and wanting to be rid of him to take up with someone else. Certainly it did seem to put the matter in a rather different light, but still. . . .

"Are you suggesting, Mr. Pettigrew," said his lordship suddenly, "that this witness murdered the deceased?"

From the point of view of the defence, it was the wrong question, asked at the wrong time and in the wrong tone of voice. A plan of campaign, thought out with infinite pains and being executed with great skill, was violently disorganized. Pettigrew had set himself to instil into the jurors' minds by slow degrees a suspicion which might lead them to a rational doubt of his client's guilt. Sooner or later, the accusation against the wife would have to be made, but not until her composure had been sapped by a multitude of cleverly designed attacks, her credit weakened by a score of forced admissions on minor matters. By then, the jury would have been prepared to believe the worst of a woman already exposed as a worthless character. But at this point, the naked accusation, abruptly plumped down before them, obviously shocked and frightened them.

"My lord," said Pettigrew with such calmness as he could command, "it is no part of my duty to suggest that anybody is guilty of this offence. My submission will be, at the proper time, that the prosecution have not proved to the reasonable satisfaction of the jury that the prisoner is guilty. I am entitled to put such questions to the witness as will assist the jury in coming to that conclusion."

"No doubt," said the Shaver drily, "but certain suggestions have been made to this witness that, to my mind, at least, can lead only to one result. In justice to her, if to nobody else, they should be made plainly. However, if you are reluctant to put the question, I will do so myself: 'Mrs. Ockenhurst, did you kill Palmer?' "

"No, my lord."

"Very well. Go on, Mr. Pettigrew."

And Mr. Pettigrew, sick at heart, went on. The art of cross-examination is pre-eminently the art of timing. The question that would be deadly if asked at its proper place in the sequence falls completely flat if interjected out of its turn. That was what had happened here. Moreover, the Judge's interposition had forewarned the witness what was coming. She had time to brace herself to meet the blow, and when it came she met it with perfect composure.

And that, as Pettigrew and Babbington, talking over the case afterwards, agreed, was the real turning point of the trial. It continued to be hard fought up to the end, but the jury never forgot, and Barber in his summing-up did not allow them to forget, the impression that a baseless accusation had been made against a wronged (and, incidentally, extremely good-looking) woman. Next to his wife's evidence, perhaps what really contributed most to Ockenhurst's conviction was his own. She had made an excellent witness. He, ugly, hulking, slow-witted and obviously insincere, was a very bad one. None the less, the issue still hung in the balance when the concluding stages of the trial were reached. Babbington's final speech was a masterpiece. It was reasoned, cogent and perfectly fair. Only in its closing passages did he insensibly allow his leaning for the dramatic to get a little the better of him. There was a trace too much warmth in those periods, too much energy in those gestures to be quite in place for counsel for the Crown. It was not Babbington's fault, it was the way he was made. With whatever good intentions he might start, by the time he had been long on his feet the old daemon would take possession of him, and he would once more be Babbington of Magdalen, President of the O.U.D.S. and destined, so everyone believed, to a tremendous career on the boards.

Pettigrew, jotting indecipherable notes on the paper in front of him, wondered whether he dared to use the exordium with which he had once blown Babbington sky high in a libel action:

> *As in a theatre, the eyes of men*
> *After a well-graced actor leaves the stage,*
> *Are idly bent on him that enters next——*

He looked at the jury. No, they wouldn't relish Shakespeare. They would think it flippant, too, and for once he must abjure flippancy. Damn it, this case was serious, in all conscience. It was absurd, at his time of life, to feel nervous about a case, but on this occasion he positively did. He wished he didn't want so desperately to get his man off, and he wished too that he didn't feel that he was battling against odds, one man against three—Babbington, now mopping his face after his exertions, the prisoner himself, his villainous face his own worst enemy, and the Shaver, sitting tight-lipped above him.

Wisely, he made no attempt to outdo Babbington in eloquence. The amount of rhetoric which any audience can absorb at a given time, as Pettigrew well knew, is strictly limited; and this particular audience was drugged not only by the flow of words to which it had been subjected, but by the foul air which it had breathed for the last three days. If he had subjected them now to an emotional appeal, the jury would merely have sunk back in a bemused trance from which they would have emerged with a deep respect for the learned gentleman's gift of the gab but no notion of what the defence was. Some great reputations have been made by speeches delivered in like circumstances, but a surprisingly high proportion of those on whose behalf they were made have been executed. So on this occasion the usual roles of prosecutor and defender were reversed. Pettigrew was dry, unemotional, at times almost conversational. And before long, he was aware that his method was having its effect. The jury, disappointed at first that they were not going to be treated to another fine speech, began to sit up and take notice. They found to their own surprise that they were beginning to think. And little by little, in plain, commonplace phrases, Pettigrew spun a thread that led them to think upon the lines he wished.

And then came disaster—disaster in such trivial, unheroic guise that probably not more than half a dozen people in Court knew it for what it was. Pettigrew was discussing the evidence of the threats alleged to have been made by the prisoner against the deceased, and dealing seriatim with what he suggested were a few hasty words, recollected long after the event by unreliable witnesses and exaggerated out of all recognition in the telling. "And then we come," he said, "to Mr. Greetham's evidence. He said, you will remember, that he met the prisoner outside his forge on the Monday before the night of the tragedy, and——"

"Tuesday," interjected Barber suddenly. "It was on the Monday that Mr. Rodwell saw the knife. Mr. Greetham's evidence relates to the Tuesday, the day following."

"I'm obliged to your lordship," said Pettigrew, somewhat nettled by the interruption. "Members of the Jury, you will recollect the incident of which I am speaking. Monday or Tuesday, it makes no difference, but Mr. Greetham——"

"I think it does make a difference," Barber persisted. "In a case of this gravity, it is important to be accurate above all things. My note distinctly says Tuesday: Sir Henry, do you recollect which it was?"

Sir Henry, with deep regret, did not, and said so.

"My note says Tuesday," the Shaver repeated. "Of course, I may be wrong, but——"

At this point, Mr. Greetham himself rose from his seat in the obscurity at the back of the Court and tried to make an observation, but was indignantly shushed into silence.

"My lord, whether Monday or Tuesday——" Pettigrew began.

"I think it would be as well to ascertain exactly what the witness did say, since we seem to be at variance. Mr. Shorthand Writer, will you be good enough to turn up your notes of Mr. Greetham's evidence and give us his exact words?"

There followed an embarrassed silence while the shorthand writer struggled with a mass of paper and finally, after several false starts, succeeded in finding the passage he wanted.

"It was on a Monday or a Tuesday, I am not sure which but I think it was Tuesday," he read in a thin Cockney voice.

"Ah! 'I think it was Tuesday.' Thank you, Mr. Shorthand Writer. Proceed, Mr. Pettigrew."

The whole incident had not lasted more than two or three

minutes, but it had been enough fatally to break the thread of Pettigrew's discourse. Worse still, it had broken the invisible thread that binds speaker and listener together. The relationship which with such care he had been building up between himself and his hearers was dissipated and all was to do again. It would have mattered less if he had been less nervous, less anxious not to put a foot wrong on the difficult path which he had to tread. That the interruption had been so irrelevant and unnecessary added to his annoyance. The fact that it had come from Barber, of all men, irritated him profoundly. He had appeared in his time before judges who simply could not stop talking. Words bubbled from them irresistibly, whether in the middle of the speech for the defence on a capital charge or on less grave occasions. For them he had learned to make allowances, to bear with equanimity a burden which fell upon everybody's shoulders as much as on his own. But Father William was not ordinarily a talkative judge. During the course of this particular trial he had said little, and that to the point. This meaningless and aggravating incursion might have been made expressly for the object of putting him, Pettigrew, out of his stride.

It was a badly rattled Pettigrew that resumed his speech when the question of Mr. Greetham had been settled at last. And a badly rattled man does not make a good speech. Having once allowed himself to be caught out in a minor inaccuracy, he became nervously anxious over small points of detail, and in consequence naturally found himself making further blunders of equal insignificance, each of which was gravely corrected from the Bench. The jury, he was aware, began to lose interest. He could feel them slipping away from him as the clock ticked on. If he had had at his command Babbington's mighty organ stops of eloquence, it might still have been possible to recover them with a burst of fine phrases in his peroration. But he could not do it. He gave them all he had—sincerity, plain speaking, an argument closely knit. He had done his best, but he sat down at last, discouraged and with a sickening sense of inadequacy.

Barber's summing up was a masterly performance. Pettigrew, who read and re-read it later when he was seeking to find grounds on which to launch an appeal, had to admit that, technically speaking, it was faultless. Yet nobody who heard it delivered could doubt that essentially it was a strong recommendation to the jury to convict. And the recommendation was conveyed largely by means which did not appear on the shorthand note—by subtle inflections of the voice, by pregnant pauses, by expressive glances.

Perhaps the most deadly moment in the summing-up, from the point of view of the defence, came near its end. The Shaver had reserved till the last consideration of the theory that the prisoner's wife was in fact the guilty person. He discussed the suggestion in clear, cold phrases that, read afterwards, seemed quite colourless and academic; but the tone of scorn which he injected into them left no doubt as to what he thought of it, and what he desired the jury to think. Finally, with the only dramatic gesture that he allowed himself during the course of his observations, he picked up from the desk in front of him the home-made dagger which had figured so prominently in the case and displayed it to the jury.

"It has been argued," he grated, holding up the wicked little object, its blade still rusty with poor Fred Palmer's blood, "it has been argued that this is not the kind of weapon that one might expect a blacksmith to use if he were minded to commit murder. You are twelve reasonable men and women of the world, and you can judge for yourselves whether that is a reasonable argument or not. This at least you do know, because it has been proved in evidence and the defence has not sought to deny it, that it is the kind of weapon that a blacksmith might make, and that this

particular blacksmith did in fact make this particular
weapon. For what purpose? You have heard his explanation, and it is for you to say whether it satisfies you. And
you may go further, and ask yourselves whether it is the
sort of weapon that Mrs. Ockenhurst, whom you have seen
in the witness-box, would be likely to use; or whether she
is the sort of woman likely to use a weapon of any kind. It
is entirely a matter for you, but if you are satisfied upon the
rest of the evidence that the prosecution are right in pointing to the prisoner as the man responsible for the death of
the deceased, I do not think that you will attach much
weight to the circumstance that the means by which he
elected to fulfil his criminal purpose, instead of being one of
the hundred and one means that might have been chosen,
happened to be—this."

The dagger fell to the desk with a little clatter.

A few general words completed the summing-up, and the
jury retired.

Three quarters of an hour later, all was over. The
crowded court had emptied itself, the jury were on their
several ways home and the prisoner was on his way to the
condemned cell. The Clerk of Assize was wrangling about
the costs of the prosecution and the witnesses in the case
were impatiently waiting until the wrangle should have
settled itself and the County Treasurer be at liberty to pay
them their expenses. Babbington and his Junior were
gossiping over the case in the robing-room and the Judge
was enjoying the cup of tea which Greene had ready for
him in his room behind the bench. In the court itself the
police officers in charge of the case were clearing up the
débris of the trial.

"That's all the lot, then," said a cheerful sergeant, cram-
ming a bloodstained waistcoat into a bulging suitcase. "All
except Exhibit 4. Have you seen Exhibit 4 anywhere, Tom?"

"Which is that, Sergeant?" asked his assistant.

"Why, the blinking knife that made all the trouble, of course. Where is it?"

"Must be up on the bench still. His lordship was waving it about when I saw it last. I'll have a look."

But the bench was bare of everything except a few torn scraps of paper.

"I expect it got mixed up with his books and things," said the sergeant. "Ask that clerk of his if he's seen it."

Beamish was sent for, and made his appearance in very ill-humour.

"Everything that came up on to the bench came down off the bench," he said testily. "It's no part of my business to dry nurse the police. There aren't any exhibits up here, nor in his lordship's pockets neither. You must find your own nasty knives. I'm off home."

"That's funny, then," said the sergeant good-humouredly, after he had gone. "I could have sworn the Judge had it last. Not that I mind what's become of it, but we ought to account for it. Perhaps Sir Henry took a fancy to it?"

But Sir Henry, who was caught just as he left the Court, was equally ignorant, though a good deal more polite about it than Beamish had been.

"I remember now," Tom said. "I heard Mr. Pettigrew's solicitor asking him whether he'd like it for a souvenir."

"That's it!" said the sergeant. "I saw him going up to the bench when the Judge went out after his summing-up. I'll just ask him to make sure."

But Pettigrew was not to be found anywhere. He had left the court immediately after the jury had returned their verdict and subsequent inquiries showed that he had left the town also.

"Well, that's that," said the sergeant resignedly. "Wherever it is, it's gone. It isn't worth worrying about, and I don't expect anybody will ever ask any questions about it."

Events were to prove him a false prophet.

Chapter 19

THE END OF THE CIRCUIT

═══════

There was an end-of-term atmosphere at dinner in the lodgings that evening. The peripatetic little household, so often dissolved, so often renewed against a fresh background, was now to break up for good and all. It was an occasion at once joyful and mildly sentimental, to which each member of the party reacted in a different way. Savage, without going so far as to be cheerful, laid aside his usual cloak of gloom. Greene, after being presented by Derek with the guinea which immutable custom prescribes as the due of the Marshal's man, had become positively talkative about the near approach of Christmas and waited at table with the air of a kindly ministering angel. Derek himself had his own reasons for being glad that his period of exile was over.

For Hilda, although she doubtless had troubles enough to look forward to, the fact that the Circuit with all its dangers and misadventures had ended without disaster was, she confessed to Derek, the one thing that mattered. She felt that it was a result upon which they could properly congratulate themselves and each other and one which had earned a mild celebration. Mrs. Square, without seeking for reasons, rejoiced that her ladyship had at last seen fit to order a dinner that was a dinner, and the resulting meal, if not quite on the lavish scale of her banquets at Markhampton and Southington, was a good deal more in the true Circuit tradition than its predecessors for some time back.

After dinner, one of the last rites of the Circuit remained to be performed. This was that known as "settling the circuit accounts". Among his other multifarious duties, a judge's clerk on circuit acts as what in even more exalted circles is known as a Comptroller to his employer. The degree of responsibility enjoyed by him in this capacity naturally varies with the individuals concerned. With Barber, as careless of his personal affairs as he was punctilious over legal technicalities, settling the accounts had been reduced to a very simple formula. On the last day of the Circuit, Beamish would leave upon his desk a neatly kept account book and a bundle of receipted bills and cheque counterfoils. With them would be a short balance sheet, showing the amounts expended, cheques cashed during the progress of the Circuit and the sum now necessary to balance the account. The Judge would glance at this last, groan heavily, sign the cheque already drawn for him, and return the whole mass of documents to Beamish. The whole process usually took about a minute and a half.

This time, however, matters did not go according to precedent. The fact that she had allowed herself a certain extravagance over dinner had not blinded Hilda to the pressing need for economy which had obsessed her for so long. Rather it had by reaction stimulated her to an even livelier appreciation of the value of money than ever. Consequently, when on entering the drawing-room she saw the usual little pile of papers neatly laid out with the cheque awaiting signature beside it, she forestalled her husband before he could reach for his pen and said firmly, "I'll go through these first, William, if you don't mind."

Barber uttered a mild protest, to which no attention at all was paid. A minute later Hilda was sitting at the desk, subjecting every item of the accounts to a severe and rigid scrutiny. For nearly half an hour she toiled, checking figures and verifying additions with the air of a professional auditor. At the end of that time she looked up, and said:

"William, there are one or two items here which I don't altogether understand."

The Judge reluctantly put down the book he was reading and came over to her side. As he did so, he gave Derek a look that said: "This is the kind of thing one must expect when women start concerning themselves in matters they don't understand." Such at least was the interpretation which Derek, who was beginning to feel himself an expert in meaning looks, put upon it. It cannot be positively asserted that Barber succeeded in conveying this rather complicated sentiment by expression alone.

It is always a little embarrassing for a third person when a married couple discuss their financial affairs in his presence; and Derek scrupulously refrained from listening to the colloquy that ensued. But he could not avoid hearing a good deal of it, and it was only too apparent that from the start the Judge was undergoing something very like a stringent cross-examination. Moreover, before very long it was borne in on Derek that he was not standing up to it very well. Clearly, there were quite a number of things that were wrong in the accounts. Equally clearly, they were things which his lordship was quite unable to explain. Finally, Hilda reached an item near the end of the account which caused her to exclaim: "But this is outrageous!" And the Judge had nothing to say in reply but:

"Well, my dear, I know that I gave Beamish a cheque."

"You gave Beamish a cheque!" said her ladyship scornfully. "You mean, you signed whatever he chose to put before you!"

"But, I was going on to say, I certainly didn't think it was for as much as that. I think", he went on, in a rather firmer voice, "that this is a matter which Beamish should be asked to explain."

"Wait a minute, before you do anything else. Have you got your paid cheques here? You should have."

"Yes. You will recollect that you asked me to get my passbook from the bank while we were at Whitsea. I have it here."

"Let me see." Hilda took the book, and turned rapidly over the bundle of paid cheques. She pulled out one and scrutinized it carefully. "This cheque has been altered!" she pronounced. "Do you see? the 'ty' of sixty is in a different coloured ink from the rest, and an extra nought has been added on to the figures. When Beamish gave you this to sign it was for six pounds only. Now it reads for sixty. He has defrauded you of fifty-four pounds and faked the account to hide it. And if I hadn't insisted on going through the figures——"

"Marshal, will you touch the bell?" said the Judge with awful calm. "And Hilda, you will please be good enough to leave me to deal with this matter myself."

Savage answered the bell, and was ordered to tell Beamish that his presence was required immediately. It seemed to those who waited quite a long time before Beamish made his appearance. When he came in he had a rather dishevelled air and his face and hands were dirty. But more than this, Derek noticed something about his expression which put him in mind of the occasion at Rampleford when he had been so unexpectedly confiding. And when he spoke there was a distinct trace of huskiness in his mellifluous baritone.

"I must apologize for being so dirty, my lord," he said. "But I've been packing up the books and things."

He advanced with steps that were rather too carefully steady towards the desk, where the cheque to balance the account should normally have been awaiting him.

"Beamish!" said the Judge in a tone that brought him up short in his tracks. "Will you be good enough to explain the meaning of this?"

And he extended at arm's length the paid cheque for sixty pounds.

"This cheque, my lord?" Beamish said flatly, taking it from him. He looked stupified, standing in the middle of the room, turning it over and over in his dirty hands.

"I wish to know how it comes about that that cheque is made out for sixty pounds."

"I'm sure I couldn't say off-hand, my lord. It's all in the account there, I've no doubt."

"Do you desire any time to consider your answer? If so, you are at liberty to take these papers away with you and give such explanation as you can to-morrow. I must tell you now, however, that the cheque you are holding bears signs of having been altered. Do you wish to consider?"

Beamish did not lift his eyes. He was still studying the piece of paper, which he held in one hand while with the other he ruffled his normally sleek dark hair. By now, he was visibly swaying on his feet.

"No," he muttered in a low voice. "I don't think it would be any use."

"Do you mean that you have no explanation to offer?"

This time Beamish lifted his head and answered in a loud, almost defiant voice, "I mean just that, my lord."

"You are dismissed," said Barber in a tone in which sorrow and sternness were mingled.

Beamish opened his mouth as if to say something, evidently thought better of it, and walked with faltering footsteps to the door.

And there the ugly little episode might have ended if Barber had not been moved by some evil genius to speak again.

"Beamish!" he said just as the clerk reached the door.

Beamish turned and stood silently looking at him. He still wore the same dazed expression, but the colour was beginning to come back into his cheeks, and his mouth was set in a firm, hard line.

"I am not at all sure," said his lordship, "that it is not my duty to prosecute you. But I do not propose to do so. I do not wish to add to the punishment that you have brought upon yourself by your criminal misconduct. You have betrayed the trust—the implicit trust—which I, perhaps foolishly, have placed in you over a number of years. Whether this is an isolated incident or not, I shall not seek to determine. The blow that it has been to me to find faithlessness where I had expected faith is not to be measured by the amounts or the numbers of your defalcations. Neither shall I inquire into the reasons which led one in your position to jeopardize everything a man should hold dear for the sake of——"

"That's enough!" Beamish shouted suddenly.

There was a horrified silence.

"You're not going to treat me to one of your blasted sermons," he went on truculently. "I'm not in the dock now, and if I ever get there, it won't be you that tries me, that's certain, thank God! I'm sacked, I know that. Well, what of it? I'm not the only one that's due for the sack, that's all. I shouldn't have kept this lousy job for another six months anyway, and you know it! You're a fine one to talk about not prosecuting as if it was a favour. You ought to be in the dock yourself, and if there wasn't one law for the rich and one for the poor, that's where you would have been."

"Be silent!" roared the Judge.

"Prosecute me?" Beamish went on, undeterred. "You daren't! Just you try it, that's all. There's a lot I could say about the goings on on this Circuit if you did, about you and that fine lady of yours who put you up to this. And you won't be a judge by the time my trial comes on, don't you forget it. I'm not the only one that knows things, I can tell you. I——"

"Leave the room at once!"

"All right, my old cock, I'm going. But just don't you forget this. You've had plenty of warnings, and here's the last of them. *You've got something coming to you!*"

And the door banged behind him.

It was a subdued party that returned to London next

day. It would be hard to say in which part of the train the atmosphere was more oppressive—in the third class carriage where Savage, Greene and Mrs. Square discussed the downfall of their colleague in shocked whispers, or in the first class one where Derek, Hilda and Barber sat in embittered silence. The tension was aggravated by a number of minor mishaps which marred the normally smooth transit of the King's representative from one place to another. Such mundane matters as the taking of tickets, the provision of porters, the proper bestowal of luggage, which had been managed with such slick efficiency by Beamish that they had appeared to be performed of themselves, now obtruded themselves with disagreeable insistence. Savage, when appealed to, protested with humility but firmness that it was not his place to do a clerk's work, and Derek in the end had to attend to most of these affairs himself. He made a number of minor blunders, which the Judge, wrapped in a gloom alleviated only by slabs of milk chocolate, did not seem to notice and which Hilda bore with martyred resignation.

The journey was over at last. Derek had seen the pair into a taxi and watched them drive away—a worried elderly gentleman and his young and handsome wife. The Commission was over and His Majesty's alter-ego was no more, until the next Circuit—if there was to be another Circuit.

His train home was from the same station, and he had an hour or so to wait. He told his porter to put his luggage in the cloakroom and was just moving in that direction when a quiet voice spoke at his elbow:

"I wonder whether you can spare me a moment or two, sir?"

Derek turned round in surprise. A moment before he had been looking in that direction and he could have sworn that nobody was there. Moreover, in the bare expanse of the station, there was no cover to hide anyone, let alone the huge man who now strolled beside him. He seemed to have materialized out of nowhere. It was a disconcerting habit of Inspector Mallett, and one of which he alone knew the secret.

Derek explained that he had some time to kill.

"I thought you would be catching the 12.45 if you were going straight home," observed the inspector. "That will just give us time for a quiet chat, if you've no objection."

Mallett's tone was so casual that it did not strike Derek at the time as at all remarkable that his probable movements should be known to Scotland Yard. When, later on, he realized it, he was conscious of an uncomfortably cold feeling down his spine. But by then it was far too late to do anything about it.

He walked with the inspector to the cloakroom in silence. He wondered where in the echoing din of the terminus it was proposed that they should have a quiet chat. But Mallett had thought of this also.

"The stationmaster has been kind enough to lend us his room," he said, and led the way into a quiet little office.

"I saw your little party got back all right," he went on, as he sat down and began to fill his pipe. "All except the Judge's clerk, I noticed. What's happened to him?"

"He isn't the Judge's clerk any more. He was dismissed last night. For embezzlement."

Mallett's face, so far as it could be seen through a thickening cloud of tobacco smoke, showed no surprise.

"That would explain it," was his only comment.

He smoked in silence for a moment or two. Then he said, "Well, Mr. Marshall, the last time we met we were discussing unpleasantness on the Circuit of a rather different kind. Lady Barber was decidedly anxious about it then. I haven't heard anything further about it since from her. But it did occur to me to wonder whether anything had happened at all abnormal during the rest of the Circuit, and I thought perhaps you could help me."

"I'm not sure that I know what you mean by abnormal,"

said Derek. "You see, I've never been on a Circuit before, so I hardly know what to expect."

Mallett took the evasion in good part.

"Oh, well, you know the sort of thing I mean," he said. "There was that anonymous letter at Rampleford, for instance——"

"You know about that?"

"Surely. In fact, I've got it about me somewhere, I think." He pulled out a wallet bursting with papers from the inside pocket of his coat. "The Judge sent it back to the Rampleford Police as soon as he got to Whitsea and they sent it on to us."

"I didn't know he'd done that," said Derek.

"Didn't you? Well it's only to be expected that he should. He's been just a little nervous of anonymous letters ever since Markhampton, you see. But there's no reason why he should mention it to you, after all. I dare say there was a good deal that went on which you wouldn't know about."

"I should think I knew a good deal more than the Judge about what went on," said Derek rashly.

"Well, it's very satisfactory to hear that," said Mallett. "Because, after all, that's just what I was after. What exactly did go on?" Then, seeing that Derek was still hesitating, he added, "I shall be having a talk with her ladyship shortly, of course. Only I thought it would be a good plan to get the point of view of an outsider, so to speak, and by catching you now I can get it while it's still fresh in your mind."

Derek had had a vague idea that he should not, in Hilda's absence, say anything to anybody about the misadventures of the latter part of the Circuit, but the inspector's last words effectually loosened his tongue; and by the time that his train came in he had told him everything that he remembered. Indeed, as he settled back into the unaccustomed discomfort of his third-class carriage, he had leisure to reflect with surprise on how much he had remembered.

Under the inspector's tactful guidance he had found that all sorts of details had returned to his memory which left to himself he would never have thought of. Not that any words had been put into his mouth. On the contrary, nothing could have been less like a cross-examination than was the friendly interview just concluded. It was simply that by some kind of instinct Inspector Mallett seemed to know exactly what was missing from any description or account, for all the world as though he had been there himself, so that his questions always came pat to stimulate the sluggish memory. And the questions had been surprisingly few. For the most part he had been content to listen in silence. To Derek's surprise, he had taken no notes. None the less, he was perfectly certain that nothing he had said would go unremarked. He had had the impression of feeding facts into a sort of machine, which would in due course produce—what sort of finished product, he wondered?

About the same time next day, Mallett was making his report to the Assistant Commissioner who ruled his department.

"I saw Lady Barber this morning, sir," he was saying. "Her story is very much the same as Mr. Marshall's, with one or two variations."

"That's to be expected," said the Assistant Commissioner. "But were any of the variations at all important?"

"Only one seemed to me significant. She made no mention at all of the dead mouse incident."

"Indeed? Did you ask her about it?"

Mallett smiled.

"No, sir. On the whole I thought it better not to."

"I suppose it did happen? Or do you think that boy could have invented it?"

"No, I shouldn't say he has a very inventive mind. I think it happened all right."

"Then why should she have suppressed it?"

"I think, sir, mainly because it didn't fit in with her theory about the rest of the affair."

"Well, that's only human nature, I suppose. What is her theory, exactly?"

"It isn't one theory precisely," Mallett explained. "There are several. Her favourite one is still that all these different incidents are the work of Heppenstall."

"Then you didn't tell her——?"

"No, sir. If you recollect, we agreed at the time that no mention should be made of Heppenstall's arrest until after the Circuit was over. I ventured to extend the time a little so far as these two persons were concerned, because I thought it would only start putting ideas into their heads—and after all, it is facts we're after just now, and not ideas, isn't it, sir?"

The Assistant Commissioner nodded. Then he said, with a sigh, "It's an odd position altogether. You don't think it advisable to try to get a statement from the Judge himself?"

"In the circumstances, no, sir. There is only one other person I should like to talk to—for various reasons."

"You mean Beamish, I suppose?"

"Exactly, sir. I dare say we shall be able to pick him up before long. He must be short of money."

The Assistant Commissioner smiled and glanced at a file of papers in front of him.

"Yes," he said. "I've just been going through the report on the affairs of Corky's Night Club. The raid there must have hit him pretty hard."

"I fancy that was where all his savings, legal and otherwise, have been going for a long time," said Mallett. "It's a funny sort of sideline for a judge's clerk, isn't it? He certainly covered his tracks pretty well. Even the manager didn't know who his principal was. I think that the closing of the club has left him badly in debt, and that would explain why he tried to help himself to a slice of the Judge's money in the rather crude way he did."

"No doubt. Well, that's a side issue, really. What I am mainly interested in is this series of attacks on the Judge. What is your theory about it?"

The inspector was silent.

"You have one, haven't you?" said his superior reproachfully.

"Well, yes, sir, I have," Mallett said hesitantly. "Only I'm afraid you'll think it rather ridiculous. I mean, I think I know what the facts are, but I can't understand the reason for them. And without the reason, it just makes nonsense. Logically, it's sound, but psychologically it's all wrong. Unless, of course, we're dealing here with one of these funny mental cases which——"

"That's enough!" said the Assistant Commissioner. "We're policemen, not mental specialists. Cut the cackle, and tell me what your notion is."

Mallett did so.

"Absurd!" was the comment.

"Yes, sir," said Mallett meekly.

"Quite absurd!"

"I agree, sir."

The two of them contemplated the absurdity together in silence for a full half minute.

"And suppose you are right" said the Assistant Commissioner abruptly, "what is to be done?"

"Nothing, sir."

"Nothing?"

"Nothing at all, sir. Logically, it seems to me to follow that all these threats, attacks and so forth which have recurred so regularly all through the Circuit will stop now that the Circuit is over, and the particular—er—predisposing cause is removed."

"I only hope you're right. We can't afford to take any

risks where a man of this sort is concerned. You really think he is safe from now on?"

"No, sir. I don't go so far as that. I wouldn't care to say that of any man, let alone Mr. Justice Barber. All I do say is that if any danger does threaten him it will be from a different quarter altogether. Unless, of course, there's some element in the whole story which we don't know about. But you are the best judge of that, sir. I've given you all the facts and I think they are complete."

"Thank you, Mallett. You have told me a most extraordinary story, and propounded a most ridiculous theory to account for it. I accept the story, of course, and I'm hanged if I can see any flaws in the theory. That being so, I can only hope that your prophecy is equally sound. What about Mr. Justice Barber's next Circuit, by the way? Have you any prophecy about that?"

"I understand that he is one of the judges to stay in town next term," said the inspector. "And after that——"

The two men looked at each other with pursed lips and understanding eyes. Both were well aware that Barber's judicial career hung upon a thread.

Chapter 20

TOUCH AND GO

———

About two months later, Derek Marshall was walking eastwards along the south side of the Strand. He was just opposite the Law Courts when he noticed Pettigrew crossing the road towards him, accompanied by his clerk. Pettigrew waved to him to stop and a moment later reached the pavement at his side.

It was the first time that they had met since the end of the autumn circuit, and each looked at the other as though to see how he had fared in an interval that was nearly as long as their previous acquaintance had been. Pettigrew was pleased by what he saw. Derek looked older, more assured. There were unfamiliar lines about his face that seemed to tell of long hours of hard work, but at the same time he looked decidedly happier than he had been dancing attendance on the Shaver. Derek, on his side, noticed that Pettigrew was looking extremely pleased with himself. There was a jauntiness in his gait which was matched by the demeanour of his clerk, who was grinning broadly beneath the burden of a large bundle of papers and half a dozen calf-bound books.

"Well," he said after they had exchanged greetings, "and what are you up to now? To what fields have you carried your idealism?"

"I've got a job," said Derek proudly.

"So much I gathered from your almost aggressive air of importance. What is it? Obviously you must be adorning some Ministry or other. I always knew that you were born to write ingenious little minutes on official files."

"I'm in the Ministry of Contracts," Derek explained.

"I breathe again. For a moment, I was afraid you were going to say the Ministry of Information. And what are you doing just at this moment?"

Derek explained that he had come out for lunch.

"The office is just round the corner," he said. "And as I don't know this part very well, I thought I would go and try the ——"

He named an establishment which journalists are fond of referring to in print as "a celebrated hostelry" but which in practice they are careful to avoid.

"That place!" said Pettigrew in horror. "My dear fellow, it is obvious that you don't know this part of London. It's bogus, completely bogus! Even the Americans had begun to tumble to it before the war. No, I can't allow that. You must celebrate the new job by lunching with me."

"It's very kind of you," Derek began, "but——"

"I won't listen to any objections. Do you always have to have hospitality forced on you in this way? Besides, this will be a double celebration. I too have my little triumphs, ephemeral though they be. This morning", he said proudly, as he led the way beneath an ancient brick archway, "I've been upsetting Hilda."

"Upsetting Hilda?"

"Precisely. In the Court of Appeal. Don't tell me you have forgotten the great cause at Southington Assizes? Between you and me and this gatepost—which, by the way, is not Christopher Wren's, as the guide-books will tell you, but James Gibb's—Hilda's judgment, as rendered by Father William, was perfectly sound, but I contrived to persuade their lordships otherwise. Here we are."

Derek had never been in the Temple before. He gaped like any tourist at the mellow, placid Courts, ghost-haunted by the illustrious dead, which next year were to vanish into ugly heaps of charred timber and brickdust. After a lunch eaten beneath the famous carved rafters of Outer Temple Hall, he fell in with Pettigrew's suggestion of a digestive stroll twice round the as yet inviolate garden, which sloped down towards the river. The charm of his surroundings, his congenial company and the excellent meal combined to loosen his tongue, and before they had completed their first circuit he had confided to Pettigrew the reason why, apart from his new-found employment, he found life particularly good at the moment.

Pettigrew was ideally sympathetic.

"Engaged!" he exclaimed. "Engaged, as well as employed! You certainly don't do things by halves. My congratulations! You must tell me all about her."

This Derek, in halting tones but with suitable enthusiasm, proceeded to do.

"Splendid, splendid!" Pettigrew ejaculated at intervals as the portrait, admittedly imperfect, of a she-seraph gradually unfolded itself. "Splendid! All the same——" he stopped abruptly and looked narrowly at his companion. "I may be wrong, but you don't look to me quite as cock-a-hoop as in the circumstances you should. Care sits upon that brow. Are the minutes at the Ministry really as troublesome as all that? Or can it be that there is a snag somewhere?"

Derek, at once annoyed at having given himself away and relieved at being able to share his anxieties, admitted that in truth a snag existed.

"It's nothing to do with Sheila, really," he hastened to explain. "It's her father. You see, he's in rather bad trouble. With the police."

Pettigrew clicked his tongue sympathetically.

"That sort of thing doesn't make matters easier with one's own family," he observed.

"No, of course not. Though Mother's been awfully good about it. Anyhow, it's not anything dishonest, or really bad like that. But he knocked a man down with his car——"

"Well, well! Even judges have been known to do that, as we know."

"Yes. But this is worse in a way, because now the wretched man has died, and they are going to prosecute him for manslaughter."

"Bad luck—very bad luck. But I shouldn't let it worry you too much. There's many a slip, you know. Any lawyer will tell you that the percentage of convictions for motor manslaughter is lower than for any other offence. Besides, juries in wartime don't consider human life quite so important as in times of peace. And who shall blame them? Still, it's an unfortunate business, and you have my sympathy. Which reminds me," he went on, as though anxious to change the subject, "have you been approached to give evidence in the Markhampton affair?"

"Yes," said Derek. "I had a letter from some people called Faraday something or other. I told them I didn't want to have anything to do with it."

"A mistake. You'll only be subpœnaed. Do as I did and give an identical statement to both sides. But mind you, the action won't ever come into Court. It'll have to be settled, *pro bono publico*."

Derek flushed angrily.

"It's all wrong," he muttered.

"What is?"

"That Sheila's father should be prosecuted, and that man get off scot free, just because——"

"My dear chap, we had all this out before, you remember! Don't let your ideals run away with you, or Heaven knows what contracts you'll be sanctioning at the Ministry. Besides, don't forget this sort of thing cuts both ways. I shouldn't mind betting that the Shaver is going through a worse time at this moment than your father-in-law elect. Let that comfort you. There are rumours floating round the

Temple that—— But we'll talk about that another time. I can see that you're champing to get back to your files. And I ought to be in my Chambers. After this morning's miracle, anything might happen. Even a new client calling with a brief wouldn't surprise me."

Pettigrew was right. The anxieties of an ordinary man expecting a charge even of a serious nature in the criminal courts probably seldom reach such acuteness as those with which Barber awaited the prospect of a civil action for negligence. The action indeed was not yet started. By one means or another, Hilda, to whom in his misery he had virtually surrendered the conduct of the affair, had so far succeeded in postponing the evil day. By proposal and counter-proposal, by every device of delay and temporization, she and her brother contrived to keep the matter hanging on from month to month. It was certainly a fine delaying action, fought out with skill and tenacity, but it could be no more than a delaying action. He knew only too well that the struggle could end in only one of two ways— either in a resounding scandal in the Courts, or in a settlement that would completely ruin him.

Since his return from circuit, the sequence of threats and misadventures which had followed him had abruptly ceased. Always indifferent to personal danger, he positively re-gretted the placidity of his life. Possibly it was with this in mind that he firmly insisted on the withdrawal of the two Scotland Yard men who for the first few weeks of the new term ostentatiously dogged his footsteps to and from the Law Courts. It made no difference. Nobody, it appeared, thought it worth while to threaten his life any more, and he continued, unhappy and unmolested, to carry out his judicial duties in a mood that grew ever more embittered and morose.

During this period, as the hard winter began to give place to the lovely, agonizing spring of 1940, he became acutely aware that by now his misfortune had become more and more generally known. Since his memorable encounter with his brother judge in the Athenæum, nothing whatever had been said in his hearing which remotely hinted at the affair, but with nerves made more sensitive than usual by unhappiness he could feel the knowledge of it ever present. He was conscious of embarrassment among his fellow Benchers at the Inn when he joined them at the High Table at lunch. He felt certain that the very ushers in his court looked at him in a peculiar way. His new clerk—and he had experienced unexpected difficulty in replacing Beamish —seemed to show less than the proper respect due to him, as though he knew that he had taken service on a sinking ship. And from time to time, as he made his way about the Temple, he had caught sight of Beamish himself, no doubt haunting the precincts in search of a job, and at the same time busily engaged in spreading the poison of gossip among his former associates.

Gossip, however widespread, takes some time to permeate to official quarters. Or possibly it may be that those who move in official quarters prefer not to notice gossip until it has been confirmed by discreet inquiry. For whatever cause, it was not until the last week of the law sittings that Barber knew that his fall from grace had passed beyond the stage of gossip to become a matter of concern to persons of high importance. He had long been aware that this was bound to occur sooner or later, but this did not in any way lessen the shock when a very exalted Judicial Personage sought him out and tactfully broached the question of his resignation.

The Personage was extremely considerate about it. He did his best to soften the blow. He referred several times to Barber's health, which, indeed, had distinctly deteriorated under the strain to which he had been subjected during the past few months. At the same time, he made his meaning only too clear. A man in Barber's position could not continue to be a judge. If this unhappy affair could be settled quickly and finally, well and good. The scandal might still be hushed up and forgotten before public confidence in the administration of justice was hopelessly shaken. But if an action should be commenced, or the matter allowed to leak into the press—well, the Personage could not answer for the consequences. On the whole, the Personage, who seemed surprisingly well informed, thought the chances of an immediate settlement very remote. Would not the best solution be to resign now, before the rot had time to spread further? Surely Barber must see that in the interests of the Bench as a whole, indeed of the whole fabric of British Justice. . . .

The hapless Shaver found himself pleading desperately for a reprieve. He could not resign now, in the middle of the legal year. To do so, he argued, would almost amount to a public confession of misconduct. It would provoke the very scandal which everyone was so anxious to avoid. Besides, he still had hopes of meeting his opponents half-way—indeed, he was sure that the matter would be settled amicably at quite an early date. In any case, he must have time to consider. . . .

The Personage continued to be considerate. He had, he protested, no desire to exercise any undue pressure on Barber. "Indeed," he pointed out, "constitutionally I have no power to do so. At the same time. . . ." It boiled down to this. Subject to no writ being issued, when the position would obviously become immediately untenable, Barber might remain at his post until the end of the summer term. Unless by that time the Sebald-Smith affair was dead and buried beyond all chance of revival, then his resignation would be expected during the vacation following.

"They can't make you resign!" Hilda's defiant words came back to him as he made his way homewards. Couldn't they? Perhaps not, if you were as tough and indomitable as Hilda. Not for the first time, as he dragged his weary feet up the steps of his house and let himself in at the front door, he wished he had her vitality, her indifference to anything but her own ambitions and well-being. In his heart he knew that they could. Of what avail were the constitutional safeguards, the Bill of Rights, the cherished inviolability of his position, against *them*, whose weapons were the irresistible pressure of public opinion, the unwritten laws by which he and his predecessors were governed and which they transgressed at their peril?

He ate a solitary dinner, wrapped in dejection which only increased as the evening wore on. Hilda, as it happened, was away for the night. She had gone down to the country to attend the wedding of her brother's daughter, and at the same time, he suspected, to discuss with him once more plans for the appeasement of the implacable adversary. The house seemed cold and silent. Barber drank two glasses of port, looked at the decanter and decided that one more glass would about empty it and that it was not worth while preserving such a small quantity. He found that he had underestimated the remaining contents of the decanter by more than one half, but he finished it all the same. The effect of the drink was only to depress him still further. When it was finished, he sat long, staring into the mouldering embers in the grate, thinking of his future. What future was there for an ex-High Court Judge, retired under a cloud? When Sebald-Smith had taken his pound of flesh, how was he to live? The Personage had made it perfectly plain that at the present juncture it would be out of the question to ask the Treasury to sanction the payment of a pension after only five years' service. Perhaps it would have been different if he had been popular, like poor old Battersby, and not merely a good judge. And he had been a good judge, he told himself in angry defiance, ten times as capable as Battersby had ever been. Nobody could deny that. And now, just because of a ridiculous accident that might happen to anybody, the whole of his career was to be shattered, and he could starve for all that anyone cared.

The hypocrites! he thought angrily, apostrophizing the whole legal system, from the Personage down to the lowliest clerks in the Temple.

The spurt of anger died down, to be succeeded by a mood of yet deeper depression. "This is the end," he told himself, over and over again. "This is the end." He sat on over the remains of the fire, no longer thinking but simply enduring, his mind a blank to everything except the fact that his world had collapsed about him. And then, quite suddenly, he knew what he had to do.

At the last moment Hilda decided not to stay the night away after all. Subsequently she declared that it was her instinct which told her that she should be at home. Nobody could ever disprove this assertion, naturally, but it is possible to suppose that in this case instinct was reinforced by her strong dislike for one of the relations who had also been asked to stay and who had been given the best spare bedroom. Whatever the cause, she left her brother's house immediately after dinner and caught the last train to London. She had some difficulty in finding a taxi at the station, and did not finally reach home until nearly midnight. To her surprise, the electric light was still burning in the drawing-room. Going in, she found her husband unconscious in his arm-chair. An empty glass was on the floor beside him and on a table near by were two letters in his handwriting. One was addressed to Hilda herself, the other to the coroner.

The doctor whom, after maddening delay, she was finally successful in summoning declared subsequently that without question Hilda's promptitude and presence of mind alone saved her husband's life. By the time that he arrived on the scene, everything that an unskilled person, fortified only by recollections of the First Aid Manual, could do had been done. It was touch and go. For half an hour she worked desperately at artificial respiration and was almost at the point of physical collapse when signs of life flickered back. Even in the reaction that followed the knowledge that victory had been gained she did not lose her head. Pale but calm, she assisted the doctor with all the steadiness of a professional nurse, and when all was over had sufficient control of herself to tell him a coherent and plausible story of how the affair must have occurred. Her husband, it appeared, had been sleeping badly. He had formed the habit of taking sleeping draughts. His shortsightedness had led him on more than one occasion to misread the directions on bottles of medicine. Obviously on this occasion he had taken an overdose by accident. Did not the doctor agree?

The doctor, more impressed than ever, agreed whole-heartedly. None the less, before he visited his convalescent patient next morning, he thought it his duty to report the matter at the local police station. He was an elderly prac-titioner, called out of retirement to take the place of younger men on war service, but he had his wits about him. And he had noticed out of the tail of his eye the letter to the coroner which Hilda had left on the drawing-room table.

Chapter 21

END OF A CAREER

Hilda capped her triumph in saving her husband's life by another, less spectacular but more difficult. By the beginning of the next term, the Shaver was back on the bench, carrying out his duties to all outward appearance as though nothing had happened. The tongues which had wagged everywhere when it was published that Mr. Justice Barber was suffering from indisposition were abruptly stilled. Everybody who professed to be in the know had read into the announcement a forecast of his impending resignation. His reappearance had the effect of stifling the rumours for the time being.

By what means Hilda succeeded in injecting into her husband sufficient vitality to enable him to carry on his normal life under the shadow of a threat which had utterly overwhelmed him remained her own secret. It was certainly not by appealing to the Bill of Rights. Barber had given his word to the Personage, and he intended to keep it. Whether she had contrived, against all the evidence, to persuade him that the position might yet be restored by a last minute change of heart on the part of Sebald-Smith and the woman who controlled him, or whether it was merely that she had convinced him that the manlier course was to play the game out to the end, the fact remained that she succeeded. The result was not obtained without some cost to herself. During the next few weeks it was remarked that she had grown pale and listless. It was as if she had surrendered some of her own vital force to animate the automaton who still went daily to and from the Courts, sat and heard argument, gravely gave judgment as though his position was as secure as that of any live judge, with ten years between him and his pension.

Accordingly, on a fine April morning, while the British public was anxiously discussing remote Norwegian place-names that had with terrifying suddenness become household words, Barber, still Mr. Justice Barber, was driven in a hired car to the Central Criminal Court, where it was his turn to be the presiding Judge. He did not care for the place. The synthetic atmosphere of the Court, he would complain, always ended by giving him a headache. For some reason of his own he even took exception to the traditional posy of flowers, with which the City still protects its lawgivers from the menace of gaol fever. In previous years, he had seldom let a visit there pass without some covert expression of his distaste. On this occasion he said nothing at all. He was being taken to occupy one more judgment seat, to try one more case, and it was of little consequence to him, under suspended sentence of death, where or what it was.

Hilda, who sat beside him, was as silent as he. She regularly went to Court with him now, as though afraid to let him out of her sight. That morning she had hardly glanced at the newspaper. The map of Norway had been spread before unseeing eyes. All her attention had been given to a letter which had come by the first post. She had read it without comment before folding it up and carefully putting it away. Barber had asked no questions about it, or shown any sign that he was in any way interested. Now, however, as the car crossed the traffic lights at Ludgate Circus, he suddenly broke silence.

"You had a letter from your brother this morning, didn't you?" he asked.

"Yes," said Hilda flatly.

"What does he say?"

"Faradays have made a final offer. It is exactly the same as their last one."

"Yes?"

"They give us until the day after to-morrow to accept it. If not they issue their writ," Hilda went on, as the car turned the corner into the Old Bailey. "Michael says they mean business this time."

Barber sighed. It sounded almost as if a weight had been lifted off his shoulders. He said no more until just as the car was drawing up at the Judge's entrance in Newgate Street. Then he said very quietly, "In that case, Hilda, it rather looks as if this will be the last Old Bailey Sessions I shall ever have to attend."

The policeman who opened the door of the car for him nearly forgot to help his lordship to dismount. The appearance of her ladyship, as he said afterwards, gave him quite a turn. She looked as though she was about to faint. But she recovered herself and walked into the building with a firm step.

The dock in No. 1 Court at the Old Bailey is an enormous affair. It occupies so much floor space that from the seats behind and beside it it is difficult to get more than a partial glimpse of what is going on at the business end of the Court. Derek Marshall, without influence, or the wit to employ what influence he could have mustered, had not been able to find a seat in front of the obstruction. By attaching himself to a friendly barrister's clerk he had managed to get inside the Court, and here he squeezed into the end of a row rightly reserved for jurors in waiting. He could hear well enough, but it was maddening not to be able to see better. Above all was it maddening to be utterly out of touch with Sheila, who was with her mother in places reserved for those with a legitimate interest in the case. Sheila had forbidden him to come with them, and he had perforce obeyed, but he had counted at least on being able to give her encouragement from afar.

"Let Herbert George Bartram surrender," said the clerk, and Derek was treated to a fine view of the back of his future father-in-law's neck as he pleaded not guilty to the charge of feloniously killing Edward Francis Clay. Then, after the usual preliminaries which he knew by heart, he heard a rustle in the far right-hand corner of the Court as counsel for the Crown rose to open what, from his experience, Derek told himself sounded like a pretty bad case of motor manslaughter.

At the end of the day, the case was still unfinished. Derek had a fleeting glimpse of his adored as she went away on the arm of her father, whose bail had been renewed. On the whole, he considered, it had not gone too badly. Remembering what Pettigrew had said to him, he felt that the chances of an acquittal were good. He had not realized until he came into court who the presiding judge was, and it had been a shock to him when he heard those familiar tones creaking across the air. An insane impulse had seized him to get up and protest that this man of all men was not fit to try such a case. But on reflection he had to admit that, so far, the conduct of the trial had been perfectly fair and impartial. If anything, the Judge had leaned towards the defence. Perhaps after all it was a blessing in disguise that had brought the Shaver to these Sessions. Would he not, would not anybody in his position, feel that there but for the grace of God——? This thought comforted him until he remembered Pettigrew's account of the trial of Heppenstall. With that, his anxieties began to return.

"Excuse me, my lord, but could your lordship allow me just a few minutes. Just a short interview, my lord ——"

Barber, on the pavement outside his house, looked round slowly. It was some time before he could drag himself from the abstraction which had settled upon him the moment he rose at the end of the day's sitting. He looked at the man who addressed him with eyes that were perfectly blank and expressionless. He might have been seeing a complete stranger. Indeed, it was not until the pressure of Hilda's hand upon his arm recalled him to himself that he recognized who had spoken to him. Then in a dry, flat voice he uttered eight short words.

"I have nothing to say to you, Beamish."

It was as if a corpse had spoken. There was a dreary finality about his tone that froze the carefully prepared supplication upon Beamish's lips. He took one look at the weary, withdrawn face and hurried away. Not until he had turned the corner did he so much as remember to swear. It must be recorded that when he did he amply made up for lost time.

"I have nothing to say." It seemed to epitomize Barber's attitude towards existence ever since he had seen Hilda reading the fatal letter that morning. After all their arguments and wordy discussions, the ultimate decision was taken in the fewest words possible.

"I shall send in my resignation at the end of the week," he said. "It would inconvenience everybody if I were to retire in the middle of a session. The work should be ended by then, and I can arrange with the Recorder to take anything in my list that may be left over."

"Yes," she said. "That sounds the best plan."

Later he broke silence to remark, "You had better tell Michael to enter an appearance to the writ. It may be the cheapest way out not to take any further step and leave a sheriff's jury to assess the damage."

"I'll ask him what he thinks."

Later still, as they were going to bed, he said in a tone that was almost tender, "I'm sorry it has ended this way, for your sake, Hilda. It might have been better if you had let me——"

"Don't say that, William!" she answered quickly, and turned away so that he could not see her face.

By arriving early, Derek was able to secure a rather better place for the concluding stages of George Bartram's trial next morning. The evidence had been finished overnight, and there remained only the speeches and the summing-up. The effect of these was to increase his confidence in the result. The defence was in the hands of John Fawcett K.C., an impressive speaker, whose weakness was a tendency to be overwhelmed by his own volubility. Derek was reminded of a jest of Pettigrew's at the expense of "the faucet in full spate", as one crashing period succeeded another, without pause for reflection, or, as it seemed, even for breath. But so far as he could tell it was having its effect on the jury, and the summing-up that succeeded it seemed tame and ineffectual in comparison. The Shaver, indeed, spoke like a tired man, almost as if he had lost interest in the case. As the jury filed out, Derek was able to catch Sheila's eye. She too seemed to have lost her strained look of anxiety, and they exchanged a glance that spoke of a hope almost amounting to certainty.

The jury was out for over half an hour. During that time, Derek, afraid of losing his place, was compelled to listen to the opening of another case in which he could not feel the smallest interest. Sheila and her mother meanwhile were engaged in close confabulation with their solicitor in the corridor outside. At last the jury returned. Derek strove to read in their faces what their decision could be, but in vain. They looked as wooden as all British citizens contrive to do the moment they undertake jury service. The proceedings in the succeeding case were interrupted. Mr. Bartram was reinstated in the dock while his jurors propped themselves uncomfortably in front of the box now occupied by their successors.

A moment later the suspense was over. The foreman in a

firm voice had pronounced the blessed words, "Not Guilty", and the Clerk, as though to make assurance double sure, had echoed, "You say that he is not guilty and that is the verdict of you all." Derek felt like cheering. He could see Sheila with her handkerchief to her eyes, and Mrs. Bartram turning round to wring Fawcett by the hand.

Then ensued a pause which Derek did not at first understand. Instead of ordering the prisoner's discharge, the Judge was indulging in a whispered colloquy with the Clerk. Counsel for the prosecution was exchanging words with Fawcett. What had happened? Then Derek remembered that he had heard Mr. Jenkinson, the solicitor for the defence, say something about a second indictment, some minor charge to follow the main one. In the excitement of following the trial for manslaughter he had quite forgotten about it. He had not been told what it was, and, indeed, nobody had seemed to take it very seriously.

The Clerk, having finished his conversation with the Judge, turned round again. The jury, who had been lingering disconsolately, looking rather like a troupe of actors who, having finished a play in which the curtain refused to come down, were told that their services were no longer required. The second indictment was then read to the prisoner. It charged him with having on such and such a day driven a motor-car at such and such a place without possessing a valid certificate of insurance against third party risks. He pleaded Guilty.

Little was said by counsel on either side. The offence was undisputed and the facts had all been thoroughly threshed out during the preceding trial. Fawcett ventured to remind his lordship of what he knew already, the important war work which his client was performing at the time of the offence, the strain which everybody was undergoing at the present time and which might well lead anyone to overlook the requirements of the Road Traffic Acts, and the defendant's immaculate character hitherto, both as a man and a car-driver. The court fell silent while the Judge considered his sentence. Looking up, Derek saw that Barber's usually pale complexion was faintly pink. Suddenly he began to feel very much afraid.

"George Herbert Bartram." The voice sounded harsher than ever. "I cannot take the view that has been represented to me that the offence to which you have pleaded guilty is a merely technical one, such as can be passed over lightly. On the contrary, I regard it as a very serious offence indeed. The consequences of the breach of this section of the Act. . . ."

The voice grated on. Derek began to think that it would never stop. It seemed as though Barber was deliberately working himself up to a pitch of anger as he rehearsed and enlarged upon the heinousness of the crime. Knowing what he did, it seemed to him a monstrous parody of justice. He wondered why somebody did not get up and denounce this hypocrisy. In that moment he hated Barber more than he had ever hated anyone in the world.

If Derek had happened to be a trained psychologist, and not merely a very young man very much in love, he could perhaps have understood the inner meaning of the Shaver's intemperate tirade. For it was not Bartram that he was denouncing, but himself. In his mind's eye he was the culprit whose delinquency he was reproving. It was in a mood of self-abasement that he magnified the grossness of his own offence, and at the same time he was bitterly aware how small was the penalty that he could inflict compared with the one that he was called upon to undergo. How willingly would he have changed places with the man in the dock before him! But Derek could know nothing of this. So far as he could tell, Barber was simply being grotesquely unjust. As for the prisoner, it is to be imagined that the only matter which concerned him was that he was finally sentenced to the maximum amount prescribed by law, namely a fine of £50 and three months imprisonment.

Derek met Sheila outside the court. Her rather prominent blue eyes were dry, and there was a glassy look in them which he had never seen before. Her pale face was set and her mouth was a thin, hard line. Derek had for some time been aware that his fiancée was a young woman of determined character, but on this occasion there was a look of angry resolution about her that positively frightened him. She was alone.

"Where is your mother?" he asked.

"She's down—down there with Daddy. I wouldn't go. It would only upset him. She'll be going back to the hotel afterwards. Mr. Jenkinson will look after her. I want to talk to you, Derek. No, not here. You must give me lunch somewhere."

Derek began to explain that he had only had one day's leave from his office and that he should be getting back, but in face of Sheila's determination he saw that it would be useless to persist. Even at the risk of hazarding his hard-won job he could not leave her now.

They fed miserably at the first restaurant they could find. Although she had said that she wished to talk to him, he could not for some time get a word out of her. When the meal was over, she looked at him for the first time.

"What are we going to do, Derek?" she asked. She said it in a way that made it sound less like an appeal than a challenge.

"It's not going to make any difference to us," Derek assured her, for the twentieth time.

"Oh, us!" Sheila said impatiently. "I'm thinking of Daddy."

"I expect he'll appeal," said Derek. "It's a monstrous sentence. He ought never to have been sent to prison."

But Sheila's thoughts had taken another turn.

"What made that brute of a judge behave in such a beastly way?" she exclaimed. "Anybody would have thought that Daddy was a real criminal. Listen, Derek, you know him, don't you? Can't you see him and tell him that he's made a horrible mistake? Tell him the sort of person Daddy really is and that he's simply got to change his mind and let him out?"

"But Sheila, I couldn't possibly! It's—it's simply not done, that sort of thing."

"Not done!" Her tone was scornful. "What does it matter whether it's done or not? I thought you cared for me, and I'm asking you to do it for me, now."

"But Sheila, honestly, I can't!"

"You mean you won't. All right. I know what that means. It's all very well for you to say that this won't make any difference to us, when you won't do the least thing to help."

Derek realized with a sinking heart that Sheila really believed what she was saying. He saw too that in her present mood it would be quite impossible to explain to her the hopeless impossibility of what she proposed. Desperately he cast about in his mind for some argument that would convince her, and in an evil hour he found it.

"Look here, Sheila," he said. "You know I'd do anything in the world to help you. If talking to Barber would be any use, I'd do it like a shot, whatever anybody thought about it. But it's just because I do know him that I can see it would be hopeless. You see—you don't understand just how rotten it was of him to say the things he did and pass that appalling sentence. And I don't expect anybody in court knew either, except just me and him."

"What on earth are you talking about?"

"Just this." And Derek in the fewest words possible revealed exactly what had happened on the night of the circuit dinner at Markhampton.

"Of course," he concluded, "I promised not to say a word about this to anyone, and I haven't up to now, but——"

"That's all right," Sheila interrupted him. "I'm not going to tell anybody else, if that's what's troubling you.

But I'm very glad you told me." She was breathing hard and looked more fiercely determined than ever.

"So you see it wouldn't be much good my trying to do anything."

Sheila did not answer. Instead she got up abruptly from the table.

"Let's go, shall we?" she said.

Derek offered to find her a taxi, but she shook her head.

"Aren't you going home?" he asked in surprise.

"No. You needn't wait, Derek. I know you want to get back to your old office."

"But what are you going to do?"

"Never you mind. If you can't help me, I'd rather be alone. Oh, Derek, darling, I know that sounds horrid. I don't want to be a beast to you, but if anything's to be done, I can see I must do it myself. No!" she went on hastily, as he began to speak, "please don't ask me anything. I don't know what I'm going to do. Go away now and leave me. Only say that you love me, whatever happens!"

This Derek proceeded to say several times and sufficiently loudly to surprise a number of passers-by, before he caught a west-bound bus, leaving her standing, a forlorn but resolute figure on the pavement of Holborn. He did not, however, go back to his office. He knew that he was quite incapable of doing any work that afternoon. In his angry, unhappy, bewildered state he would be unable to give his mind to anything outside his own affairs. He might as well be hung for a sheep as for a lamb, he thought, and take the day off altogether. But equally the prospect of spending the afternoon in solitary idleness appalled him. Suddenly, he felt the urgent need of confiding in someone, who would help him to see his troubles in their proper perspective. Acting on impulse, he got off the bus at the top of Chancery Lane and walked down to the Temple.

He met with disappointment. Pettigrew, the clerk informed him, was out. He could not say exactly when he would return, but he expected him in any moment. Perhaps Mr. Marshall would wait? And wait Mr. Marshall did, for what seemed an endless time, in those dusky, dusty Chambers, until he could bear it no longer.

When he finally decided to go, he left in what Pettigrew's clerk thought at the time a most unreasonable hurry. As if he had suddenly remembered a pressing appointment, he fairly sprinted out of the place, with a purposeful expression on his face, in odd contrast to the aimless manner in which he had entered it. The Law Courts' clock was striking four as he crossed the Strand. He waited impatiently for a moment or two for a bus, and then, as none appeared, turned and set off down Fleet Street as fast as he could walk.

By the time that he reached the Old Bailey, a steady procession out of the main doors told him that the Courts were "up". He looked round everywhere for Sheila, but she was not to be seen. Inquiring from a doorkeeper, he learned that No. 1 Court, in which the Judge sat, had risen a good ten minutes ago. The present exodus was from the two other courts, which had just finished their business. The Common Serjeant was still sitting, he believed. Derek was not interested in the Common Serjeant, except to wonder for an irrelevant instant how he came by his uncommon title. He pressed on to the top of the street and turned to his right round the angle of the great building. On this front three doors from the Courts give into Newgate Street. From one, a few black-coated men were emerging—counsel and their clerks, obviously. From another, providing access to the public galleries, came a stream of those odd beings who find free entertainment in contemplating the misfortunes of their fellows. They crowded the narrow pavement and momentarily obstructed Derek's view of the third door, the Judge's entrance. Then he caught a glimpse of what he thought to be Sheila's hat ahead of him and quickened his footsteps.

As he approached, he saw a car drawn up outside. Somebody, evidently Barber's new clerk, ran out, deposited a bundle of papers in the car, and disappeared again. A moment later, just as Derek came level with the door, Mr. Justice Barber, his wife close beside him, stepped out and across the pavement.

The police subsequently took statements from thirty-three individuals who claimed to have been eye-witnesses of the events of the next few seconds. After eliminating from these the inevitable half-wits, publicity-seekers and deliberate or unconscious liars, they arrived at the conclusion that twelve sane and sober persons, including two police officers, had in fact seen some part or another of what occurred. Not one of these selected statements agreed exactly with any other; and indeed this was to some extent a guarantee of their truthfulness. By careful checking, however, they succeeded at last in arriving at a fairly reliable account of the order of events during those crowded moments.

The pavement was full of passers-by at the moment when Judge and lady emerged from the building. A constable on either side held up the traffic to form a narrow lane between the door and the waiting car. It was the kind of thing that happens daily when the Central Criminal Court is in session, and it may be inferred that to neither of these men was their duty more than a matter of routine. The Judge was half-way across the pavement when the first abnormal event occurred. From under the arm of the officer holding up the pedestrians on the east side of the entrance a small, stout man wriggled his way forward and approached the Judge. This was made the more easy for him because, as the constable pointed out, that arm was at the moment quite properly raised in salute. He was heard to say a few words beginning, "My lord, I must insist——" He had got no further when police officer number two, from the west, made a dive at him and seized him by the arm. At this point, as if profiting by the interruption on her side, a young woman ran forward from the opposite direction. Dodging round Lady Barber, who was standing close behind her husband's left shoulder, she reached the Judge unobserved. She was heard to say something. Reports were at variance as to whether this was, "Listen to me, you beast!" or "Take that, you beast!" but at least one reliable witness observed that her hand was seen to be upraised. Whatever she said, it was immediately followed by a cry of "Sheila, come back!" This apparently came from a young man, who, perhaps finding his approach in front blocked by what was now an excited crowd, had slipped round on the outside of the pavement and suddenly appeared between the car and the Judge, forcing him back towards the door from which he had come. The young man reached the girl at the same moment as the two officers, who had made a concerted dive towards her. There were a few moments during which the Judge and Lady Barber were the centre of a violent struggle. Both policemen had hold of the girl and the young man had hold of all three. Each was pulling in a different direction. A tall, middle-aged man had somehow become inextricably mingled in the confused group. The young man was heard to say, apparently to him, "Pettigrew, don't let them——" Then superior weight and training told and he and the girl were dragged by main force away from the car. The fat man who had begun the disturbance had disappeared while the officer who had seized him was otherwise engaged. The crowd which had surged in from both sides parted for a moment. Then a woman screamed, and those nearest to him heard Mr. Justice Barber utter a low moan and saw him pitch forward and fall to the ground in a crumpled ungainly heap.

Chapter 22

THE FORCES IN CONFERENCE

Three days later, Inspector Mallett was summoned to the room of the Assistant Commissioner in charge of his department at Scotland Yard.

"I've rather an unusual job for you," he was told.

"Sir?"

"I think that you know all about Mr. Justice Barber?"

"I know that he has been murdered, sir, naturally," said Mallett non-committally.

"Well, somebody in the City Police seems to have an idea that you know a little more than that. Anyhow, I've had a formal request that we should lend you to them to assist in their investigations."

"*Sir?*"

Mallett's astonishment was genuine and profound. The relations between the City of London Police and the Metropolitan Force were at that moment, as it is to be hoped they always have been, correct, friendly and even cordial. But they were definitely the relations of two distinct, if allied, Powers. For the City to ask for the assistance of Scotland Yard in the matter of a murder committed literally on its own doorstep was a portent, even in the age that was to produce the Lend Lease Act.

The Assistant Commissioner was smiling.

"Well?" he said.

"Of course I shall go, sir, if I am wanted," said Mallett.

"I should hardly have thought I would be of any use in a case like this, but——"

"Have you seen this?" his superior interrupted him, holding up a photograph.

Mallett looked at it.

"Yes, sir. I understand that was the weapon employed in this case. An unusual looking object. The photograph has been circulated widely, I believe."

"Exactly. And it has now been identified. A report has come in from the Eastbury police to say that it is identical with the dagger used by a man named Ockenhurst to commit a murder in their part of the world last September."

"Eastbury!" said the inspector. "Was this man tried there, then?"

"He was. And this knife was naturally an exhibit at the trial. And when the trial was over it had disappeared. *And* it reappeared between Mr. Justice Barber's shoulder blades outside the Central Criminal Court. Therefore," concluded the Assistant Commissioner, who believed in rubbing things in, "it occurred to somebody in the City C.I.D. that this business might have something to do with what happened on the Southern Circuit. And it further occurred to him that you knew rather more about that than most people."

Mallett said nothing. He was standing, very square and solid, in front of his chief's desk, pulling vigorously at the long points of his moustaches and frowning. His gloomy appearance impressed the Assistant Commissioner.

"Well?" he said sharply.

"I'll go, of course, sir," said Mallett. "This afternoon."

The Assistant Commissioner looked at the clock on the wall.

"It is now 10.32 in the morning," he said reproachfully. "You are usually quicker off the mark than that, Mallett."

"It's no use my going down to the City empty handed, sir," Mallett pointed out. "With your permission, I propose to spend a few hours assembling all the information bearing on this matter that I can."

"Quite so. And then there is your lunch to be considered, isn't there?"

Mallett sighed.

"Lunch is hardly worth considering these days, sir," he said. "I'm positively losing weight every day."

Superintendent Brough, of the City of London Police, made Mallett welcome at Old Jewry. He was a level-headed, broadminded man, who seemed positively to enjoy the prospect of working with Scotland Yard. It was even rumoured that in his very early youth he had been heard to suggest that it was ridiculous to maintain two entirely separate police forces in the capital, but he had managed to live down the memory of this subversive remark, as his subsequent promotion showed.

"First you'll want to see what we've got, and then we'll see what you've got," he began briskly, laying before the inspector a pile of neatly arranged witnesses' statements.

Mallett sighed as he looked at the mass of paper.

"You've got plenty," he said. "But I understand you have something more than this, haven't you? Three persons n c ustody, I'm told."

"Yes. All three remanded in custody for a week from yesterday. Charged with breach of the peace and obstructing the police. It seemed the best thing to do with them. Besides, it really was a breach of the peace all right. One of my constables has a beautiful black eye. They have all made voluntary statements. Perhaps you would like to look at them first. One in particular will interest you very much."

He pulled out three sheets of paper.

"Here you are. Beamish, the girl Bartram and Marshall."

Mallett read them one after another. Beamish's statement was florid in style but succinct enough. Having explained that he had lost his position through an unfortunate misunderstanding which he was anxious to clear up with his late employer, he went on to describe the vain effort which he had made on the previous day to speak to him. Then, according to his account, despairing of any other means of attracting his attention, he had formed what he described as "the desperate resolve" of accosting his lordship outside the court and so attracting attention to his just grievance. He deeply regretted the disturbance of which he had been the cause and desired to plead guilty to the charge. As to the death of his lordship, which had shocked him beyond all measure, he was as innocent as the babe unborn.

"Yes," said Mallett gravely, as he put down the paper. "By the way, did you know that Beamish was known as 'Corky'?"

"No," the superintendent confessed. "I didn't."

"Corky's Night Club, you know. That's him. And that reminds me of something—something——" He beat upon his forehead with the knuckles of his fist. "Lord! My memory's going! It must be because I never get any proper meals these days. Never mind! I'll think of it soon. Meanwhile, let's see what Miss Bartram has to say."

Sheila's statement was quite short. Like Beamish, she admitted the offence of obstructing the police and disturbing the peace of which they were the guardians. Like him, but in simpler terms, she denied all knowledge of, or connection with the Judge's death. As to her part in the affray outside the Old Bailey she said:

"I was frightfully upset about Daddy being sent to prison and I thought I would see the Judge and tell him he must change his mind. I had been told it was the wrong thing to do, but I couldn't stop myself. When I came close to him and saw his face I knew it wouldn't be any good appealing to him and I'm afraid I lost my temper. I think I called him a beast, but he didn't seem to take any notice. There was a lot of noise going on behind me and I was afraid someone would stop me before I had done anything, so I hit at him with my fist. Then a policeman got hold of me and there was an awful mix up. I was winded and my hat was knocked over my eyes. I don't really know what happened after that."

Mallett put the document down without comment, and extended his hand for the third statement. He read the first sentence and whistled aloud.

"I thought that would interest you," said Brough with a grin.

The statement opened with the words: "I killed Mr. Justice Barber."

"You haven't charged him with murder yet, have you?" Mallett asked in a tone that sounded almost anxious.

"We have not. You see, we considered—— However, read the rest of it, and tell me what you think."

Mallett read on.

"I killed Mr. Justice Barber. I was disgusted with his outrageous conduct at the Old Bailey to-day. Knowing what I do of him, I considered his attitude towards Mr. Bartram a travesty of justice. After thinking the matter over during the afternoon I procured a knife and went to the Judge's entrance. I arrived there just when he was leaving. I saw my fiancée, Miss Bartram, endeavour to speak to him. She was seized by a constable before she could get near him. This made me lose my head completely, because I knew that he was solely responsible for the trouble in which she was. Acting on an impulse, I took the knife and stabbed him between the shoulders. I told nobody of what I was going to do, and I am solely responsible for all that occurred. I did not know that I should see Miss Bartram there. She has nothing whatever to do with the Judge being killed. I decline to say where the knife came from. I am quite prepared to take full responsibility for what I did."

"Very interesting," said the inspector.

"Interesting and rather puzzling too," Brough remarked. "You see how full of contradictions it is. First he says that he was disgusted with the Judge's behaviour, and therefore got a knife 'after thinking the matter over' and went to the Court—with the intention of killing him, presumably. But then a moment later he is saying that he lost his head because he saw his young lady being held by an officer and acted on impulse. It can't very well be both."

"True," said Mallett. "And you will have noticed, no doubt, that he goes out of his way to say that Miss Bartram never got near the Judge. Whereas we know from her own admission that she got close enough to strike him."

"Exactly. The whole rigmarole has just been made up to shield Miss Bartram, if you ask me."

"I quite agree."

"Which doesn't of course mean", Brough pursued, "that he isn't necessarily responsible."

Mallett did not answer. He was studying the document afresh.

"'I decline to say where the knife came from'," he repeated.

"The knife! Yes," the superintendent put in. "We've got some very interesting information about that from the Eastbury police. Let me show you what they——"

"Wait a moment, Super! Let's have one thing at a time, if you don't mind. Tell me something else first. Was Marshall told that this was the Eastbury knife?"

"No. We hadn't found that out at the time this statement was taken."

"Of course not. Well, was he shown the knife?"

"No. It was being examined for finger-prints, I remember. Incidentally, there weren't any."

"I see. Well, I suggest it would be rather a good plan to see him again, show him the knife, and ask him if he recognizes it. If he doesn't, tell him what it is and where it comes from. Then see what his reactions are."

"And what do you expect them to be?"

"If this confession is a fake, made up because he thinks Miss Bartram is guilty, he'll withdraw it."

The superintendent looked puzzled, and Mallett went on:

"Because, you see, he'll tumble at once to the fact that

she couldn't possibly have got hold of it. She wasn't at Eastbury Assizes."

"But he was," Brough objected. "He might have given it to her."

"Granted. But that's not the point. If he did give her the knife, then she is probably guilty, with or without his assistance. In that case, he'll stick to his story. But if he didn't, then he'll know that she must be innocent. And he'll change his tune at once."

"But suppose his story is true, and he really did kill the Judge?"

"All the more reason for changing it. He won't want to hang himself any more than the next man, once he knows that there's nothing to be gained by it. You see, if I'm right, and he denies it, it won't prove his own innocence, but it will prove hers. And we shall be that much further on, by eliminating one suspect straight away."

Mallett pulled his moustaches in a satisfied manner.

"And now," he said with a sigh, "I suppose I'd better tackle this little lot." And with the superintendent assisting him to separate the wheat from the chaff, he rapidly mastered the accounts given by the eye-witnesses of the tragedy. Over only two of them did he linger. The first of these was Hilda's. It was short and uninformative enough. Like everybody else, she had had her attention distracted from her husband by the successive appearance of Beamish, Sheila Bartram and Marshall. The last of these had, she thought, separated her from the Judge, although she had tried to keep hold of his arm. Then she had got into touch with him again, and at that moment she felt him stagger and he had collapsed in her arms. That was all.

"We couldn't very well ask her any questions about it," the superintendent explained. "She was very distressed. But I doubt whether in any case she would have much to add to her story."

"Quite," said Mallett. "By the way," he added suddenly

and after a pause, "I wonder whether you happen to know whether she had been in Court that afternoon?"

"As a matter of fact, I happen to know that she wasn't. I got a routine statement from the attendant in the Judge's room, and he mentioned that she was waiting there all the afternoon until his lordship rose."

"I see. Now the other statement that interests me is *this* one."

"Mr. Pettigrew's? Well, it's certainly rather more intelligible than most of them. But he didn't really see more than the rest—less, if anything, being mixed up in the middle of things, so to speak."

"It's Mr. Pettigrew himself that interests me more than what he says. Also what he doesn't say."

"For instance?"

"Well, you will note that he doesn't say what he was doing there. His statement just begins: 'At about 4.20 p.m. on the 12th April 1940, I was outside the Judge's entrance of the Central Criminal Court'."

"They all begin that way, more or less," Brough pointed out. "The officer who took the statement would probably ask a leading question to get the witness going. In any case, Mr. Pettigrew is a member of the Bar, and I suppose the neighbourhood of a court of law is where one might expect to find him."

"But I've never heard that Mr. Pettigrew had any practice at the Central Criminal Court," Mallett objected. "He's certainly not a member of the mess there. Of course, anybody might happen to have an odd case there now and again, especially in wartime, with so many regular practitioners away, but I shouldn't have expected to find him at this particular place at this particular time. I think it will be worth looking into."

He made a note, and continued:

"Now about this knife. You've got a report from the Eastbury police, haven't you?"

"We have, and a very good one too. Read it for yourself."

"It comes to this," the inspector said, when he had read and re-read the papers which Brough put before him. "This nasty little tool was an exhibit in the trial of Ockenhurst at Eastbury last December. After the hearing it disappeared, and turned up four months later between Mr. Justice Barber's shoulder blades. The last time anybody can positively speak to having seen it was during the Judge's summing-up and then it was on the Judge's desk. H'm. And they very thoughtfully give a list of the people on the bench at the time. From left to right—Captain Trevor, Chief Constable; Beamish, Judge's clerk; Marshall; the Judge in the centre; then Sir William Candish, the High Sheriff; Lady Candish; Lady Barber; and the Under Sheriff, who was—*phew*!"

"What's up?" said the superintendent.

"I dare say there's nothing in it, but it gave me quite a start. Mr. Victor Granby is the Under Sheriff. That will be the senior partner in Granby and Co. of course. They are the principal solicitors for that part of the world, I remember. He has been Under Sheriff for years."

"What of it?"

"Only that the firm used to be Granby, Heppenstall in the old days. Heppenstall senior died, and young Heppenstall took his capital out of the firm and set up on his own in London. That's all ancient history. You remember the Heppenstall case, of course?"

The superintendent nodded. "And——?" he said.

"And Granby married Heppenstall's sister. That's all. But it won't do, of course. The Judge has been in that circuit half a dozen times since he sentenced Heppenstall and Granby doesn't seem to bear him any malice."

"We'll have his movements for the day in question looked into, to be on the safe side," Brough said. "But I can't see why, if he took the knife to kill the Judge with, he should wait four months to use it."

"And that applies to every soul in court that day," said

Mallett. He paused, and said deliberately, "Tell me why the Judge was killed on the 12th of April and I will tell you who did it."

"Well," he went on. "What else do the Eastbury fellows tell us? Oh, yes. Entry and exit to the Bench immediately behind the Judge's desk. That means that anybody leaving the Bench would pass by the place where the knife was last seen and would have an equal opportunity of picking it up. Others who might have had an opportunity of getting hold of it without attracting comment—Counsel on both sides, namely Sir Henry Babbington and his junior, Mr. Pott, and Mr. Pettigrew; the solicitors instructing them; the police themselves, who hunted for it afterwards and couldn't find it; and the Clerk of Assize, Mr. Gervase, who sat just in front of and beneath the Judge. I don't think we need worry about old Mr. Gervase. Oh, yes! and Greene, the Marshal's man, who served the Judge his tea, and was flitting about between his lordship's room and the Bench after the case was over. That's the lot."

The superintendent was doing some calculating.

"Of the people who could have taken that knife," he said, "the following, so far as we know, were within striking distance of the Judge when he was killed with it: Marshall, Pettigrew and Lady Barber."

"And Beamish," Mallett added.

"No," Brough corrected him. "All the evidence goes to show that at the exact time when the Judge collapsed, Beamish must have been some distance away. In fact, he never got within arm's length of him. He was the first, you remember, and the constable pounced on him as soon as he appeared."

"Quite right," said the inspector. "He freed himself when the officers were going for the other two, but he never seems to have got any closer. So it looks as if——" He stopped suddenly, and then exclaimed in a tone of immense satisfaction, "*Darts!*"

"Eh?"

"I've just remembered. That's what Corky's club was famous for. They had a lot of dart boards there. It was quite a centre for the sport, if that's the right word for it. The London championships were held there. Now suppose Corky himself was an expert dart thrower? What easier than to throw this little knife at a few feet's range, while the police were dragging the other two away? In doing so, they made a clear space on the pavement, remember. The Judge filled it up when he fell."

Superintendent Brough did not believe in displaying emotion. If he was excited at the new suggestion, he did not show it.

"Very well," he said. "Then we add Beamish to the list. That makes four altogether. I think we know more or less all we want to know at the moment about Marshall and Beamish. What about the other two?"

"Pettigrew and the Judge had been on notoriously bad terms for years," said Mallett briefly. "Lady Barber was—well, she was his wife. As I expect you have heard, Barber was supposed to be on the brink of having to retire because of that scandal at Markhampton. I'll tell you all the details of it directly. She may well have thought it wasn't much catch being married to him if he was going to lose his job. She was also an old friend of Pettigrew's. They may have been in it together."

There was something cursory and unenthusiastic in the way in which he recited these facts that made the superintendent look up at him with a question in his eyes.

"But . . . ?" he said.

"But, perhaps someone will tell me why, if all that is so, her ladyship should put herself to enormous trouble to save his life when he tried to commit suicide only a few weeks ago?"

"Suicide?" said Brough. "This is new to me. What was the motive, do you know?"

"I have every reason to suppose that it was because he couldn't face the prospect of having to leave the bench, and the scandal I was talking about just now. We can verify that by further inquiry from her ladyship, no doubt."

"You're sure it was a genuine attempt? If his wife really meant to get rid of him, she might perhaps have faked something——"

"Oh, it was genuine all right. You see—— But I'm putting the cart before the horse. All this relates back to the very odd things that happened while the Judge was going circuit last autumn. I understand that's what you called me in about, wasn't it?"

"Quite right," said the superintendent. "Let's hear all you have to say."

What Mallett had to say took up some considerable time. His account of the troubles that had pursued the Judge during the progress of the circuit interested his colleague a great deal. The conclusions that he drew from the facts interested him even more. They also surprised him very much indeed.

"Frankly," he said. "I don't quite see what you are getting at."

"Equally frankly," Mallett answered, "neither do I. I have given you the facts, so far as I know them, and I fancy they are pretty accurate. Also, I feel fairly confident that I have interpreted them accurately. But I still don't see where they are leading me—or rather, if I let them lead me in the direction they seem to point, I come up against a plumb absurdity. So what?"

"I'm beginning to wonder," said Brough, "if we're not exploring a blind alley all this time. As matters stand, we have a signed confession by Marshall. Suppose it is true, and neither the girl nor Pettigrew, nor anyone else had anything to do with it? In that case, this crime was quite unpremeditated, and all that happened between October and the day before the murder is quite irrelevant."

"If this was unpremeditated, why did he pinch the knife at Eastbury?" asked Mallett.

"As a souvenir, very likely. After all, whoever took it can hardly have been intending to commit a crime with it four months later. I think he made up his mind to kill the Judge that afternoon, and then, remembering the knife in his possession, went and fetched it——"

"Where from?"

"I expect from his home. We will try to get some evidence of that, of course."

"Do so. He's in lodgings in Kensington, isn't he? We ought to be able to establish whether he came back there during the course of the afternoon. But don't forget that you are going to show him that knife and see what effect it has on him."

"That will be done this evening. What is your next step?"

"My next step," said Mallett, "will be in the direction of Mr. Pettigrew's chambers. There are several matters I want to discuss with him. I have a strong feeling that he is the clue to the whole matter. Ring me up at the Yard this evening when you have seen Marshall again and that may help me as to what line I take with Pettigrew."

And upon this, the detectives parted.

Chapter 23

INQUIRIES IN THE TEMPLE

Mallett was at Pettigrew's chambers early next morning. He was received with a grave courtesy, not unmixed with suspicion, by John, Pettigrew's elderly clerk, who told him that his master had not yet arrived. The inspector amiably said that he would wait, and set himself to occupy the time in conversation with John.

"We've had a young man from the City Police round here already," the latter said in a somewhat aggrieved tone. "It's a bit unpleasant for us, being mixed up in this kind of thing, you know."

"I can quite understand that," said Mallett soothingly.

"As if it wasn't a nasty enough shock for us," John went on, "we being such an old friend of her ladyship and all. It's a bit too bad being brought in as a witness as well."

"Very bad luck," the inspector agreed. "But these things will occur, you know. It was just Mr. Pettigrew's misfortune that he should happen to be at the Old Bailey that afternoon. I suppose he was holding a brief there?"

John looked at him with suspicion.

"And I suppose if I said 'Yes', you'd want to look at our engagement book," he said. "Well, I'll save you the trouble. He was not. Yesterday afternoon, he was doing a little arbitration over the way. We thought it would be finished by half-past three or earlier, but it wasn't till just gone four o'clock that he came back."

"Four o'clock! Then he must have gone straight down to the Old Bailey from here?"

"It's no part of my business to tell you where he went to. For another thing, I don't know because I didn't inquire."

"But he did leave from here to go somewhere as soon as he came back?"

"I wouldn't say as soon as. We had a bit of a chat after he came in. About the arbitration, and appointments for the next day, and who had been in while he was out, and so on."

"And had anyone been in?" Mallett asked at random.

"There'd only been one caller that afternoon. Mr. Pettigrew just missed him. That was a young gentleman who had been here before. Marshall, the name was."

"Marshall. What was he doing here?"

"I'm sure I couldn't tell you, except that he called to see Mr. Pettigrew. It was none of my business to ask him."

"But this may be important," the inspector insisted. "You know that Marshall is in custody for assaulting the police at the Old Bailey when the Judge was killed?"

"Indeed?" said John in apparently genuine surprise. "No, that's news to me. You see, I don't much care for reading the reports of police courts in the papers, unless we happen to be professionally concerned. I find them rather too low for my taste, if you'll excuse my saying so. But that is interesting, as you say, really very interesting indeed."

"What did he do while he was here?"

"Why, nothing in particular. He just hung about most of the afternoon, and then, just before four, he left in a hurry. If he'd waited another five minutes he'd have seen Mr. Pettigrew."

"Did he go into Mr. Pettigrew's room at all while he was here?"

"Certainly, I let him sit there. It's got the only comfortable chair in the chambers."

"You didn't happen to miss anything after he had gone?"

"Miss anything? Certainly not! Mr. Marshall is hardly the sort of gentleman you'd expect to miss anything after he's been. I shouldn't have let him into Mr. Pettigrew's room else, I can tell you."

"You're quite sure?" Mallett persisted. "Mr. Pettigrew hasn't mentioned to you that he has lost anything?"

"He has not—and if you want to pursue that inquiry you had better ask him yourself," John added, as a footstep was heard outside the door. "Good morning, sir!"

"Morning, John," said Pettigrew, entering at that moment. "Good morning, Mr.—Mallett, is it not? Did you want to see me?"

"If you can spare me a few minutes of your time, sir."

Pettigrew preceded Mallett into the shabby but comfortable room, and sat down behind his desk with a sigh. He looked tired and dispirited.

"Well?" he said. "You have come about this wretched Barber business, I suppose? You have seen the statement I gave to the police immediately afterwards? If so, I don't think there is anything I can add to it."

"There is only one point in your statement which I should like amplified," said the inspector. "You didn't say exactly why you were outside the Old Bailey on that particular occasion."

"Quite right, Inspector, I didn't. It did not appear to me to affect the value of my evidence one way or the other. And", he added as the detective was about to speak, "it still does not appear to me to do so."

"You decline to answer the question?"

"Yes."

Mallett said nothing for a moment or two. Then he asked abruptly,

"You remember the case of Ockenhurst at Eastbury Assizes?"

Pettigrew raised his eyebrows.

"Of course," he said.

"Do you know that the knife with which Mr. Justice Barber was murdered has been identified with the knife that was exhibited at that trial?"

"Oh?" said Pettigrew slowly, his nose wrinkling.

"After the trial, the knife could not be found. The Eastbury police were under the impression that you might have taken it. I have been speaking on the telephone to-day to the officer in charge of that case, and he tells me that he looked for you, but you had left the Court, somewhat hastily, it seems."

"Yes, I remember. I wanted some exercise and I went for a walk before catching my train. I wanted to walk off my bad temper."

"Your bad temper with the Judge?"

"Certainly," Pettigrew smiled. "I was in a shocking temper over that case."

"Did you take the knife with you, Mr. Pettigrew?"

"No."

"Mr. Marshall spent a good deal of the afternoon of the twenty-second in this room. From here he went down to the Old Bailey."

"Yes. I saw him there."

"He has since made a confession that he killed Mr. Justice Barber."

Pettigrew's face took on an expression of pain.

"The poor boy!" he said. "The poor, wretched boy! This is really horrible, Inspector!" He was silent for a moment or two, and then added, "In that case, there seems to be no reason why I should not now answer the question you asked me just now. I went down to the Old Bailey because I had a suspicion that he might do something silly."

"Indeed?" said Mallett.

"Yes. You see he had told me some time ago about this case, and I knew that he was in rather a state about it. Yesterday morning, I happened to see on the notice board in the Cloisters that it was being heard in No. 1 Court, where I knew that Barber was sitting, and this morning I saw that it was part heard. I took no particular interest in it until at lunch-time when I happened to sit next to Fawcett in hall, and heard from him that Barber had—not to put too fine a point on it—behaved outrageously. That worried me quite a bit, because I am really quite fond of young Marshall, and I knew he would take it badly. Then when I got back here in the afternoon, John told me that he had been trying to see me. He told me, too, that he was obviously in a very nervous and excited state, and had left abruptly just before four o'clock. I suddenly had a horrible feeling of anxiety about him. I remembered his absurd idealism about judges and justice—rather engaging in its way, but confoundedly dangerous—and it crossed my mind that he might have gone back to the court, and that if so, I really ought to try to head him off. So, on the spur of the moment, I took a taxi and dashed down there. I was just too late, as it turned out. Poor chap!"

"Thank you," said the inspector. "And now, Mr. Pettigrew, having told me so much, would you like to reconsider another of your answers?"

"I don't quite follow you."

"If I am right, you declined at first to tell me why you went to the Old Bailey because you were afraid that by doing so you might throw suspicion on Marshall?"

"Quite right."

"I was wondering whether you denied having had possession of that interesting souvenir from Eastbury for the same reason."

"I am afraid I am very dense this morning, but I still don't understand."

"If you had taken it as a souvenir," the inspector explained, "it might have been expected to be lying about somewhere in this room—on your desk, for example, as a paper-knife. What more likely than that the sight of it should have suggested to Marshall how he could get even with the Judge and sent him hurrying down to the Old Bailey just ahead of you?"

"I see," said Pettigrew slowly. "Very ingenious, if you will allow me to say so. But it won't do, I am afraid. I can assure you that young Marshall didn't get that knife from this room."

Mallett nodded. "I am not altogether surprised to hear that," he said. "You see, Marshall was shown the knife last night for the first time since he was taken into custody. He was reminded what it was and where it came from, and as soon as he saw it——"

"Yes?"

"He immediately withdrew his confession."

"Withdrew his——! Really, Inspector! Have you been making a fool of me?"

"I hope you won't think that, Mr. Pettigrew," said Mallett apologetically. "You see, I was really anxious to know your explanation for being at the Old Bailey that afternoon. In fairness to yourself, some sort of explanation had to be made. And I thought the quickest way of getting it was to lead you to believe that it was no longer necessary to shield anybody else."

Pettigrew seemed to be undecided whether to be annoyed or amused.

"This is most immoral," he said finally. "And now will you tell me what induced Marshall to behave in this way?"

"I think that he made his confession originally because he was under the impression that the police suspected Miss Bartram."

"Miss——? Oh, of course, the young lady of his affections. That must have been the blonde person I last saw indulging in an all-in contest with the two Roberts. And the reason why—No, don't tell me, let me work it out for myself. Marshall knew that she could not have had the Eastbury poignard because she wasn't there to take it, unless he had given it to her himself and he knew he hadn't. *Ergo*, she was innocent, to the knowledge of the police. Hence the necessity for protecting her disappears. Am I right?"

"Quite correct."

"There seems to have been a lot of unregulated quixotry about this case. I suppose the young woman hasn't dashed forward to shield her fiancé with a bogus confession, by any chance?"

"No," said Mallett gravely.

"I thought not. The female of the species usually has a more realistic outlook in such matters, I fancy. Meanwhile, it still remains possible that Marshall, not knowing that you had identified the dagger, really had—but you have worked all that out for yourself no doubt. Who am I to do Scotland Yard's cerebrations? By the way, I understand that friend Beamish is also in custody?"

"He is."

"One tip about him I can give you. I am tired of shielding people, and it's time I took a hand in giving my fellow man away. He's a perfectly miraculous dart thrower."

"I thought as much," said Mallett. "But I'm interested to have positive evidence of it. Have you actually seen him play?"

"I have, indeed. It was a most impressive sight."

"When was that?"

"Oh, quite a long time ago now. The night of a certain motor accident. The night when it all started."

A long pause succeeded the remark. Mallett stared into the fireplace, pulling at the ends of his moustaches, as though uncertain how to proceed. Pettigrew was lost in reverie.

"Well, that's that!" he said at last. "I think we have covered the list of suspects, have we not, Inspector? I suppose, for form's sake at least, I must include myself among them?"

"Yes," said Mallett absently. It was not clear from his tone which of the two questions he was answering. "I was wondering," he went on, "about what you said just now—

'the night that it all started'. That was Lady Barber's idea, you know, that all the unpleasant things that happened to the Judge on the circuit were in some way connected—including the motor accident at Markhampton on the 12th of October 1939."

"How precise you detectives always are," said Pettigrew. "I couldn't have given the date to save my life. Well, there's no doubt that it was the accident that put the Judge in the very nasty hole in which he was at the time of his death. This is a breach of confidence on my part, Inspector, but I think it is justified in the circumstances. Barber was virtually ordered to send in his resignation during the vacation, and he was so upset at the prospect that he actually attempted to commit suicide."

"I knew it already," said Mallett. "That is to say, I was aware of the attempted suicide. I had guessed at the cause, but I didn't know the precise details."

"Well, you can verify them for yourself, if you care to refer to certain exalted quarters. I had rather you didn't quote me as your source of information, however. I heard of it in strict confidence from—from the person chiefly concerned."

"Quite," said the inspector. "There is no doubt, according to the medical evidence, that Lady Barber saved her husband's life on that occasion. It is a pity she was less successful on the other."

"I don't want to seem callous," Pettigrew observed, "but to me it is nothing less than astonishing that any woman could be married to Barber for so many years and still want to save his life." He glanced hastily at the detective and went on, "At all events, in the circumstances, I am extremely glad for her sake that she did."

Mallett nodded silently and rose to his feet.

"I have taken up a great deal of your time, Mr. Pettigrew," he said, "and I must thank you for bearing with me so long."

"Not at all. It has been a most interesting chat, for me, at any rate, but not, I fear, very useful to you. I don t honestly think that I can give you any further assistance. , could let you have a list of people who disliked Barber sufficiently to want to put him out of the way, if you like. It would be a very long one, and would contain some quite distinguished names, but I dare say you have enough suspects already, and except to save my own neck I don't want to cause anybody else any trouble."

"I should be quite satisfied," Mallett replied, "if you could give me the name of one person who had a motive for killing the Judge on the 12th of April 1940, long after the circuit was over—if the circuit had anything to do with it, beyond supplying the knife."

"The 12th of April!" said Pettigrew. "So it was! Dear me, yes! Well, good-bye, Inspector. Let me know if I can help you any further."

He held out his hand. Mallett did not take it. Instead he looked searchingly at the barrister.

"Yes, Mr. Pettigrew," he said. "The 12th of April. May I ask what there is about that date that impresses you?"

"Nothing," Pettigrew assured him in some confusion. "Nothing at all. It was only that—that you detective fellows are always so precise about your dates, as I said just now."

"But there seemed to be something about this particular date that attracted your attention," the inspector persisted.

"No, no," Pettigrew protested. His usual self-assurance seemed to have deserted him entirely. "To-day's the sixteenth, isn't it? I was surprised that it should have been such a short time ago. It seems longer. This business has been a fearful shock to me, as you can imagine, and I had quite lost count of the days. . . ."

His voice trailed off uncertainly. Mallett looked at him for a moment in silence, and then with a curt, "Good day, sir!" turned on his heels and left the room.

After he had gone, Pettigrew went back to his desk. He

consulted the calendar as though to make certain of the date. Then he went to a bookshelf and pulled out a volume of law reports. After studying this for a moment he sat down and wrote a very short letter, which he took out to the post himself.

Mallett meanwhile was in a telephone kiosk. He rang up Old Jewry and was immediately connected with Superintendent Brough.

"That's you at last, Inspector?" said Brough excitedly. "I've been trying to get hold of you all morning. This is important. I've just ascertained that Granby was in town during the whole of April the twelfth."

"Sorry, but I'm not interested," said Mallett. "But can you find out for me the name of the firm of solicitors acting for Mr. Sebastian Sebald-Smith?"

Chapter 24

EXPLANATIONS IN THE TEMPLE

———

Pettigrew was late at his chambers next morning. John, who was a stickler for punctuality, whether the work in hand necessitated it or not, greeted him with reproachful looks and was barely propitiated by the explanation that the Underground train by which he had travelled had been for some reason or another held up outside South Kensington station for three quarters of an hour. Grudgingly John admitted that there were no appointments that morning and only one set of papers which had come in over night and were not pressing. He had hardly left the room before he was back again.

"That Mr. Marshall is here, wanting to see you, sir," he announced. "He has a young lady with him."

Pettigrew, who had arrived at the chambers looking more harassed and care-worn than seemed warranted even by a breakdown on the Underground, cheered up at once.

"My dear fellow!" he cried, as the door opened to admit Derek and Sheila. "This is an unexpected pleasure indeed. I thought you were still in fetters. And Miss Bartram too—the last time I saw you, you were looking distinctly dishevelled. Congratulations on your release. Or are you only on bail?"

"No," said Derek. "It's all over and done with so far as we are concerned. I thought I must come round and tell you at once. We both came up before the Lord Mayor this morning. The case didn't take more than a minute, and he was really very decent about it. He fined me forty shillings and Sheila was bound over."

"Gross partiality. If I had been called as a witness I should have had to say that of the two of you Miss Bartram was far the more determined in her assault on the police."

"The one snag about it all is," said Derek, "that I'm not likely to keep my job at the Ministry after this."

"We must do something about that. I have a few friends at court, you know, and it so happens that one of them is a high-up in your show. I think I can save your services for your country yet. But tell me about Beamish. Was he dealt with in the same charitable spirit?"

"No." Derek looked serious. "His case was put back for seven days. They said something about a further charge being preferred."

"I suppose that means he killed that beastly old Judge," Sheila put in.

"H'm. I shouldn't jump to conclusions about that. I've a notion that quite a number of charges could be preferred against Beamish. It would be rather a sell for the great British public, all agog to hear a man accused of murder, if he's only run in for dispensing drink without a licence at Corky's night club, or something like that."

"But then who did kill him?" Sheila asked.

Pettigrew did not reply. His ear was cocked towards the door behind which sounds of altercation could be heard. Presently John came into the room, a pained expression on his face.

"Excuse me, sir," he said, "but the inspector from Scotland Yard is back here again. He's got another man with him and they want to see you at once. I told them you were engaged, but——"

Pettigrew's face was rather white as he replied. "Show them in, John. If Mr. Marshall and Miss Bartram like to stay, perhaps it would be as well."

Mallett and Superintendent Brough entered. They both looked grave and purposeful.

"You know this lady and gentleman, of course," Pettigrew said to them. "I think that they will be interested to hear what you have to say. In fact, if it is what I expect, I'm not sure that they haven't a right to hear it."

The superintendent looked at Mallett, who nodded his head slowly, pulling at his moustache. Nothing was said for a moment, and then the inspector, clearing his throat, spoke abruptly.

"I have come to tell you, Mr. Pettigrew, that Lady Barber threw herself under an electric train at South Kensington station this morning."

Pettigrew, who was standing beside his desk, felt with his hand for the chair behind him and then collapsed into it.

"So that's why my train was late this morning," he murmured.

"I'm afraid this is rather a shock for you," said Mallett sympathetically.

Pettigrew raised his head.

"On the contrary," he said, "I am very much relieved. I was afraid you had come to tell me that she had been arrested."

"A note was found in her handbag," Mallett went on, "I think it is in your handwriting?"

Pettigrew glanced at the slip of paper which the inspector placed before him.

"Yes," he said. "It is. I suppose I am responsible for what has happened."

"It is a very heavy responsibility," said Brough, speaking for the first time.

"I recognize that," Pettigrew replied. "But I am quite prepared to face it. That is—I suppose you were intending to arrest her for murder, weren't you?" he asked almost anxiously.

"Our inquiries were not complete," said the superintendent. "But in the normal course, I should probably have applied for a warrant during the next few days."

"Then I did right," Pettigrew said firmly. "Because, God help me! I loved the woman."

"Are you telling us," Mallett put in, "that this note was the cause of Lady Barber making away with herself?"

"Certainly." Pettigrew's brief outburst of emotion had passed, and he was once more his controlled, sardonic self. "I thought our discussion had been upon that basis."

"Because if so, I should like to know what it means."

Pettigrew glanced at the note again and smiled wryly.

"It is a little cryptic to the layman, I agree," he said. "But to anyone who could understand it, it is very much to the point. It simply refers to—— But aren't we putting the cart before the horse, Inspector? And worse, aren't we talking in riddles in front of Mr. Marshall? He has been trying to read this document upside down for the last five minutes, and he still can't make out what it's all about. As one who was very recently a self-confessed murderer, I think he should know the whole story, and you are certainly the only person who knows it. I can add my little piece of exegesis at the end if you wish."

Mallett hesitated for a moment.

"You will understand, of course, that all this is entirely confidential?" he said.

"We do, indeed. So far as I am concerned, Mr. Marshall will tell you that I long ago impressed upon him the virtue of hushing things up. He didn't altogether agree with me at the time, but I think that subsequent events have rather tended to change his views on the matter. As for Miss Bartram——"

"I shan't breathe a word," said Sheila earnestly.

"I trust not. Your chances of a wedding present from me depend entirely upon your discretion. I hope the threat is sufficient. Now, Inspector, make yourself comfortable and light your pipe if you wish. We are all ears."

"It is a little difficult to know where to start," said Mallett. "But perhaps the best way to begin is to explain how this case struck me when I was called upon to consider it the first time. You will recollect sir,"—he turned to Derek —"that when Lady Barber asked me to come to her club to discuss the unpleasant events that had occurred at the first three towns on the Circuit, she was rather annoyed with me for suggesting that she might be wrong in supposing that they were all due to one cause. My reason for so thinking was that there was one incident which quite clearly did not fit in with the others. I mean, of course, the chocolates filled with carbide which were sent to the Lodgings at Southington. I had very little doubt that the two anonymous letters, sent one before and one just after the motor accident, were the work of Heppenstall, whom we knew to be in the neighbourhood at the time. There seemed every reason to believe that he was also responsible for the assault on Lady Barber at Wimblingham."

Mallett paused and tugged at his moustache points. He looked embarrassed.

"As a matter of fact, I proved wrong there," he said. "Not that it made any difference to the argument, as it turned out. But Heppenstall was entirely innocent of what occurred at Wimblingham. He has succeeded in satisfying us of that beyond any doubt."

"Then who was it?" asked Derek in some eagerness.

Mallett smiled.

"You were perfectly right in your guess, Mr. Marshall," he said. "It was the person who kicked you so severely in the ribs that morning."

"Beamish?"

"Yes."

"But you said yourself that if he had wanted to attack anyone at night he would have put on rubber shoes or something like that," Derek objected.

"Quite. But Beamish didn't want to attack anybody. His

assault on Lady Barber was really in the nature of an accident. He only committed it in order to get away from the corridor before his identity could be discovered."

"What was he doing there at that time in the morning, then?"

"We have been at a good deal of pains to discover that. He was simply making his way back to bed after breaking into the Lodgings. You see, he had been——" Mallett glanced at Sheila and coloured slightly—"*elsewhere* most of that night, if you follow me. I am afraid his moral character was——"

"Well, well," said Pettigrew tolerantly. "We mustn't be too hard on him. After all, the beds in Lodgings were notoriously uncomfortable. One can hardly blame him for seeking softer lying somewhere else. But go on, Inspector."

"As I was saying," Mallett resumed, "I thought that I could refer all the other events to a single source. But not the affair of the chocolates. That was a totally different type of crime. In fact, it was less like a crime than a particularly malicious practical joke.

"Now in the ordinary way, practical jokers are very difficult to detect, because the whole essence of the game is irresponsibility and absence of motive. But in this case, there was this much to go on. The Judge was already involved in a trouble unconnected altogether with Heppenstall's release from prison—the motor accident in which Mr. Sebald-Smith was injured. Simply because on the balance of probabilities it was more likely that he should have two ill-wishers than three, I set about connecting the affair of the chocolates with the accident. I made some discreet inquiries about Mr. Sebald-Smith, ascertained his connection with a lady named Parsons, satisfied myself as to her character and that she would have a certain degree of familiarity with the Judge's taste in confectionery, and as a result came to the conclusion that she was the person responsible for that episode."

"Apart from that, you took no steps in the matter?" Pettigrew asked.

"No. There were really no steps to take. I had no evidence then on which to arrest Heppenstall, and I knew that I could keep an eye on him and see that the Judge came to no further harm through him. As a matter of fact, we pulled him in a few weeks later on a charge of fraud, but that was incidental. So far as the lady was concerned, I didn't look on her as a potential danger, although she might prove herself a nuisance from time to time.

"That was the position up to the end of Wimbling-ham Assizes. During the rest of the Circuit, I received reports from the police forces at the various towns, which worried me a good deal. I therefore took the opportunity of seeing Mr. Marshall immediately on his return and getting an account from him while the facts were still fresh in his memory. This time, the incidents which had to be considered were, successively, the dead mouse in the parcel, the Judge's fall downstairs and the third anonymous letter, all at Rampleford and finally the gas escape in the Judge's room at Whitsea. There was in fact another incident which was not reported to me until long after but which proved to be the most sinister of all—the disappearance of the knife from the court at Eastbury. But I doubt whether I should have been much the wiser if I had been told of it.

"The dead mouse, of course, gave no trouble at all. It fitted in perfectly neatly with the poisoned chocolates, and confirmed me in my views about them. But the other matters were altogether different. They fitted in with nothing at all. Most emphatically, they did not fit in with the incidents on the earlier part of the Circuit. And above all in contrast to those incidents, they seemed to me on examination to show every sign of being bogus."

"Bogus?" said Derek. "What made you think that? After all, the Judge was twice in quite serious danger. He did fall downstairs and he was nearly gassed that night at Whitsea.

Nothing that happened before came anything like so close to killing him as that."

"Exactly," said Mallett. "They both looked like quite determined attempts on his life. But they both failed. In each case, Lady Barber was at hand to save him—and to save him before witnesses, too. The fact did not of course prove that she was responsible for them, but it did look as though whoever had made these pretended attempts had so arranged matters that somebody would be at hand to see that they failed in their object. The next thing I noticed about them, of course, was that while the earlier incidents *might* have been the work of a member of the Judge's household, these almost certainly *must* have been. As for the anonymous letter, it seemed to prove the point up to the hilt. It was found at the Lodgings, you will remember, after the Judge's party had left. Now no outsider, going to leave a letter of that description, would hand it in at the door when he could see for himself that the person it was intended for had gone or was in the act of going. The writer of that letter meant it to be found at the last possible moment, but in time for it to reach the Judge before his train left. I concluded that in all probability it had been left on the hall table by one of the party while actually leaving the house. In the hurry of departure it would be very easy to do, especially if the writer arranged to be one of the last to go."

"I remember now," Derek put in, "Lady Barber kept us all waiting while she ran back into the house for her bag, which she said she had left in the drawing-room. She insisted on going herself, although I offered to get it for her."

"No doubt that was how it was managed," said Mallett. "Well! There I was left with a very odd case on my hands. On the one hand, I had been appealed to by Lady Barber to protect her husband against attack from outside, and on the other I found somebody inside engineering a series of sham attacks, and, after a careful process of elimination, I was driven to the conclusion that that somebody was Lady

Barber herself. Yet I was quite convinced of the sincerity of her appeal in the first place, and from what Mr. Marshall told me I was equally convinced that during the second part of the Circuit she was still genuinely doing all that she could, with his assistance, to guard her husband against any further assaults of what I may call the Wimblingham type. Why?

"In seeking for some explanation, I naturally tried to find something which one could mark as a turning-point between the two phases. I thought I could distinguish it in what appeared at first sight the most trivial incident of all—the dead mouse which came through the post at Rampleford. From what Mr. Marshall told me and from my own inquiries, I determined that up to that point Lady Barber had hopes of settling the action which Mr. Sebald-Smith was threatening on terms which would not ruin her husband completely. After that, it was apparent to her that Miss Parsons was not going to allow her to do any such thing. The thought crossed my mind that in such circumstances she might decide that it was better to kill her husband and live on what he had to leave her rather than allow his whole estate to be swallowed up in the enormous damages which Mr. Sebald-Smith was demanding."

"Aha!" said Pettigrew.

"The theory left a good deal unexplained, of course. If that was right, why should she be going to such immense trouble to safeguard her husband's life, and why should she be careful to see that her own attempts were unsuccessful? I thought, however, that all this might be put down to a very elaborate scheme to distract suspicion, and I decided that the theory was worth pursuing. But first I had to make sure that it was really to Lady Barber's interest to kill her husband. I made inquiries from our legal department and I found out that if the Judge died, there was nothing whatever to prevent Mr. Sebald-Smith from pursuing his action at the expense of the estate, so that by killing her husband she would be no better off financially. That is the result, they told me, of a fairly recent change in the law."

"Law Reforms (Miscellaneous Provisions) Act, 1934," Pettigrew interjected.

"Thank you, sir. Unfortunately, as it turned out, I didn't pursue my legal inquiries quite far enough. But with that information before me, it seemed to me that my theory must be wrong. For some reason or another, Lady Barber was pretending to try to kill her husband, while all the time only too anxious to keep him alive. Only two explanations seemed to me possible. Either she was deliberately interested in frightening him, for some obscure purpose of her own, or she was suffering from some kind of mental strain. The second alternative seemed to me the better of the two. I don't know much about such matters, but I could well imagine that a rather highly strung woman, genuinely afraid for her husband's safety, losing her sleep in watching for the assault that never came, might in the end be so mentally affected as to start faking attacks upon him as though to justify the trouble that she was putting herself to. If I was right, I thought, then as soon as the strain of the Circuit was removed, and she was living a more or less normal existence in London again, all these odd manifestations would stop. And so it turned out.

"At the same time, I was not absolutely easy in my mind about the matter at first. Then, as time went on and there did not seem to be the least sign of any danger threatening the Judge, I felt that I must have been right. Heppenstall had been put out of harm's way, and the first series of threats and attacks had stopped. Lady Barber had returned to London, and immediately the second, faked, series had stopped also. It all seemed too easy. Then, as though to clinch the matter, came the Judge's attempted suicide. There was no doubt that it was a real attempt, and equally no doubt that Lady Barber had done everything in her power to save his life. Indeed, the doctor told me that but for her promptitude he would infallibly have died. That cleared my mind of my last, lingering suspicion. There could be no doubt that so far from desiring his death she was prepared to go to all lengths to preserve his life.

"Then, only a few weeks later, the Judge was killed, in circumstances with which you are all familiar. There were five obvious suspects. Three of them are in this room. The fourth was Beamish. The other, of course, was Lady Barber. The fact that the crime had been committed with a particular weapon which we could identify with the one last seen at Eastbury Assizes, led me to eliminate Miss Bartram at once and, after a little further inquiry, Mr. Marshall also. But that merely put me in this difficulty—that in so doing, I had eliminated the only two people with a motive for committing the crime *at that particular moment*. Yet it was plain that whoever had done so had taken a very considerable risk. The whole thing spoke not only of considerable daring and efficiency—how different, you will notice, from the half-hearted, bungling attempts on Circuit!—but also of great urgency. It looked as if the murderer had been under a compulsion to seize that one momentary chance rather than wait for a better opportunity. Looking at the three remaining suspects, two of them with not inadequate motives for murder, I could not find any such compulsion, and so far as Lady Barber was concerned, there was the added absurdity that an anxiety to keep alive must have been suddenly changed into what I have called a compulsion to kill. And yet, on the grounds of opportunity alone, it was impossible to shut one's eyes to the fact that she was by far the likeliest of the three.

"That was my state of mind yesterday, when you, Mr. Pettigrew, gave me the key to the whole mystery, by drawing my attention to the fact that the day of the murder was exactly six months after the day of the accident at Markhampton."

"Any competent lawyer could see the point of that," said

Pettigrew. "But I must say I was astonished that you tumbled to it so quickly. Quite candidly, I hoped you wouldn't."

"I didn't see the point of it," said Mallett modestly. "But I did see that there was a point somewhere. The date of the murder was in some way connected with the date of the accident. Very well. The only thing to do was to start all over again from the beginning, and find out what I could about the accident. Accordingly, on leaving you, I went straight to Faradays, Mr. Sebald-Smith's solicitors. And there, almost the first question I asked brought the explanation which I had been seeking for so long. I asked what stage the action against the Judge had reached at the time of his death, and the partner whom I interviewed told me that in fact it had never got beyond the stage of negotiations. The writ in the action was actually to have been issued on the day after the Judge died. I noticed that he seemed very upset about it."

"I bet he did," said Pettigrew. "Are Sally and Sebald suing the firm for negligence?"

"He indicated that there was a possibility of that occurring."

"An odd little epilogue to a murder!"

"But I don't understand," said Derek. "What had all this to do with the murder?"

"The answer," said Pettigrew, "is in Sub-section three of Section one of the Act of Parliament I quoted just now. Put into non-technical language, it amounts to this: You can maintain an action against a chap for running you down even if he's dead. *But* to do so you must fulfil one of two conditions. Either you can start your action while he is still alive, in which case John Brown's body can moulder in the grave, but your case goes marching along and you cash in on the executors. Or you can start your action with J.B. already mouldering, but in that case you have only got six months to do it in, counting from the time his car hit you. If you choose to spend six months palavering about the rights and wrongs of your case before you kick off and the man dies on you, then your action descends into the grave and moulders also. And serve you right."

"And that is what happened in this case?"

"That is what happened in this case. And it happened because Hilda—God rest her soul!—meant it to happen. She was a lawyer, you see, and it so chanced that her pet study was what is known as the Limitation of Actions—a subject I used to think dull, but never will again. She knew that Sebald-Smith's action would ruin her husband completely if it was fought. She knew also that if he died, she would be ruined by it just the same. So she set herself to keep him alive and the plaintiff's solicitors at bay until the six months were up. That was why she had to stop him from committing suicide last month. And that was why, the moment the period had gone by, she had to kill him before the writ could be issued. She must have thought it all out as soon as she was certain that Sally meant to have her pound of flesh—that day at Rampleford when the fatal little mouse turned up in your pocket, Marshall. I apologize, Inspector," he added. "I'm afraid I've taken the words out of your mouth."

"Not at all," said Mallett. "You have put it all much more clearly than I could have done. I think that that is the whole of the story—except for *this*, Mr. Pettigrew." He indicated the note on the table.

"That? My little footnote to the Act of Parliament? Well, it's a very succinct missive, is it not? A mere reference to the Law Reports."

He took the paper and read aloud:

"Dear Hilda,
(1938) 2 K.B. 202.

F."

"That, my lord and members of the jury, is simply the

reference to the case of *Daniels v. Vaux*, which decided a different point of law altogether, but in which the facts were rather similar to these. A well to do young man, who had omitted to insure himself, ran into a policeman and injured him badly. There was no real defence to the policeman's claim, and the solicitors on both sides settled down to argue the amount of the damages. They were on the point of agreement when the young man himself was killed—how, history does not relate, but since all this happened in pre-bomb days, I assume either by his own car, or someone else's. That occurred six months after the first accident, and nobody had thought of starting an action. And so the poor plaintiff had none. You will find all that set out, as my hieroglyphics indicate, in Volume Two of the King's Bench Reports for the year 1938, at page two hundred and two. I happened to refer to it yesterday morning, and that was why the coincidence of the dates struck me so forcibly."

Pettigrew's face, which had been animated during his exposition, suddenly looked very tired. He reached for the note and tore it slowly into pieces.

"I suppose," he said bitterly, as he dropped the fragments into the wastepaper basket, "I suppose that it is the first time on record that anyone has ever been driven to commit suicide by a quotation from the Law Reports."